Cara Luecht

This is a work of fiction. All characters and events portrayed in this novel are either fictitious or used fictitiously.

SOUL PAINTER

WhiteFire Publishing
13607 Bedford Rd NE
Cumberland, MD 21502

ISBN: 978-1-939023-24-7 (print)
       978-1-939023-25-4 (digital)

To David
Thank you.

Chapter I

Chicago, 1891

The bricks crumbled under her feet. Down by the docks, repairs to the infrastructure of the thick, stretching city were considered more luxury than necessity. Walking in the dark hours, after the fog slipped up from the churning lake and gave body to every shadow and mass to every lamp, walking then, when even the air closed in around her, she could move freely.

Her long wool skirt blended with the fog. A hooded cape, buttoned at the chin, molded to the back of her head and fell over her face. The heavy folds draped her shoulders.

It had been years since someone had looked directly into her gray eyes. She wrapped that knowledge around her like the fog, wore the isolation like a second cloak, let it melt into her pores as she navigated the city.

Her feet knew every cobble, every crack. She counted the steps. At step nineteen, the brick gave way to yellow, desperate patches of grass. Six steps later, she turned behind a fence, again counting the steps to the streetlamp burning at the base of the cathedral stairs. A statue of the Virgin glowed in the muted light. The Virgin's robes were faded to gray and a crack scarred her smooth complexion. It crawled from her hidden ear, across her lips, and toward the inner corner of her eye. The crack never lengthened. It was almost as if the Virgin had decided when the pain should stop.

Miriam loved the Virgin. She loved how her stone-carved hair was pulled tight under her cascading veil. Miriam imagined her own brown hair becoming one with her colorless cape and falling to the ground. On damp nights it wicked up the moisture from the stones, and, if she stood still enough, clung to the street. For as much as she avoided the crowds, she was as much a part of the city as the immoveable, silent Virgin.

The church towered overhead. She knew the stonework, the carved faces of the saints, and every piece of stained glass. The windows of her rooms in the upper levels of the warehouse faced the cathedral, and although she had not stepped a foot inside since childhood, she could remember every detail: the sputtering candles to the right of the heavy oak doors, the pool of water that never rippled, and how the sun cast pieces of color across the heads of the penitent, kneeling parishioners.

She hadn't stepped inside since her mother's funeral. Her father had sat in the front pew, stone-faced, clenching her eight-year-old fingers. His hand trembled, once. They followed her mother's casket out of the doors, down the stone steps, and watched the men load her into the wagon. When they returned from her grave, they turned right, into her father's warehouse. He carried Miriam up the stairs, past his offices, and into her new nursery, where he kissed the top of her head and handed her over to a motherly nurse.

They never returned to the glittering townhouse where her mother had hosted parties for the city's elite. As far as she knew, her mother's brushes still sat, a decade later, on her dressing table with her tangled hair wrapped around the bristles.

Miriam looked up to the carved façade of the cathedral. She could only make out the details to the bottom of the second row of windows. There, the light failed.

When her father died, his solicitor knocked on the door. Miriam watched him from her rooms above the warehouse. Eventually, the bespectacled man gave up and mailed the letters. She instructed him through correspondence to leave all as it was, to make deposits into her trust at regular intervals, and to send her the balance sheets. He complied and left her in peace. The few men who worked in the offices were paid generous pensions.

And Miriam locked the doors.

Down by the docks, the city was never akin to the rich, planted gardens where she'd spent the years in her mother's arms. But they had a flavor of their own. A reality she could smell and taste from her windows above the streets. The changing landscape of people passing, hurrying, every day, gave her an unlimited source of new faces to capture on canvas.

The church was the center of her world even if she never stepped inside. She gave, via her solicitor, and in return was rewarded with glimpses into the lives of the devoted, the employed, and those on the periphery. They were close to the docks and the shipbuilders. While some sailors populated the stone steps to wait for a priest to hear their confessions, others used the deep shadows that ran through the alleyway and found reason to confess.

Miriam stepped around the Virgin and out of the illuminated mist. There would be no one in the alley at that hour, and she was tempted to change her path, to veer down the narrow walkway, to see where it all happened. She didn't. Instead, she counted her steps back to the warehouse door, pulled her key from her pocket, inserted it into the well-oiled lock, and turned it. The lock opened without hesitation, as relieved to find her as she was to find it, and she stepped into the dark, dusty room. She closed the door, locked it behind her, and turned to the stairs. She didn't need to light a lamp.

Once upstairs, she made tea. She sat in her living room with her feet up on cushions and her back pressed deep into the upholstery of her chair. Her father's chair still sat on the other side of the room, with his imprint permanently registered in the sawdust stuffing. Miriam never sat in the chair herself, nor had she ever thought to remove it. It filled the corner of the heavily decorated room as if it had grown there of its own volition, and she would no more extract it from its place than she would chop down some unsuspecting country tree. There simply was no reason.

The cushion under her feet was red, with gold stitching and tassels in a rainbow of colors. On its own, it would have appeared ostentatious, gaudy even. But in Miriam's room, an echo of her father's younger years spent in the orient, it was completely at home.

She watched from her lead-framed, factory-grade windows until the sun glinted off the cathedral's stained glass panes. When it reflected and caught the crystals hanging from the lampshade next to her, she rose, rinsed her cup and saucer, set in on the counter to dry, and found her bed where she would sleep until the bells of the church chimed and the school spilled its children into the streets. The children's faces were her favorite, had been since she was a child herself, watching them from above.

They wore their day like a mask. Over the years she watched as that mask slowly became their adult face, just as hers did in the mirror. But she painted, painted the children when the mask was still a mask. Painted the child, and then added layers of brush strokes over the child's face, predicting with color the person they would become.

John had made the habit of watching for her before the sun burned off the fog. As a deacon in the cathedral, he woke before all the others in order to prepare for the morning mass. It was a congregation consisting primarily of aging mothers praying for wayward sons, and wayward sons who had exhausted every other resource. Of course, there was never an opportunity to match grandmother with son.

The strong coffee he poured from the pot did little to add to the early hour, so he turned off the lights and watched the street through the barred windows. He knew she would be by. The fog had come in heavy that night and had only thickened during the pre-morning hours.

She stopped as he knew she would. Once again he took a step nearer to the pane of glass. He could see a shadow of what appeared to be fine, small features. Under the shadow of the hood he failed to make out the color of her eyes.

He wasn't sure why it mattered. It shouldn't. She was a soul, like the countless other souls that passed by every day. She was a soul who never stepped a foot into the church. He knew he should turn away, should review the passages for that morning's service, should make sure everything was ready. There were more pressing matters, more urgent needs. People walked by every day, desperate, hopeless, yet she filled his thoughts.

Maybe it was the way she paused to face the statue. Her motionless lips open with her exhale, as if she might start up a conversation. He thought of her lips. Wondered if they had ever felt the pressure of a man, wondered how much she had in common with Mary.

Mary. That's what he called her in his mind. She was called by other names. The school children whispered about her. They called her the factory witch. The eldest priest called her "that poor creature." John never questioned his superior about her real name. He didn't trust himself enough to maintain the proper demeanor of concerned, but casual indifference.

Mary she was.

Ione shivered. She hated the fog. Hated the way it hid the men. Hated the way she could hear their work boots slosh in uneven stumbles before she could see their approach. But they always knew where to find her.

She waited at the entrance to the alley and watched the strange, quiet fog-woman pause mere feet from where Ione stood. Ione shifted behind the hedges at the entrance to the alley. The solitary woman with the ghostly white skin unsettled her far more than the men who claimed her time. A drip of water fell from a low branch and traveled down her bare shoulder, into the void between her breasts. Ione shivered again.

The clock struck four chimes. But even that bold, bronze beacon was dampened by the ever-thickening blanket that suffocated the docks. It was time to go home, to crawl into bed with her younger sisters, and to look in on her mother. She moved her toes against the night's earnings wadded in a cloth under her stocking. The coins were taking on the chill of the concrete. Her bed would be warm, her sisters' limbs smooth and soft. So unlike the rough, groping hands of the men that held her still, then trembled as they fastened buttons and dropped the coins into her hand—sometimes with a mumbled apology, sometimes with a sneer. Her mother was too sick to ask where the money came from.

Ione looked up from her hiding place. The fog-woman had slipped away. Ione stepped out of the shadows and into the damp light of the streetlamp. In the morning, after her sisters

11

had left for school, Ione would go to the butcher—to the back door, but to the butcher, nonetheless—and she would buy soup bones. The good ones, with meat still tucked in the crevices. She would buy the bones and boil them to a rich broth, and her sisters would come home to something hot and good. She would spread the marrow on a cracker for her mother, and maybe her mother would eat. Ione wiggled her toes against the money one more time before stepping off the curb and into the street. It had been a profitable night.

Jenny passed by—a white girl with dirty hair and gapped teeth. She was on her way home too, only Jenny lived with her father, one who knew how Jenny spent her nights. They made quick eye contact without slowing down. Jenny nodded her recognition before turning down the alley that led to her storefront rooms. Ione continued into the fog.

Chapter 2

Miriam counted out the exact change, tucked it in an envelope, and folded it securely. The money was for the errand boy.

He had red, red hair, and the face of an eight year old, although Miriam knew he had to be closer to fourteen. She counted the steps down to the warehouse floor as she calculated how long he'd had been delivering her groceries. Soon he would have a job on the docks, and then she would have to find someone else. The potential for a younger brother was always there. That would be acceptable.

One table sat next to the exterior door at the base of the stairs. Miriam kept it uncovered and dusted. Transom windows spaced evenly down the high factory walls let in sufficient light. She checked the time and decided she was early enough to walk the inside perimeter of the huge building. Boxes and crates lined the walls under the windows. Tables, chairs, conveyor belts, and heavy machines she knew nothing about were stacked on top of one another and pushed toward the center of the room. They were covered with tarps that draped to the floor. Miriam's heart beat faster as she rounded the final, tight corner. Anyone could be hiding under a table, concealed by tarps and shadows, and Miriam would never be the wiser. She quickened her pace back to the table by the door.

She pulled the envelope from her pocket, placed it in the exact center of the table, unlatched the door, and rushed to the dark under the stairs, where she sat on a crate to wait.

She checked her pocket watch again—her father's watch, really. Dug it out of her waistband and pressed the warm gold button that flipped it open. The second hand never stopped. She clicked it closed without registering the time.

The door latch lifted.

"Why do you do this every week?" A whiny, young female voice echoed through the warehouse.

"Because I get paid." Adolescence razed the boyish answer. Miriam smiled to herself, considering the color she would mix for his cracking voice. "You can come in, you know."

"Nuh-uh."

"Well, you can't stand in the street by yourself."

"Yes I can."

Miriam heard the door scrape open to the furthest extent the rusted hinges would allow.

"No you can't," the boy argued.

Light from the open door flooded the room in an uneven rectangle. Through the stairs, Miriam watched the boy take a step in and hold the door open with his back for his younger sister.

"Is she in there?"

"Of course not." He slid across the door and set the heavy brown bag on the floor to hold it open. "She's never here. She just leaves the money in an envelope."

The girl took a tentative step over the threshold and looked toward the stairway, her blue gaze trying to discern shapes from the shadows, but Miriam knew she was hidden well enough.

"Why does she live in here?" She squinted into the dark.

"I think she must live up there." The boy gestured toward the top of the stairs.

"I don't like that."

"You don't have to. Now, hold the door open for me."

"I hear congratulations are in order."

John jumped and turned from the window.

"I apologize. I didn't mean to startle you." Father Ayers floated into the room, his black robe reaching to just above the carpet. It hovered there as he came to a stop, assisted by his generous waistline. "Anything interesting down in the alley?"

John cleared his throat. "No. Of course not." He took a few steps away from the window. "Is there something you need me to do?"

"No, I just wanted to congratulate you. I received notice you'll be taking your vows next month."

John nodded. He had read the notice days before but hadn't mentioned it to anyone. He rubbed his sweaty palms against his modest robe and tried to embrace the anxiety as excitement.

"Are you feeling well?" A concerned look clouded Father Ayers's gaze, but not too much. John envied him for his mastery of a false, simple demeanor. His discrete question, alluding to health, dispersed any questions of intent, and released John from explaining his gaze into the unholy, narrow space running from street to street.

"I'm feeling quite well," John lied. The elder priest didn't look away. John pulled a chair out from a small round table next to a bookcase and sat, heavily. "No, I'm sorry. That wasn't the truth. I'm not fine." He ground his elbows into his knees and dropped his head into his hands, closing his eyes against the vision of the worn, red rugs.

Father Ayers pulled a chair from the other side of the room and sat down, facing John, remaining silent until John looked up.

"What's troubling you?"

"Do you ever have the feeling that something is dreadfully wrong?" John sat back, slouching against the hard wooden back of the chair. His long legs stretched under his robes, his knees straining the fabric.

"Wrong with what?"

"That's just it. I'm not sure. I keep watching out the window."

Father Ayers looked down to his own clasped hands. "Are you afraid of your own feelings? Is this about your vows?"

"No. Maybe. I'm not sure." He let his breath escape in a rush and paused to feel the emptiness before taking in another. "I see the same people come in and out of the church and the alley. I pray for them, even those who knowingly live in sin. Then I worry about them, and I watch for them, and I stand by the window waiting to see if they are back for another night of torture."

John stood and crossed back to the window. The orange light of dusk fell on his hands as he leaned against the sill. "I see things. Things I don't want to see. And I wonder why I watch." He turned back to the priest and smirked. "It's a fine line between longing and praying."

Father Ayers measured him. "You're where you need to be." He stood, picked up the chair, and put it back where it belonged. "It's the students who don't understand that line that have difficulty later." He moved back to the doorway. "Watch over your flock. They live in a meadow of temptation and sin. The meadow feeds them, but it also hides the dangers. What kind of shepherd would you be if you failed to watch over your charges because you feared for your own life?"

"But I thought I was supposed to keep my thoughts pure." John gestured toward the ground outside the window. "It's pretty hard to do when watching that." His eyes fell to the concrete below.

"You'll know if it switches from about them to about you." The elder priest slipped out of the room.

John leaned his forehead against the cool glass, hoping Father Ayers was right but unable to shake the expanding evening dread. He wanted to see Mary, wanted her to walk down the alley. Wondered if her serene spirit could accomplish more than the pathetic, curious disgust he mustered, safe on his perch in God's house.

A lone woman in bright colors walked from the back of the alley. John marveled. They never thought to look up. Even when dropping to their knees, they never looked up.

What he would do if they did, he had no idea. They knew what they did was wrong. Knowing a church leader watched would only add guilt. But he wished to meet their eyes, to tell them to run, something bad was coming.

The girls were tucked in and asleep. Ione pulled a Mason jar from behind the stack of mismatched plates. She reached to the bottom for the coin she would press into the doctor's hand.

He ducked out from behind the curtain and paused. "I'm sorry." He frowned. "I've done all I can do." He set his brown leather bag on the table and tightened the buckle before meeting Ione's eyes. "It won't be long."

Ione nodded, glancing toward her sisters' bed. She hadn't even told them yet.

"Here." Ione held the coin out for the doctor to take.

"No, there's nothing I can do. I'm not going to charge you just to give you bad news." He pulled up the leather strap and tightened the buckle further.

"But you still came. You were the only one who would," she whispered, meeting his eyes.

The doctor took a step nearer and settled his stark white hand over Ione's, closing her fingers around her precious coin. His skin was warm, and his fingernails were trimmed perfectly.

He held her hand in his. "I'm sorry I was the only one who would come." His eyes bored into hers, his sincerity evident in his scratchy tone. He dropped her hand and turned toward the door. "You'll let me know if there is anything you need?" He hesitated, his hand on the knob. "Is there something?"

Ione looked down to the wide plank floor, to the one nail that had worked itself out of a board. "What do I do—I mean, when she..." She let the question die off.

"I'll come back in the morning to check on her. We can talk about it then."

Ione nodded, not trusting her own voice. She closed and locked the door behind the doctor. She wouldn't be working that night.

Her sisters snored softly—Maggie, twelve, and Lucy. Lucy rolled over and pulled her arms out from underneath the quilt. Her hands had lost their baby roundness over the last year. Ione tucked her back in and brushed her cheek with the back of her fingers. At four, she would only remember snippets of their mother.

Ione trailed her fingers across their fine quilt. The stitches were perfectly spaced; their mother's competence as a seamstress displayed in shades of green. Ione hoped to teach her sisters just as their mother had taught her. She would protect them from her truth. If she'd never left in the first place, she wouldn't be living as she was now. She'd paid for her rebellion. Ione straightened and turned away from her sisters' bed.

She was still paying. She could only hope her mother knew how sorry she was.

But it was a sacrifice worth making, and it would only be a little longer. Her mother had a warm bed. Her sisters still went to class. They had food. Ione slipped behind her mother's curtain.

The room was sweet-smelling, the air still. Ione could hear her shallow breathing. Her chest rose in trembles, and her distended stomach strained against her nightshirt. She hadn't even woken for a taste of the doctor's sticky pain syrup.

Ione knelt at the edge of her mother's bed, the wood floor biting into her knees. "It's fine, Mama," she said. "If you need to go, you can. We'll be fine." She reached up and brushed her mother's dark hair. Her mother grimaced, as if even that small disturbance hurt. Ione pulled her hand away and laid her forehead against the thin mattress.

In the wee hours, Ione woke. Her mother was cold. Ione covered her face, pulled the curtain closed, and waited for her sisters to stir. She would let them sleep one last night, one last night with a mother.

Chapter 3

Miriam dropped her brush into the jar of turpentine and glanced out the window toward the church. He still stood there. His fascination she understood, but his approach she did not.

He liked to be near the people. He often walked out the heavy wood doors, greeting people on the street, stooping to smile at a child. That's how she'd been able to see his face.

Miriam studied the painting on her easel. She'd captured the side of his face as he'd turned away, and then blurred it into the dark unknown. It was a close painting. One shoulder almost filled the frame, and she'd cut off most of his hair. But the black-viridian of the night was evident, as was the zinc-white illuminating his skin from underneath. She'd captured his glow.

He never walked into the alley, though; never sullied himself with their sin. Miriam swished the brush around the jar as she gazed out the window. She knew her painting would be much different if he had frequented the paved path. But as it was, so he was—a man who watched over his flock, literally.

The white woman, cloaked by dusk, found her way to the entrance. She casually glanced to make sure no one watched, and then ducked behind the untrimmed hedge at the gate. Miriam looked up to the window in time to see him back away. He never watched like Miriam did, but then, her view was blocked.

The streetlamps flickered to life. Miriam twisted the tin tubes closed for the night. She glanced out again, but in the direction of the river. There would be no fog—too much breeze coming off the lake. She sighed and leaned on the window sill, waiting for the other woman, the dark-skinned girl who always wore the striped dress. In truth, it was more costume than dress, designed to conceal and reveal at the same time. The woman painted her face, too, rouge over her dark skin, but Miriam still recognized her. It was her lips. They were full and red and hadn't changed since childhood. In fact, the girl's face was the only childhood face Miriam had painted whose future she'd painted wrong.

Miriam watched until the streetlamp glowed in a circle on the pavement, making all else disappear into the night. There was almost no moon. If the fog rolled in tomorrow, it would be a black night, indeed.

John paced, unable to sleep, and unable to bring himself to look into the alley. The dark-skinned woman hadn't appeared. He tried to think back to when she'd last abandoned her post, but he couldn't remember a single evening she hadn't crept into the shadows. More men than usual walked past the gate and gazed into the blackness. They were looking for her.

John wondered what she did to so entrap them, then pulled his rosary from his pocket and prayed for forgiveness. They weren't entrapped by her, it was their own longing. John knew what that was like.

Mary wouldn't be out. There was no fog. John paced back to his bedside table and flipped his Bible open. It was too dark to read. Instead, he lay back against his pillows and placed his hand on the thin, gilded-edged pages, closing his eyes to his own thoughts.

A muffled scream echoed up from the alley. John jumped off the bed and slammed the window sash open. It banged against the exterior bricks, but the pane remained unbroken.

"Hello?" he yelled into the darkness. "Who's there?"

Silence.

"Does anyone need help?" The empty concrete cavern revealed nothing.

John glanced to the clock across the room as he pulled on his boots. It was nearly four a.m. Past the time when most of the girls had gone to wherever they called home, past the time for the stumbling, drunken sailors. It was the hour of unconsciousness, the hour when darkness began to sense the coming sun and finally capitulated.

He burst into the hallway, expecting to find disturbed nuns, or at least the elder priest, but was greeted by emptiness. The hall was black. No one stood, concerned and uncomfortable in their night clothes. No light escaped from underneath the doors of those who might have been woken by the unfamiliar sound and, in turn, sought the comfort in a flame. Nothing.

John knew he hadn't imagined it.

In darkness, he stumbled down one of the many hidden stairways descending into the bowels of the church. Finally feeling the cool steel door in front of him, he found and pulled the bolt open. John heaved against the strength of the rusted hinges until they gave, bit by bit, shrieking with every push. He squeezed into the dark silence of the alley.

"Who's here?" Only his own, obscenely loud echo answered.

His boots clomped against the stained concrete as he walked the length of the church. He dodged reeking buckets of garbage and rainwater and puddles of things he didn't want to consider. There was no one. He reached the lamplight. A small pool of what looked like blood dripped into and out of the light—possibly the evidence of an innocent fight between two seamen.

John released a loud snort at the thought of anything in the city being innocent. Chicago was the antithesis of innocence. Everything was corrupt. Even charity in the city was somehow perverse. Every time he stood on the ladle side of the soup kitchen, he felt a creeping guilt that had nothing to do with serving his fellow man.

Had he imagined the scream?

He stepped into the light and looked at the tall factory wall across the street. Gray brick. Everything was gray or dying or wishing it was dead. Leaning against the light pole, he listened to the sounds of the city: trickles of water running into the sewers, the distant air horn of a ship coming into port, the wheels of a wagon lurching over broken cobbles.

He raised his eyes to the factory windows and saw a shadow disappear into the darkness behind her. Mary had been watching him. She probably saw him come out of the alley. He knew what she would think, and he laughed at himself, because somehow the city had a way of making even the desire to protect look like usury.

21

John pushed off the lamppost in disgust. Mary's conclusions about him ate at his sour stomach more than they should. The city would wake soon. He walked around the overgrown hedge that had forced its way through a crack in the concrete. Bunches of closed, white buds hung heavily from the branches.

The city would wake soon, but it would never be alive.

Ione stabbed the sizzling bacon with a fork and flipped it in the cast iron pan. Her sisters were on the other side of the room, shrugging into their night clothes.

The news was not as much of a surprise to them as she had anticipated. They handled it with dignity. They made her proud, although she had no right to be proud of siblings she had abandoned. She'd been such a fool.

In the wee hours, Ione had washed her mother's face and arms and put her nice apron over her nightshirt. When they woke, and after she had explained, she'd pulled the curtain back for her sisters to say good-bye. They cried, and then they walked in the spots of sunlight that fought its way to the dirt paths between the small shanties on their street. They picked the flowered heads off the weeds and tucked them into their mother's apron pockets.

The doctor had brought a minister with him that morning. Ione's mother hadn't attended church since her father had died right after Lucy was born. The minister was nice enough. He said a proper prayer, and they sang "Amazing Grace" while the driver of the wagon waited with the horses. He said he would check in on them later in the week. Ione wasn't sure what that meant, or what they could do, but it sounded nice.

If they found out what she was doing, they wouldn't be sending anyone over.

They had no money for a burial, so they did the best they could. Now the tiny house seemed too big and the coins in the jar too few.

Of course, after they took her, Lucy asked every half hour or so when Mama was coming home. Maggie just busied herself with chores. Tonight, Ione would tuck Lucy into bed and keep Maggie up to discuss things. There was a haze of concern in every move

Maggie made, and Ione needed to reassure her. Maggie was too old not to worry.

The bacon was the last of their meat, and there was only enough money to pay the next week's rent and to buy food for the three of them. Ione slid the bacon out of the pan onto a plate and dropped three spoonfuls of biscuit dough into the grease. She was almost out of flour too.

She would never tell Maggie how she fed them.

School was almost over for the year. Just a couple more weeks. After that, they would be home during the day. They would be involved in her life. After school ended, there would be no hiding her true occupation. She had to arrange things now.

"Come and eat," Ione whispered. They'd been whispering all day long.

Her sisters shuffled to their places at the table and sat quietly on their stools. They both took an intense interest in the worn, gray, wood grain. Their mother's stool was enormously empty.

Ione forked the biscuits and bacon onto their plates. "Eat up. We don't want it to go to waste."

"I'm not really hungry," Maggie picked up her tin fork and speared the bacon. She brought it to her mouth and chewed.

Lucy picked up the biscuit and held it in her fisted hands.

"Take a bite, Lucy," Maggie urged.

Lucy looked up at Ione. Tears threatened to spill over and run down her round face.

"Come here." Ione held out her arms. Lucy ran to her on the other side of the table.

Maggie looked down at her plate. "What are we going to do?"

Lucy rubbed the top of her head into the crook of Ione's neck. "Do you want to go to bed early?" Ione whispered into Lucy's ear.

She nodded, and Ione carried her to her bed on the other side of the room. She pulled the quilt under her chin and kissed her forehead, breathing in the scent of her hair. They were hers now to take care of.

"What about the prayer?" Lucy said, just as Ione was turning back to Maggie.

Ione didn't remember it.

Maggie walked over and knelt next to Lucy. Foreheads touching, they whispered the words together. Lucy smiled up at

Maggie before closing her eyes and turning toward the wall.

"What will we do?" Maggie crossed to the table and sat.

"I have a job for a little while longer." Ione paused at her half-lie. "It's in the night, though." She glanced up at Maggie.

"What kind of a job is at night?"

"I'm entertaining people."

"How?"

"Don't you remember me singing to you before I left?"

Maggie nodded. "But do you make enough money?"

Relieved that the answer satisfied Maggie, Ione picked up her biscuit and took a bite. "We'll have to be very careful. And I'll need you to stay in here at night with Lucy. I should be able to make enough. During the day, when you are at school, I plan to visit Mother's old customers. I think I still remember where most of them live." Ione looked into the corner of the room where the washtubs were stacked upside down. "She taught me how to do laundry and how to mend. There's no reason we can't pick up where she left off. Then I can stay here with you in the night."

"What happened?" Maggie asked.

"What do you mean?"

"Why did you come back?"

Ione closed her eyes and sighed. She'd never explained it to anyone. By the time she'd gotten back to her mother, she had been so ill that no one even asked what had brought her home. "He was a bad man."

"I'm going to lay down with Lucy." Maggie pushed her stool away from the table and walked to the other side of the room.

The words "bad man" didn't even begin to describe him. Within a month, Ione had been bruised from head to toe. She still sang with him in the seedy little saloon. But there wasn't enough money in it. They were both hungry when the owner offered them a room in exchange for her services. Too proud to go back to her mother, she considered it a sacrifice for their future. When he started bringing other men to her, she'd had enough.

Ione picked up the dishes and dropped them into a bucket of cool water, still shocked that, coming home, she'd run into exactly what she'd run away from.

She dried her wet hands on her apron. There would be an end, though. A couple more weeks, she promised herself.

Chapter 4

It had been a few days. She hoped she hadn't been away too long. Ione peered out of the alley to see if any other customers haunted the shadows. The alley was well suited for this sort of thing. Ione let out a short, cynical breath. She was sure that was not what the cathedral's architects had intended. She scanned the empty street again. The glowing lamp at the entrance promised she would at least see their faces for the few seconds before they entered the shadows. And it was dark enough that if she chose not to serve them, she could hide—a welcome comfort for a moonless night.

Jenny wasn't around. It wasn't as if they were close friends, but at least it was someone.

She kicked a crate upside down and sat on it. It was a slow night.

Possibly her customers had gone elsewhere. She should have been back the night before, but she didn't want to leave her sisters. Leaving them alone was difficult. Lying to them was harder. The fear of Maggie finding out was nearly unbearable.

Two more weeks.

Maggie had promised to keep the door locked, to answer it for no one. Still, Ione hadn't left the house until much later than usual. She took a slow breath. The evening was almost over. Then she would crawl in bed with her sisters for a couple of hours before getting her things together to offer her services as a seamstress.

She picked a string off the hem of her jacket. It was double-breasted. The buttons were fake brass, and showy, and harkened back to the days when she would sing for a living. But the costume had more fabric then. It had sleeves. She ran her hands down her bare arms. The thick, wet fog didn't make her any warmer.

The respectable part of her day had been successful. There was a stack of mending to tend to for one of her mother's old customers, and talk about a fall wardrobe for their youngest daughter. They wanted to see samples. Ione didn't have much to show, but it was something.

Ione had begun a list of needed supplies: thread, good needles, and fabric for patches. If they wanted her to make dresses, she would need some money up front. She hoped they would understand.

"Excuse me." The words slithered through the fog.

Ione jumped and turned. She hadn't heard anyone approach. No one had come under the streetlight.

"I apologize if I startled you." The voice was smooth, male, cultured.

"It's no trouble." Ione peered into the blackness.

A metal-tipped walking stick clicked against the pavement. It was slow, deliberate. Ione brought her hand to the back of her neck to rub the prickling hairs. She turned a full circle, trying to place the direction of his approach. Sound moved unpredictably in the echoing alley, and the mist concealed anything the dark didn't.

"Have I met you before?" Ione's voice, low and seductive, drew him out, gauging his distance and direction. The steady click was his answer. Her heartbeat roared in her ears.

"Who are you looking for?" Ione turned again. The smell of sandalwood filled her overwhelmed senses.

"Jenny isn't here tonight." She began to back up toward the fence.

"You'll do nicely." The voice came as a whisper from behind her. It sank in, and she froze. A finger stroked the outer edge of her ear. She turned around slowly.

"I've been waiting for you," he whispered, his voice low and gravely.

Ione swallowed and looked up, breathing a sigh of relief as she took in the quality of his clothes and his quiet demeanor.

He was tall and thin. His coat was cut perfectly. She calmed her breathing and raised her gaze up to meet his, giving time for her pulse to slow, and for her sultry mask to slide back into place.

He had just shaved. His nose was straight, and his cheekbones prominent. He reached up to remove his hat, and Ione flinched.

A slow smile worked its way across his thin lips and stopped there. Ione looked into his shaded eyes. They narrowed, and he reached, touching her face.

"What's your pleasure?" Ione used business-like tones, hoping to cool his heated demeanor. It was good for a man to want her; it meant she could charge more. It was dangerous for him to want her too much.

He studied her face, turning her chin left and right, tilting her head into the light. Ione felt as if she were standing on her grandmother's auction block. She swallowed against the rising bile. A strand of dark hair slipped onto his forehead. He released her, smoothing it back as he turned, placed his hat on the handle of his cane, and leaned it against the fence.

"Can't you guess why I'm here?" He still faced away.

Ione looked toward the lamppost. She didn't like him. She didn't like his look, or the sound of his voice. Another man would be a welcome interruption.

"It...it's getting late..." Ione focused on the light. "Maybe tomorrow..."

"I think"—he grabbed her by the hair and forced her to her knees—"tonight is just fine." His face only inches from hers, a drop of spittle flew from his mean mouth and landed on Ione's cheek. The weak light reflected off his silver buttons. Ione reached for them, wanting to get the experience over as fast as possible.

"Oh, sweet." He brushed her hands away, pulled her hair, and forced her chin up. "That's not what I came here for." A flash of steel drew her attention. "That's much too easy."

Ione pushed against his sinewy thighs. His muscles flickered repulsively under the fabric. She scrambled to get away, turning, feeling her hair let loose of its hold on her scalp. He dropped his knee into her back. She couldn't breathe. She flailed, face first in the concrete, the gravel and soot grinding into her skin.

"You needn't work so hard," he whispered from behind her, easily capturing both of her wrists in one of his cold hands. She felt his teeth scrape at her exposed shoulder. "I'm easy to please." His cajoling tone contrasted with the hard edge of steel that slowly slit the fabric of her bodice. She felt the cool metal travel up to caress the base of her throat.

"What do you think would happen if I nicked your skin right... here?"

Ione smelled blood. Felt it trickle down her shoulder. He pressed his knee in harder, and reached for her skirts.

Visions of her sisters floated into her consciousness. She turned her head and kicked against the concrete, opening her mouth to scream. Only a strangled whimper escaped her lips. She tried to suck in more air, but he dug his knee into her back—dug it in until her ribs cracked.

"That's not wise." He readjusted his position over her. The bite of the knife seared a path into her flesh. He removed it and brought the bloodied tip to her face.

He wiped it across her lips before slamming the handle into her skull.

Miriam pulled her cloak over her hair and eased outside. The fog had rolled in, thick. The warehouse and the cathedral existed only in the portions illuminated by the lamppost's circle of suspended light. Miriam imagined walking into the dark oblivion, wondered if the buildings would cease to exist. Even the typical shipyard sounds were condensed to nothingness.

She waited with her back against the brick warehouse wall. The fog floated in and out of the light in waves, the Virgin disappearing and reappearing dependent on the thickness of the mist.

Tonight she would walk the alley.

Miriam had considered it for days. It was a portion of the streets she hadn't wandered. It was dark, and the chances of meeting someone, remote. It was past the hour for the dark girl to go home. The white girl hadn't worked.

Miriam had heard the scream earlier in the week. The same scream that woke the watchful deacon. The white girl had since been missing. Miriam glanced up to the upper windows of the cathedral, but anything above the Savior's stained glass feet was eaten by the black fog.

The scream had almost changed her mind, but Miriam reasoned that the responsible party was long gone, and she needed to see the alley. Miriam couldn't paint the fear behind the white girl's eyes if she couldn't color it. And she couldn't paint her future if she didn't get the fear right. The white girl's tomorrows were still dark in Miriam's mind. Not the comforting dark, but the unknown kind. Fear against a soft, rotted fence colored differently than fear pressed up against a stone wall. If the trees overhung, then her face would be of a completely different palette. Nature buffered everything.

Miriam hoped, for the girl's sake, to find deep vines, with new-green sprouts, curling through a deteriorating wall. She hoped for lush weeds, thick with their own importance, and emboldened by brick-shielded roots. She prayed for redemption for the girl. She prayed to the God that shared a wall with the godless alley that the girl's future was an unexpected one, that when the colors came off her knife, they would be colors of hope, with deep strokes of healed pain, rather than the red blotches of persistent ruin. It was possible. Sometimes what sprouted was only a weed, but if weeds could grow, so could useful plants. But she had to see for herself. Tomorrow was the day her brush would slide against the girl's already finished portrait. Tomorrow she would cover last week's paint. Tomorrow, good or bad, it would be done.

Miriam kept to the shadows. She moved around the overgrown hedge and felt for the fence opposite the cathedral wall. She reached into the black, hands thrust ahead, taking small, stumbling steps.

Grainy wood planks jutted from the ground. Miriam walked a few feet, her fingers testing the raised grain. She turned and retraced her steps, running her other hand over in the same way. Sometimes things were different with a different hand. Back at the entrance, she turned again, reaching higher. Water dripped down, cool from the fog, and trailed to her wrist, where it wet the cuff of her sleeve. She reached higher, and leaves trembled and turned in to her palm.

Twenty steps, she rationed; if the leaves lasted for twenty steps, she could go home. Miriam's lips quivered up at the corners. If the leaves lasted for twenty steps, the girl would be more than fine.

Shades of blue the color of the sky filled her mind. *No*, she thought at step five, *lighter, like the country sky*. She counted. Step seven. Step eight. The color of the girl's complexion was losing its redness. Step seventeen. Miriam paused. The blotchiness would be gone. She pulled at the branches, still overhead, and plucked a handful of vibrating, tender green leaves. Her sleeve was wet to her elbow, but she breathed relief for the girl as the gathered mist rained down and rolled off her cape.

Step nineteen.

A hand closed around her ankle, tight.

"Help...please?" A soft, treble voice floated in the black.

Miriam ripped her ankle from the grasp and ran. She ran through the light, heedless of its implications. She hit her dark door and fumbled the keys. They jerked out of her grasp and fell into the night. Miriam let out a soft cry.

She dropped to her knees and plunged her hands into the puddles and filth until the keys rang against the bricks. Still kneeling, she reached above her head for the lock and pushed the key into place. The lock gave way, and she fell into the dusty threshold. She crawled in and kicked the door closed.

Miriam jumped up and ran toward the stairs. *Who was that?*

It wasn't the white girl. She hadn't gone into the alley, but Miriam hadn't seen anyone else.

Miriam had missed her. It was the dark woman, the one with the striped dress. She was the one Miriam had painted with a future of contentment, but had gotten it wrong. Miriam stopped. She'd been pacing. She forced herself to sit on the bottom step.

Who would help her? Miriam could send a message to someone tomorrow.

She might be dead by then.

Miriam rubbed her hands together to get the dirt off. Maybe she was really fine, and she planned to rob Miriam.

No. That kind of person was painted without color. Miriam knew she couldn't have been that wrong.

The deacon. Miriam could find him. She could knock on the door to the cathedral. But who would answer? How many would look at her? It had been so long since she'd spoken to anybody. How would she explain her presence in the alley?

She stood up, sat down, and stood again. She would have to go back in.

Miriam opened the door and listened. A train rumbled and groaned in the distance; water dripped. This time she didn't lock the door behind her. She followed the same path, straining to hear anything out of the ordinary. Slowing at step eighteen, she inched forward, holding her breath. Her foot rustled against the fabric of the woman's dress. Miriam dropped to her knees, searching for, and finding, one deathly still hand. Miriam held her breath and wrapped her warm fingers around the stranger's icy ones. She held them until the woman moaned and stirred.

Exhaling a prayer of relief, Miriam blindly forced her hands to follow the line of her bare arms and over her naked shoulders. She shuddered to feel the flesh under her fingers and drew her hand away when the blood-soaked cloth clung to her own palms.

"Take me with you. Please." The woman's breath puffed against the back of Miriam's hand. She grabbed a fistful of Miriam's skirt. Miriam wanted to scrub, to soak the filth of the alley away. "He might come back." The woman began trembling, hard.

"Who?" Miriam's voice sounded strange and loud in her own ears. She adjusted, quieting it. "Who might come back?"

The woman struggled to her knees. Miriam blindly felt for her waist and lifted her. The woman was even smaller than Miriam was. *Who would do such a thing?*

Miriam's breath came in short bursts of protective outrage. She heaved the woman's arm over her shoulders, supporting her with her own weight. A soft cracking noise filled the alley and Miriam felt unnatural movement from within the now whimpering woman's ribs. Anger held the nausea at bay.

"We'll get you to my house and get a doctor." Miriam had no idea how that would happen.

The woman made no further sounds. She dragged her feet step after agonizing step back toward the streetlamp, and into Miriam's warehouse home.

No one had come into the alley.

John watched for movement on the sidewalk in front of the church, squinting out the kitchen window. The fog made the morning sun almost too bright. The desolate sounds of trains rolling through the docks were liberally punctuated with horns. John was sure, in this soup, the conductors hadn't the slightest idea where the roads crossed the tracks. When the fog cleared, they would be clearing more than one vagrant victim.

He should be rejoicing. No one had come into the alley. But he wasn't.

Instead, he'd spent the night pulling bead after bead across the string. When he reached the end, he began again. Sometimes, with no words to pray, the rosary was the only option left, even for a soon-to-be priest.

Less than a month now until the bishop would give him his orders.

John sipped the black liquid. It burnt his tongue. He took another sip before setting it on the chipped cabinet.

There were stirrings in the rooms above. John moved the steaming pot off the stove and headed to the sacristy. The sacramental wine cabinet stood to one side, the bottle and chalice exactly where he had left it the day before. He unlocked it and pulled them from the shelf before glancing through an accidental opening in the heavy red velvet drape that separated the clergy from those who knelt in the pews. John pulled the edge over. A few in the congregation had already gathered. Most sat near the back. Three elderly women sat closer to the front, at respectable distances from one another.

The doors at the back of the sanctuary opened, and a small figure in a gray hooded cloak slid into the shadows. The wine John was holding dribbled down his hand. He let the curtain drop and set the chalice on the table.

Taking the stairs two at a time back down to the kitchen, he turned and followed the hall that led to the offices and entrance of the cathedral. At the door, he stopped and bent over, resting his hands on his knees, attempting to calm his breathing before he burst into the foyer of the church and startled an old lady.

It had to be her. No one else had a cape like hers, nor would they wear it so far over their face.

He knew he'd been up praying all night for a reason.

Chapter 5

She shouldn't have come.

Miriam huddled in the back of the sanctuary, watching the feet of those who passed by. How she'd thought she could ever get a message to the deacon, she had no idea.

She bunched up the fabric in her pockets to try to dry her sweaty palms. It was hot in the church, and her chest hurt. Maybe the girl would feel better after a bit of rest, she reasoned. Maybe it wasn't as bad as she had thought.

But Miriam knew better. The woman was broken, her face a mass of colors even Miriam couldn't have imagined. She drew her hands from her pockets and reached out to touch the bench in front of her. If she touched it, maybe she could sit in it. She turned to see if anyone was watching.

A black robe filled her line of vision. She tried to back up but was already pressed tight against a wall.

"I'm sorry." The robe took a step back. "My name is John."

Miriam nodded, her eyes still focused on the stone floor. There were nine blocks in the pattern, with the odd ones larger than the even ones. Or the even larger than the odd, depending on how you looked at them. She raised her glance far enough to see his face below his eyes. He was the man in the window.

"Is there something I can help you with?" John asked.

Miriam took a step to the side. "I don't need any help," she said to the stones on the floor. "There's someone in my house."

"A burglar? Are you in danger?" John looked around for someone he might call upon to fetch the police.

"No."

He brought his attention back to her tight face.

"There's someone else that needs help."

"Who?"

Miriam hadn't asked her name. She bit her bottom lip. She shouldn't have come.

"Do you know their name?"

"No."

"Are they hurt?"

Miriam nodded, and took a step sideways, toward the door.

John brought his hands together in front of him, as if he were about to gather a baby bird that had fallen out of its nest. He stepped to the side with her. The door opened for another parishioner to enter. He bent toward her and whispered, "Do I need to follow you?"

Miriam turned and ran.

Dodging wagons and pedestrians, he chased her across the street. He'd left the church without telling Father Ayers he was stepping out. He hoped he would understand.

"Is it one of our parishioners?" John asked, out of breath, as she paused in front of her door to insert the key into the lock. He knew she knew every member of his flock. He smiled at the thought. They were his flock.

"No, but you will recognize her."

The door flew open. He followed her to the left and up the stairs. John paused at the landing, surveying the warehouse floor below. "Does all of this belong to you?" There were tables and huge machines draped with shipping tarps. Chairs and stacks of boxes lined one wall as far as he could see.

"I suppose it does." Miriam didn't glance over her shoulder into the shadows. Instead, she turned the knob and pushed the door open.

John stepped into a world awash with color: textured fabrics, crystals that shattered into a thousand hues, and cushioned upholstery with competing patterns. Heavily framed works of art filled his senses. The four walls in the oddly shaped old office were painted, not different shades, but entirely different colors. The room smelled of tea leaves and simplicity. A small, ornately carved kitchen table stood against one wall, under a huge, industrial clock.

It was chaotic and beautiful. He swallowed. "What's your name?"

"Miriam." Her gray eyes darted to what he thought must be her places of comfort and then flickered up to meet his. Her name was Miriam. Not Mary, but he'd been close.

"Hazel," she said.

What?

"Your eyes are hazel. I didn't know what color they were."

She looked away at his confused expression. "Follow me."

He did. He followed her around the corner and into her bedroom. There was no door. But there was a woman tucked under a blanket, with her arms tight to her sides, as if she were a child.

"I had to cut off her clothes." Miriam apologized. "I couldn't tell where all the blood was coming from."

John crossed to the side of the bed. The woman's chest moved in an irregular pattern, her breathing labored. It was the dark-skinned woman from the alley.

"I don't know a doctor," Miriam explained, holding her hands out and then quickly dropping them to her side.

The woman's face was swollen to nearly twice its normal size. Her shoulder rested at an odd angle from her body. Dark blood oozed from nicks and scrapes and from one disturbingly even gash near her collar bone.

"Do you know her name?" Miriam asked.

John shook his head.

"Can you get a doctor?"

She was the size of a child. From his window view, she hadn't seemed so delicate. "How did you find her?" He was still unable to take his eyes from her limp body.

"I walked in the alley." Guilt hovered over her words.

John turned and watched her face until she looked up at him and met his eyes. "Thank God you did."

"Can you get a doctor?" Miriam asked again.

"Of course. Will you be fine here until I return?"

Miriam nodded and reached into the basin she'd left next to the bed. She pulled a washcloth from the water and wrung it out.

"I'll be back as fast as I can."

John darted through the traffic back to the cathedral. He grabbed his robes and took the stone steps two at a time.

Her eyes were gray.

The mass was nearing completion. John sat in the last pew and tried to quiet his breathing. For once, he was glad there weren't many parishioners at the morning mass. Father Ayers made eye contact with John just before the prayer. John slipped into the doors at the offices and made his way back to the sacristy.

"What happened?" The elder priest lifted the stole off his neck, kissed it, and folded it neatly on the table.

"I'm sorry I wasn't here. I really can't explain right now, but I need to find a doctor."

Father Ayers stopped and turned, his eyebrows drawn together with concern. "Who is ill?"

"It's one of the women from the alley."

"Where is she?" He looked around as if he might find her hiding behind John.

"She's in Miriam's house. I know you must have a number of questions, but I really have to find a doctor right away. She's hurt, badly." John began unfastening his own robe.

"I'm sorry. Of course." He pushed past John and started for his office. "I'll give you a name, and I'll write down where to find him."

John followed his elder into the wood-paneled room filled with stacks upon stacks of books. His desk was smaller than John would have anticipated, but the man struck him as more of a reader than a writer anyway.

Father Ayers pulled a piece of paper from his desk and scrawled a hasty note. He folded it over. On the front he wrote the name Dr. Samuel Pierce. Holding it out to John, he explained where to find the doctor.

"He works in an office attached to his house. It's a modest house, but the doctor is good, and he will not care what the girl's situation is. He will take care of her, no matter what the cause of her needs. He's a good man. Perhaps one of the best I know." Father Ayers half-smiled. "In fact, if you could figure out how to convert him, he might be nearly perfect."

"Thank you." John took the note and backed out of the room, tucking it into his pocket. "I'll return as soon as I can and explain as much as I know."

Father Ayers nodded and waved him out of his office.

The doctor's home was a small stone townhouse with a short wrought-iron gate. He opened the gate, and stepped onto the cobbled path. The door to the main house was straight up a flight of stairs. Instead, he followed the path to the right, to another door with a glass panel, with DOCTOR lettered in gold. A faded green shade was rolled up, its string hanging still in the window. A carved wood sign next to the door read, MY GRACE IS SUFFICIENT FOR THEE: FOR MY STRENGTH IS MADE PERFECT IN WEAKNESS.

John knocked on the door and turned the knob, stepping into the office to the light sound of a ringing bell. It hung overhead, like the bells in the grocer's. John smiled to himself.

A trim man sat behind a cluttered desk. His spectacles rested on the very tip of his nose, and when he looked up, they dropped off and hung from a small chain. His vest was buttoned, but his sleeves were rolled up to his elbows.

"How can I help you?"

"My name is John." He took a few steps forward to stand in front of the desk. "If you are Dr. Pierce, then I need to ask for your assistance." John pulled Father Ayers's note out of his pocket. "I was sent to you by Father Ayers." He handed over the slip of paper.

"Well, you're in the right place." Dr. Pierce smiled and opened the letter, taking time to read it in its entirety. His gray eyebrows lowered, and he looked up. "It sounds like this is urgent?"

"Yes, very urgent."

"You can tell me on the way."

The doctor stood up and crossed to what looked like a closet door. He opened it, revealing a set of stairs.

"Eliza?" he called. "I have to go out for a while."

A female voice answered as the doctor shrugged on his jacket and gathered a few of his necessities in his brown leather bag.

"How did you get here?"

"I ran."

"What do you say we take my carriage?"

"I wouldn't argue with you."

Chapter 6

John led Dr. Pierce to the warehouse door. In the carriage, he'd explained as much as he could about the situation, and told the doctor the little he knew about Miriam, but John knew no amount of description could begin to offer a picture of the strange contrast of care and neglect that made up Miriam's world. His concern was unnecessary, however, as the doctor marched through the dust and dark, up the staircase, through the lush living room, and back to the bedroom as if nothing were out of the ordinary.

"Would you please move the basin of water?" he asked a surprised Miriam, never taking his eyes off his patient. She complied. He placed his bag on the nightstand and unbuckled the straps.

"When did this happen?"

Miriam looked at John, and he nodded for her to answer. "Last night."

"Do you know when last night?" He pulled a stethoscope and inserted it into his ears. "Where are her clothes?"

"I'm sorry. I cut them off so I could see where the blood was coming from."

The doctor paused at her apologetic tone. "It's fine you did that." He looked back to the patient and listened to her heart through the sheet. "You did the right thing. When was it that you found her?"

"Around four or five in the morning."

"Where was she?"

"Lying in the alley."

The doctor held up a finger to communicate he needed silence. He moved the stethoscope from one side to the other, his eyebrows bunched together in concentration.

"She's lost quite a bit of blood. I need to examine her."

"I'll step out. Is there anything I can get?" John asked.

"No, it appears I have everything here." The doctor glanced up. "Miriam? Would you mind staying to assist?"

"I can stay," she whispered, locking eyes with John. He mouthed he was sorry, and then ducked out of the room, feeling that he had broken some kind of trust by telling Dr. Pierce her name.

The doctor began at the top of her head.

He pulled pin after pin from her hair and untied the ribbon that secured it. "I'm going to lift her head. Can you pull everything out from underneath her, and put a fresh towel down?"

Miriam pulled another towel off the pile she'd left in the room. She shook it out and set it on the bed.

The doctor lifted, and Miriam pulled everything away before flattening the clean towel beneath her. She gathered the dirty linens in a ball and placed them in a nearby basket.

Dr. Pierce began feeling her scalp for the place that still seemed to be seeping blood.

"Here it is." He knelt on the floor next to the bed. "She's going to need a couple of stitches behind her right ear."

He turned her face slightly toward his and frowned, recognition in his expression. "Would you hand me that washcloth, please?"

Miriam wrung it out and placed it in his hand. Gently, he washed the dried blood from her closed eyes. The brown water made small rivulets down her childlike face and into her ears. Miriam wanted to get a dry cloth and wipe it away. She wanted to wipe it all away. He examined the side of her face with the most significant swelling, being careful to avoid the bruises. He wiped the soot and blood from her lips and chin, all the time studying her features.

"I think she'll need stitches here too." Miriam pulled back the top of the sheet.

The doctor's face darkened at the long, smooth cut. He took the sheet from Miriam and covered her back up. "Would you please tell John I'd like to see him for a moment?"

Miriam nodded and stepped out of the room. John sat at her kitchen table, reading her paper. The folds would never be right, and for a moment, Miriam let herself enjoy the familiar panic over the problem of what to do with a paper that may not be able to sit perfectly on the stack with the others.

John looked up.

Miriam smoothed the front of her wrinkled skirt. "The doctor wants to see you."

The knock at the door startled Maggie. She hurried to the window.

They'd waited for Ione all morning. She hadn't come home.

Instead, a woman she'd never met stood at the door, balancing a covered cooking pot. A basket hung over her forearm. Her skin was a few shades lighter than Maggie's, and she had good hair. It was pulled back tight and straight, with just a few hot-comb curls hanging down. She nodded to Maggie in the window.

Maggie hesitated, her hand on the knob. Ione had told her not to answer the door for anyone, but the woman had already seen her, and, Maggie considered, she might have news about Ione. She slid the latch over.

"Hi, sweetie." The woman elbowed her way through the door. She crossed the room and set the pot on the table. Lucy watched from the bed, where she'd stayed busy braiding and unbraiding her doll's yarn hair for most of the day.

"Aren't you cute?" the woman said, noticing Lucy.

She turned back to the table and wiped her hands on her apron before pulling the cover off the steaming pot. The aroma of tender beef, potatoes, onions, and carrots filled the room. Maggie's stomach growled.

"You must be Maggie. I'm Mrs. Whitaker," she said, smiling.

Maggie nodded. "How do you know us?"

"My husband is the reverend at the church just down the way." The woman pointed in a general direction, and Maggie nodded as if she knew what she was talking about. The woman quieted her substantial voice. "He was the one who came with the doctor a few days ago."

"He was nice." Lucy had walked up behind the woman, undoubtedly drawn by the smell of luxury. Maggie held out her hand and Lucy came around to stand behind her, where she belonged.

"I wanted to say we're sorry for your loss. Well, that, and to drop off a dinner for you."

"Thank you," Maggie said, disappointed that there was no news of Ione.

"Did Ione send you?" Lucy asked before Maggie could distract her.

"No, dear, she didn't." Mrs. Whitaker turned a questioning gaze toward Maggie.

"She's just a bit late." Maggie pointed Lucy back in the direction of her doll. "We expect her home any moment."

"Well, in that case, I'll leave you two to prepare the table for your sister." Mrs. Whitaker turned to leave, pausing at the door. "You girls are always welcome at the church, you know that, right?"

Maggie and Lucy nodded in unison.

"And I live right next door to the church. If you need anything, you know you can stop by." She waited for their affirmative nods before pulling it open.

She gathered her long, plaid skirt to keep it up out of the muddy path. "I'll stop by tomorrow night." She turned back for a moment. "I'll get my pot and bring you another dinner. Will that be satisfactory?"

"Maybe you can meet Ione, too." Maggie looked up to the darkening skies.

"Yes, child. That would be nice." She took a few steps away and turned back again. "I'll be praying for you."

Maggie closed the door. "Thank you," she whispered under her breath.

"And we should pray for Ione," Lucy added, already back at the table, setting it for three.

Chapter 7

John sat in the chair next to the detective's desk. A man sat near him, slumped over and snoring. His leg was bent awkwardly, and he was blocking the aisle. Everyone who needed to pass the desk did so by brushing up against John. The officer facing the man, presumably tired of the man's drunken, open-mouthed breath, called one of the junior officers over to drag him back to a cell to sober up. The man woke enough to get one foot in front of the other, but not enough to avoid tripping over the leg of the next man he passed. Eventually the officer dragged him, smiling, out of the room.

The desks were crammed together in an odd-shaped room full of paper and smoke and straight-backed chairs occupied by either perpetrators or victims. Discerning the difference was far less simple than John thought it should be. It was almost as difficult as thinking of the reasoning behind the five, faded green walls of differing lengths. Water stains leached from the ceiling, scuff marks bordered the floor, and between the two, a chair rail of dirty body grease waved around the room.

Half of a tin can sat on the detective's desk, inches from John's arm. A soggy cigar hung from the sharp edge. The detective reached for and found it without taking his eyes off his paperwork. He brought the wet end to his loose lips and played with it for a while before sucking on it. He looked up.

"So, you say there's a woman got stabbed last night?"

John crossed one ankle over his knee and leaned forward, relieved to have a question to answer. "Yes."

"And, how did you find her?"

"Like I said before, a woman who lives across the street from the cathedral found her."

"And she came to get you?"

"Yes." John uncrossed his legs and looked around the room. There was no one else to talk to. Everyone in uniform was either similarly occupied or didn't have the look of one who would welcome a conversation. When the doctor said someone needed to see to the sisters, and someone else needed to get to the police, he should have chosen looking after the sisters.

"And what is this woman's name?"

"Miriam."

"Miriam...?"

"I don't know her last name."

The detective lifted the top sheet of paper on the pad and wrote a note on the page beneath before concealing it again with the first page. He brought his hand up to his mouth and pulled the cigar from his fleshy lips. It stuck to them, until he dislodged it and dropped it back into the can. He sat back in his chair and tapped his pen on the worn wooden surface of his desk.

"You don't know her name," he repeated.

John closed his eyes briefly, reminding himself he was wearing his robes. "I don't know her name, but look, if you can send someone with me, maybe she will be awake, and you can get the information directly from her."

"So the woman who found the victim is sleeping?"

"No. The woman who is hurt might be awake. She's at Miriam's house. Miriam found her." John looked around for a clock but couldn't find one anywhere.

"Why don't you give me a description of the victim?"

"She's small. She's a negro woman..."

The detective looked up. "What did you say she was doing out at four o'clock in the morning?"

John shifted in his chair, putting both feet back on the floor. "I've never seen exactly what she does." He stared at his shoes before meeting the detective's small, blue gaze.

The detective grunted, coughed, and tapped loudly on the desk with an unusually large index finger. "And what was the other woman doing out at four o'clock in the morning?"

"I think she said she found her a bit later."

"What was she doing when she found her?"

"Walking?" John examined the stained floor.

The detective flipped the paper up again to write something. "And no one saw who stabbed her?"

"No."

"How do you know she didn't just fall on something?"

"Because she looks like she got hit by a train." John's voice rose in frustration.

The detective's eyebrows lifted sardonically.

"Are you going to send someone or not?"

"Of course we will. Why don't you leave me the address of 'Miriam's' house, and we will get there when we can."

The officer pushed a blank scrap of paper across the desk. John scribbled down the address of the warehouse and stood to leave. The other officers looked up from their desks. No one else paid any attention at all.

John began to pick his way through the mass of people while the detective handed the file off to another officer at the next desk over.

"A whore got herself a bit roughed up...probably another one found her." The detective leaned back. "Send one of the rookies." He picked up the soggy cigar and tapped a bit of ash off the end.

John watched the other officer drop the file into the bottom drawer of his desk and, loudly enough for John to hear, say, "Priest must be new. He'll learn like everyone else does."

John ducked out. He kicked at the accumulated grime at the curb, dropping chunks of dirt and animal feces into the collection of garbage floating by. It all traveled by gutter to the lake. The smell of dead fish clogged the air, but no one noticed anymore. John wondered how much garbage could collect in one place before the consequences made inaction impossible. He turned back toward the cathedral, and back to Miriam.

They were on their own.

Before he'd left, the doctor had said she had sisters. Miriam paced outside the opening to the room where Ione lay. At each left turn, she glanced in, checking for any changes.

Dr. Pierce said she'd be fine; she didn't need to visit the hospital.

She still slept. She'd slept through the stitches, and if she woke, he instructed Miriam to give her the sleeping powder.

"Make sure she knows her sisters will be taken care of," he'd said as he gathered his instruments and placed them in his bag.

Miriam paced to her father's bedroom. She cracked open the door. It squealed on its hinges.

A massive four-poster bed dominated the otherwise industrial room. Closed curtains hung in the windows overlooking the warehouse floor. There were no outside windows, and only shadows seeped in from the hallway. Miriam wondered if she should lock the door, in case someone tried to come in, but satisfied herself with closing it and listening to the latch fall. She opened the door and closed it again for good measure.

She couldn't sleep in there.

She slid past her room, back to the living room and kitchen. She sat at the table. John had left the paper in a bunch, but Miriam had been able to fold it as it should have been. She ran her fingers over the smooth fold, and then opened it again, this time reading headlines. At the bottom of page four there was a mention of a missing prostitute. No one had seen her for two weeks. Her friends reported her disappearance to the police. They were investigating.

Miriam hoped Ione remembered something.

Before it had gotten dark, after the doctor left, Miriam had watched for the white girl. But she never came. She hadn't come to the alley for days.

Miriam stood and placed her teapot on the stove. She pulled her cup and saucer from the shelf over the sink and lined them up on the counter next to three sugar cubes. Her father had insisted on only two.

They were always taking bodies from the lake. Miriam wondered what they did if they were too decomposed, if they came out in pieces.

A slow tap began. Miriam walked back to her room, but Ione was still sleeping. The tap became insistent. It was coming from the living room window, high above the level of the street.

She sat on the kitchen chair and counted the taps. Seven, eight, nine. She lined up more sugar cubes from the bowl. Suddenly, a handful of whatever was hitting her window cascaded all at once.

She paced, her hands clenched in front of her.

A woman slept in her bed. In her bed. She might be dead in the morning, with a bloated face and open mouth. What if that man returned to finish what he started? Miriam bit her hand, grabbed a knife, and walked to the window. If he was back, he wouldn't get far, at least not without some injuries of his own.

John stood waving in the light of the streetlamp. He pointed to her door. He wanted in.

After dinner, Maggie had washed the dishes and swept the floor, although it wasn't really dirty. She put the clean lid on the pot and folded the dishcloth over the edge of the table.

Lucy slept in their bed. Maggie had promised she would come to bed too, but Ione still wasn't home, and the cathedral's clock had struck ten.

Maggie picked up a man's shirt out of the mending basket. She knew she should wait for Ione. Her stitches weren't as good as Ione's. But the shirts were supposed to be done by the end of the week, and they still had to be laundered.

The nausea Maggie had fought for most of the day threatened to send her to the bucket. She set the shirt down and rested her head on her knees. Maybe Ione had gone back with that man Mama hated.

Maggie sat up and pulled an apron from the basket. It was white, with tiny navy pin-stripes. She brought the ruffled edge to her nose and breathed her mother's fading scent. Slipping it over her shoulders, she wrapped the straps around her back. She tied it in front, and then let her face fall into her lap. Her mother's hand should be stroking her hair, whispering that everything was all right, and telling her she needed her sleep if she was going to do well in school. Maggie breathed deeply. Her mother's scent wouldn't be there forever.

A knock startled her to standing.

She wiped her face on the apron and ran to the door to meet Ione, almost tripping on the length of the fabric.

"Hi, Maggie." The doctor stood on the threshold. His hat was in his hands. "May we come in?"

"Where's Ione?"

"She's fine, but she's not going to be coming home for a while. Is it all right if we talk inside?"

Maggie stepped back to allow the doctor in. He was followed by Mrs. Whitaker and her husband, the minister. The minister was the same man who had said words for her mother. He was young, with no hair, dark skin, and the whitest of white collars. Maggie had a hole in her stocking. She could feel the worn wood floor under her big toe.

"Where's Ione?" She asked again, searching for clues in each of their faces.

Mrs. Whitaker looked down to the floor to where Maggie's mother's apron hung in a pool at her feet, and then glanced at her husband. Maggie pulled at the string of the knot she had tied.

"Your sister was hurt," the doctor began. "She's staying at a woman's house near the cathedral. She won't be able to come home for some time."

Maggie struggled with the knot, her fingers fumbling with the tight fabric. "What do you mean?" She began to pull the strings up, in hopes of slipping one of her slim arms through the waist. "How could she be hurt? She was fine." Maggie looked at Mrs. Whitaker, not even bothering to wipe away the exasperated tear that had traveled to her chin.

"Let me help you." Mrs. Whitaker gestured to the apron.

Maggie stepped back until she could feel the table pressing into her thighs.

"Will you let me help you?" She took a step closer and cautiously reached for the knotted material. "Was this your mother's apron?"

Maggie nodded.

Mrs. Whitaker sat on the chair next to Maggie and worked at the knot.

"Maggie." The doctor took a step nearer. "We think the two of you should not stay here alone."

"But I have to be here when Ione gets back. I can't leave. And we have school."

Mrs. Whitaker's thin fingers found a loop in the fabric, and she drew one end through the knot. "We thought, perhaps you would stay with us?"

Maggie looked down at the woman's perfectly smooth hair and her crisp jacket. She and Lucy only had a couple of dresses, and they weren't even clean. "I don't think that's a good idea. We wouldn't want to be a bother. We'll be fine for a few days. We even have money for food, and I think the rent is already paid for this week."

Mrs. Whitaker helped Maggie shrug out of the apron. She folded it in a perfect square and set it on the counter.

"Besides." Maggie reached for a basket of shirts. "I need to mend these. Ione will be surprised when she comes home." She smiled too brightly.

"It's going to be more than a few days," the minister said. He looked at his wife before finishing his thought. "I'm sure Mrs. Whitaker would love to help you with your duties."

"Yes. Very much so." Mrs. Whittaker glanced over to where Lucy slept.

"What about our house? Someone needs to be here." Maggie picked up the drying dishcloth and folded it over again. "How long will Ione be sick?"

"She will have to be in bed at least for a few weeks."

"A few weeks? Where is she?" Maggie walked the few steps to the door and shoved her foot in one of her shoes. She blindly hooked the buttons that ran up the side, her eyes, instead, on the doctor. "I want to see her."

"You can't see her now. She's resting."

"I don't care. I want to see her. Where is she?"

Dr. Pierce took a step toward Maggie. Mrs. Whitaker stopped him with a light touch on his arm. Instead, she knelt near her, took the button hook, and began fastening the black nubs of leather.

"You know," she said. "It really is too late to go tonight. We don't want to be walking around in the dark. But, if you come with us, we can talk about it in the morning before school." She pulled the hook from the last hole, stood, and held out her hand. Maggie grasped it. Mrs. Whitaker's skin was smooth. Not like her mama's.

"Won't we be a bother?" Maggie asked without meeting her eyes. "How will you have room for us?"

"Our house isn't big. You and Lucy will need to share a bed. But we don't have any children of our own, and I would be grateful for your company."

The minister cleared his throat. "We should probably get

going."

Maggie conceded. A few weeks meant there were no other options. She walked over to the foot of the bed and pulled a carpet bag from underneath it.

Dr. Pierce wrapped the quilt around Lucy and picked her up to carry her to his carriage. She moaned at the intrusion on her sleep but quickly adjusted to his warmth and tucked her forehead into the crook of his neck.

"Why don't you help Dr. Pierce?" Mrs. Whitaker suggested to her husband. "I'll help Maggie gather her things."

The minister walked out of the room, and Maggie tried not to watch the beautiful woman fold her dirty things before carefully stacking them into her bag.

Chapter 8

"How is she?"

"I don't know. She's the same." Miriam crossed to the kitchen counter and, with her back to John, dropped sugar cubes from the table into a porcelain dish one at a time.

"Sorry about throwing rocks at your window. I didn't know how else to get your attention."

"There isn't another way. There used to be a bell at the warehouse door, but I had it removed because the neighborhood kids liked to ring it and then run away."

"How are you?" John asked, softening his tone. Miriam turned. She shrugged. "Do you think she will be here long?"

"What did the doctor say?"

Ignoring his question, she moved past him, back toward the window he had just harassed with the rocks. She craned her neck to see if anyone was walking down the street. "Have you seen the other girl?"

He joined her at the window, leaving space between them, and looked to the lamppost. It was a clear night; even the gas flame was visible, flickering against the heavy glass. From her windows, the statue of the Virgin looked new, the cracks and pitting invisible.

"No. Not for a while." What use had he been?

"Page four of the paper said another girl is missing. I wish one of us would have seen the man responsible for hurting Ione."

John bent to sit in an upholstered chair but stopped at the sound of Miriam's sharp intake of breath. He paused there, half sitting, half standing. "Um...may I sit?"

She pointed to a different chair, offering no explanation.

He slid over to the next chair. "Will you sit?"

Miriam found a chair and sat on the very edge of the seat. She studied her hands clasped in her lap. Her skirts wavered with each small bounce of her knees.

"I don't think the police will be coming." John decided to get all the bad news out at once.

Miriam sighed, looking relieved.

He looked so uncomfortable. That wasn't her intention. There was a woman in her bed, and he'd almost sat in her father's chair, and all the conversations of the day were echoing around in her mind. She wanted him to leave, to take his hat and his big shoes, and remove himself from her space, and then she could decide what to do with Ione. Ione was a woman. And a woman in her home was tolerable.

"Didn't they believe you?" Miriam made an attempt to continue the conversation.

"Not really." John sat back and glanced toward the dark windows.

Miriam understood. She was a single woman who had found another single woman in the streets. Miriam was surprised the doctor had even suggested someone report it to the police. But men were men, and when problems landed in their lap, they tried to fix them. The problem was they expected others to respond in the same way. Women knew better. They knew their own interest didn't necessarily translate into an interest on the part of the other party, especially if that other party was the Chicago police.

John was sitting with his hat in his hands. He hadn't taken off his jacket. He had a day's growth of beard. He probably had a day's worth of work still sitting on his desk across the street.

"It's fine." Miriam said. "We'll be fine. You can go home if you like." The lamplight picked up the brown flecks in his hazel eyes. He really wasn't so bad.

He did take up a lot of room. His legs seemed to stretch halfway across the room when he sat. His large hands stayed relaxed on his knees, though, and Miriam had a difficult time finding a reason not to enjoy his presence in her home. His portrait leaned on an easel in the room just beyond the room where Ione slept. When he left, she would change the background color in his portrait to brown. It would be more truthful. He still stood against the dark, but he did more than stand against it, he changed it somehow. Miriam wouldn't be able to sleep anyway.

"Are you certain you don't need me to stay?" John paused and cleared his throat. "Or, if you prefer, I could send one of the nuns here to sit with Ione."

Miriam envisioned a snoring old woman propped up in the chair in her bedroom.

"I don't think I need anyone else here."

John studied the patterned carpet and then lifted his head. "May I check on you tomorrow?"

Miriam hesitated. It hadn't occurred to her that he wouldn't.

"I'll need some supplies delivered tomorrow. Do you think you might send someone?" Miriam stood. John followed suit, and she followed him to the door.

"Yes, I can send someone." His eyebrows furrowed and he looked at his hand on the knob. He was disappointed. A slow flush began at her chest and worked its way to her face. He was lonely.

He led the way down the stairs, unlocked the door, and stepped into the street.

"If you want to come back to check her, you may." Miriam made the offer without meeting his gaze.

"Thank you. I will."

Chapter 9

Muffled conversation hovered in the room. Ione staggered toward consciousness, noticing first the hum of a man's voice. The red of her closed eyelids followed, and finally the throbbing of her own body. It was the sun on her face that heaved her out of her dark dreams. It was morning. Her sisters were alone.

She pushed against the seducing warmth, only to be met with searing pain in her shoulder and the beckoning dark.

The voices again. This time, Ione didn't try to move. She cracked one eye open to a white ceiling. The sun was no longer on her face, but the room was still bright. Her sisters were still alone. She had slept again.

A woman's voice slid through the haze. "You were hurt."

Ione tried to speak, but only animal noises escaped. She tried to move, but her body didn't respond. She felt one tear slip down her cheek. Her sisters were alone. How long had they been alone?

A small hand reached behind her neck and gingerly lifted her head. "Take a drink," the voice said.

Cool water found its way between her lips. Ione sputtered to swallow it.

"Go slowly. It's been a couple of days."

Ione lifted her hand to fight the warm heaviness of the quilt. Stinging pain tingled down her arm. She clenched her swollen fist. She had to go. There wasn't even enough food for them for two days. Another tear slipped down a path to her ear and settled there. She pushed her eyes open again and moaned when the small hands brought the sheet up to cover her. A woman with large gray eyes hovered, settling her into the softness.

"It's fine. Everything will be fine. We've collected your sisters, and they're safe. They were alone for only a day."

Ione sunk back into the pillow. She heard herself crying but somehow floated above the emotion until the sweet dark took her down again.

Miriam stood in front of Ione's portrait; her pallet of paints balanced in her left hand, the knife in her right. She brought more brown into the humble green and added a blinding dab of white. She mixed it quickly to hide its brilliance so it wouldn't throw off the image that swam just out of reach. Ione's stoic face gazed back from the canvas. It was pleasant to know her name. Miriam dabbed the tip of her brush into the paint and touched her dark iris with the honey. There was truth in her serene expression. A depth that needed enhancing.

The dress Miriam had cut off Ione hung over the back of a nearby chair. Satin stripes in bright colors, no sleeves, and a scooping neckline all evidenced Ione's profession. Miriam's portrait of her, the future she'd painted, displayed her wearing a deep navy suit. The heavy fabric had come off Miriam's brush in velvety textures. She'd painted Ione's hair pulled back off her face. Ione's eyebrows were higher near her nose, and only slightly arched. The shape gave the impression that she was alert. The slight pull at her cheekbones spoke of intelligence.

Miriam dropped her brush into the turpentine and walked to the window overlooking the cathedral's entrance. People came and went, and when a face wouldn't leave her mind, she put it on canvas. And always, always, she repainted. Then she watched again, until they became the person her brush predicted. She was never wrong—except for Ione.

The prostitute lay beaten and stabbed in Miriam's own bed, yet she couldn't bring herself to correct the painting. Every touch of her brush on the canvas only made Ione stronger, more determined. When Miriam tried to bare her arms, the texture of the fabric just deepened. When she tried to add the unnatural color to her cheeks, the shading only made her wiser.

Miriam rubbed her hands on her apron and untied the knot at her back. Looping it over the hook next to her door, she walked

out of her studio and into her bedroom to stand by Ione and wait for her to wake.

John watched the alley again. He'd still not seen the white girl. If Ione were awake, he could ask her if she knew the girl's name.

He'd spent most of the day inundating Miriam with his presence. She tolerated him well, better than he'd anticipated. She was isolated, yes, and nervous, absolutely, but not afraid. In fact, as John thought back to the night she'd retrieved Ione from the alley, he suspected her overwhelming curiosity had somehow, for that moment, squelched her capacity to fear.

And it was her curiosity that drove her. She didn't like to go out in the day, but she read the paper, cover to cover, and knew exactly who was doing what, and to whom. Every afternoon, she stood like a sentry at the window, and she knew most of the children by the names they shouted to each other. The boy who delivered her groceries regularly exchanged books for her from the lending library. For a life so cloistered, John didn't doubt that, with only a few hiccups, she could easily pick back up in society where her father's fortune dictated she should be.

Not that she'd expressed any interest in doing so. On the contrary, her first reaction to finding humanity had invaded her apartment was to try to arrange for its removal. But she wasn't unrealistic, nor was she selfish. She'd adjusted admirably to the intrusion.

It was getting darker by the minute. Since the attack, John had slept only fitfully, and woken damp and cold with the fog as it rolled into his open window. He couldn't close it, though. He wouldn't miss another attack.

Maybe Ione had woken up. Maybe Miriam sat next to her bed and spooned broth into her mouth. John leaned out the window, looking for signs of life in Miriam's apartment. Lights were still on, and a shadow traveled behind the curtain. It lifted, and suddenly Miriam stood there in the lamp's halo, looking directly at him. Caught, he smiled a tight-lipped smile and brought his hand up in half a wave. Miriam waved him over, and a corresponding rush of heat settled into his chest. John thought it best not to scrutinize the feeling. Instead he reached out and pulled the window closed. Maybe Ione had woken. Maybe she could tell him about the other girl.

"How long have I been sleeping?" Ione asked, after sipping water from the glass Miriam held. John watched, leaning in the open doorway. Ione tried to shrug her bare shoulders further under the blankets. Miriam helped, pulling the quilt back up to Ione's chin. For a deacon, John seemed to be a bit out of touch. Miriam shot him a look. He just furrowed his eyebrows in a questioning half-response.

"For a few days." Miriam set the glass down on the bedside table. "Can you remember anything?"

"Not much. I remember leaving my sisters, and checking twice to make sure Maggie locked the door behind me. You said they were staying with the pastor and his wife?"

"Yes, and from what Dr. Pierce has told me, they are having a wonderful time."

"Maggie will be worried." Ione looked at John. He kicked up from his leaning position and took a step nearer. "I don't want them to see me like this."

"Of course not." Miriam shook her head. If there was anything she felt strongly about, it was letting children be children for as long as possible.

John stepped into the room. "Do you remember anything more from that night?"

"I remember thinking it was time to leave. Being glad it had been a slow night." Ione closed her eyes, a blush rising to pigment the skin around her bruises. "It's not like I wanted to..." Ione blinked quickly and avoided Miriam and John's eyes. "It was only going to be for a couple more weeks." She pulled the blanket tight to her chin. "Now I'm not even sure where the mending is I was supposed to finish."

"From what I understand, Mrs. Whitaker helped Maggie sew and wash the shirts. I think they delivered them yesterday."

Miriam smiled at Ione's surprised expression.

"But how did I get here? You live in the warehouse, right? Am I in the warehouse?"

Miriam nodded.

"How did you find me?"

"I was walking, and I thought it was too late for anyone to be in the alley..."

"Do you remember who did this to you?" John pulled a chair to the bedside and sat, elbows on knees and hands clasped in front.

"No."

"Was he old or young? Maybe he was tall?"

"I remember being pressed to the ground." Ione reached up to lightly touch the scrapes on her face.

"Did he say anything?"

Ione met John's eyes, apology in hers. "I don't remember."

"Did he—"

"Maybe she'd like to rest a bit." Miriam rose, interrupting the interrogation.

John nodded and stood, pushing the chair back to its proper place. Miriam ushered him toward the door. He looked back.

"Do you know the other girl who usually, um, waits in the alley?"

"That's Jenny, but I didn't see her that night."

"She hasn't been there at all in the last week," John added.

"Jenny's never gone." Ione studied the lace edge on the soft blue sheet. "Her father wouldn't let her miss a night, let alone a week."

"Do you think she moved on? To another place?"

"She only stays by the cathedral. She says the statue of Mary protects her..." She met John's eyes for a moment before dropping her gaze back down. "...and if Mary won't, then she thinks you will."

Miriam gestured for John to leave and walked back to Ione's side. She shook out another blanket and laid it across her legs. "Do you need anything else?"

"Thank you." Ione reached out and touched Miriam's hand.

Miriam drew it back quickly, the contact surprising her. She turned toward the basin of water to wash.

"I'm sorry." Ione looked away.

Miriam stopped before her fingertips touched the water. She dropped her hands back to her side, shamed by Ione's interpretation of her actions.

Gingerly, she sat on the edge of the bed. "No." She paused and examined the place on the back of her hand that Ione had touched. "I'm sorry." Then, as if from very far away, Miriam reached out and covered Ione's hand with her own and discovered the dry warm texture of her skin. "I haven't been around people much," Miriam whispered. "I'm not really used to...people."

Ione studied the space occupied by their hands. Slowly, she turned her hand under Miriam's and closed her fingers. "It's fine," she said. "I don't always like to be touched either."

They sat together until Ione broke the silence. "Jenny lives in one of the rooms above the Red Tavern on Halsted."

Chapter 10

John didn't like the street, let alone the tavern.

He stepped off the plank path and into the dried mud and horse manure. A solitary man at the door sat with his arms crossed, his chin tucked into his chest, and his hat pulled over his eyes. He rested, either sleeping or awake, snoring loudly, and propped on the two back legs of his chair.

Stale beer oozed from the dark interior. John took a shallow breath and made his way inside.

"I'm looking for a girl named Jenny," he confessed in hushed tones to the beefy barkeep.

The man looked up with raised brows. "Sure, Father, whatever you need, but Jenny ain't seein' no one right now."

"Is she here?"

"I said she ain't takin' no customers." He plunged a wet towel into a bucket of gray water and wiped down the counter. John backed up to avoid the sloppy splash.

He lowered his voice. "I'm not here to see her," he tried to explain. "I just want to *see* her—see if she's hurt."

The barkeep measured him for an inordinate amount of time.

"Is she here, or what?" John allowed a testy edge to shade his tone, gambling on the mix of it and his robe to garner him some authority.

"She's here," he admitted. "But she ain't so good. She got herself roughed up pretty bad the other night."

"Where is she?" John felt sick. She'd counted on him, depended on their walls to keep her safe.

"Her da ain't gonna like it much if I let you in her room."

John just stared at the big man.

"But I suppose, if you keep the door open... Her da's a mean

61

one. He'll be back soon too."

"What room is hers?"

The man gestured with a half-finger. He either smiled or sneered as John noticed the missing digit. "Up the stairs, through the door straight ahead, and turn left. She's in the last door at the end of the hall."

If that huge man was concerned about her father, John didn't want to be anywhere near her when he came back. He lifted his robes and took the stairs two at a time. The banister was coated in sticky grime of indiscernible origin, the sporadically bare rug likewise. Under it all, the odor of sweaty bodies rose to stifle the stale beer. Some doors stood open to the hallway, their owners carelessly sprawled on the thin mattresses.

John knocked on the last door, the pressure of his hand opening it slightly.

"Jenny?" He pushed it open further and stepped into the room.

The windows were closed to fresh air, the curtains pulled, blocking all natural light. John walked first to the window and pulled the fabric open a crack. He looked down to the slow moving carriages through the greasy pane and sent up a wordless prayer before turning.

It was her. Her hair was down and matted, her face yellow and green with fading bruises. Her blue eyes watched his every move.

"I'm sorry." John didn't know where to begin.

"Aren't you the new priest?"

"A deacon. But, yes. I'm the new one."

"What are you doing here?" She moved to sit up, catching her breath in pain.

"I was worried."

Jenny furrowed her brows and brought her hand up to her loose hair. "I got hurt."

"I know. I think I heard you." John pulled out a three-legged stool next to a small table with what appeared to be last night's dinner, drying to the edge of the wooden bowl. He sat next to it. A lone blue-green fly gloried in the feast, sedately walking over the leftover lumps of meat.

"My da says my ribs is broke. He wrapped me up." She lifted her nightshirt to show John the bandage. He looked down to the floor. "Sorry." She dropped the fabric back down and blushed.

"It's all right." John attempted a smile. Dirty laundry lay in a heap over a chair. He could make out what looked like blood stains and dirt. He opened his mouth to say something but closed it again, realizing there was nothing to say.

"How'd you find me?"

"Ione told me where you lived. She's hurt too."

Jenny appeared suddenly interested in a dark knot in one of the boards on the wall. "Was it the man?"

"What man?"

"The one with the knife." Jenny pulled at the collar of her loose shirt, exposing an angry red gash that followed the line of her collar bone. She touched it lightly with the tip of her finger and hissed through her teeth. "Still hurts."

John crossed to the side of her bed to take a closer look. "That should've had stitches. It must have bled for a long time."

"It did." Jenny pulled her shirt back over, covering the wound.

"It might be infected."

Jenny shrugged, picking at the deteriorating quilt. "He said he'd come back. Don't know where I'm gonna go, but I can't go back there. My da ain't gonna let me stay here forever."

John tried to keep the disgust from his expression. Her own father farming her out made his stomach roll. A small part of him actually hoped the man returned while John was still at his daughter's bedside. Halfheartedly he sent up a silent prayer for forgiveness for his violent desire. It didn't help. John just wanted to hear the satisfying sound of the man's nose crunching under his fist.

"Do you remember what he looked like?"

"Sometimes I remember a bit. He was rich—richer than rich. He smelled real good."

John sat back down. Jenny was pretty, in a country kind of way. He found the large gap between her front teeth and the light sprinkling of freckles across her nose to be charming.

The room above the tavern was not charming.

"How did you come to live here?"

"My ma died. Cholera. We used to live in a little house, and we stored food in a root cellar. But that's all I remember. Da came to work in the stockyards after she died. That lasted for a winter, until he broke his foot, but we moved on."

"Did you go to school?"

"I can read. Ma taught me. And I can write." She held her chin up with pride and smiled a crooked smile. "And I'm real good at figuring."

"If I said you didn't have to stay here, what would you say?"

Jenny glanced to the hazy light filtering through the cloudy window. She tapped her fingers on her knee.

"Don't know. What would I have to do?" She met John's eyes warily.

"Nothing like that." It was John's turn to blush now. "No, nothing like that." He stood and crossed to the door, checking to see if anyone was coming. "What if there was a safe place?" John didn't even know where that might be, but if she was willing to come with him, he wasn't about to leave without her.

"What kind of safe place?"

"To be honest, I don't know. But it would be safer than this." John gestured out the window to the street below.

"What kind of work would I do?"

"We can worry about that later. Do you want to leave with me?"

"I can't."

"Why not?"

"I just can't. My da's gonna be back. You'd better go."

John hesitated. She looked small enough he could carry her out. "Are you sure?"

Jenny nodded.

He couldn't force her. "You know where to find me if you change your mind." John pushed the door open with the toe of his shoe. "There's always a place for you. We'll find a place for you." He stepped out of the room and into the dank hallway.

"Is Ione okay?" Jenny called after him.

John turned back. "Yes."

"That's good."

"Are you sure you want to stay here?"

"I hope she gets out." Jenny glanced toward the window. "I hope she don't come back. She gots sisters ya know."

"Yes. They're fine. We're taking care of them too."

"Good."

With nothing left to say, John left her sitting on the side of her bed, chewing her thumbnail, looking like she couldn't be much older than twelve.

Maggie woke and started breakfast for the pastor and his wife. They were nice people, and they didn't have any kids of their own to care for, so their house was clean.

"Good morning, Maggie."

"Good morning, Pastor Whitaker." Maggie rubbed her hands on her mother's too-long apron. The strings were wrapped around her back and tied in the front.

Pastor Whitaker adjusted his tie under his perfectly white collar and set his newspaper on the table. "You made coffee?" He smiled and grabbed a cup off the shelf above the stove. Flipping it over, he poured in the dark, steaming liquid.

Mrs. Whitaker followed. "Good morning, sweetie." She wore a yellow dress with tiny rounded buttons up the front of the bodice and sleeves that flared at her wrists. Her hair was pulled back and greased so it stayed close to her head, but instead of looking severe, the style showed the soft curves of her cheeks and forehead. Maggie thought she was one of the most beautiful women she'd ever met.

"You know, you don't have to feed us every morning. We should be the ones getting up to feed you."

"It's no trouble at all." Maggie took the dishcloth off the hanger by the cabinet and wiped imaginary crumbs from the table.

Lucy groggily stumbled into the room, barefoot and rubbing her eyes.

"It smells good in here."

"That it does," Pastor agreed, opening up the paper and shaking the crease out. "That it does," he repeated into the pages.

"I started some biscuits. They're in the oven." At first Maggie had been overwhelmed with their home. It wasn't exactly like the pictures in the store windows, but it was as close as she'd ever seen. And they had food—so much food. Mrs. Whitaker seemed to have the habit of putting up anything she could get her hands on. There were jars of fruits that Maggie hadn't even heard of, yellow and red, lined up in neat rows. Beans and beets and pickles lined the shelves underneath. Sometimes when she was alone Maggie would sit in the little room with the food and count the jars.

Lucy cried every night after Mrs. Whitaker dropped a kiss on her forehead and said prayers with them. Maggie was thankful she was old enough to wait until the wonderful woman left, but Lucy's tears made it hard for Maggie to hold her own back. Lucy had been so tired the first night that she'd snuggled in the warm bed and breathed deeply, nestled in the fresh blankets. Only Maggie cried the first night.

Mrs. Whitaker folded a towel over her hand, opened the oven, and pulled out the fragrant pan. "These are beautiful, Maggie." She smiled over the evenly risen golden circles, arranged in a tight pattern. "You used the cinnamon. Good choice."

"Mama showed Maggie how to make them," Lucy pointed out, ignoring Maggie's restraining look.

"Your mama must have been a wonderful cook," Mrs. Whitaker said to Lucy. "She taught your sister well."

Lucy nodded at Maggie, at once both supportive of her skill and bolstered by Mrs. Whitaker's approval. "Humph," she added for emphasis.

From her stance in front of her easel, Miriam heard Ione stir. Dropping her brush and pallet onto a nearby chair, she rushed to flip the portraits that lined the wall underneath the windows. No one had ever seen her paintings, and she intended to keep it that way. Besides, the painting of Ione was wrong, dreadfully so.

"I didn't know you painted." Ione, pale and troubled, leaned on the doorframe for support. Her white nightgown, intended to be ankle length, fell to the floor and pooled at her feet.

"Yes," Miriam admitted while clearing a chair for Ione. "You can sit here."

"Thank you."

"Is there something you need?" Miriam's hands felt awkward now. She shoved them into the deep pocket slits in her skirt.

"Not really."

"Would you like me to get something for you? Are you feeling well enough to be out of bed?"

Ione studied her hands, folded in her lap. "What am I going to do?"

Miriam knew what she meant. The questions had been floating for days, waiting for Ione to feel well enough to fret over them. That was the trouble with life. Even in the worst of circumstances, the bad stuff would always wait its turn.

"I can't stay here forever, and I'm sure the landlord has rented out our rooms. I don't even know where my sisters are." Ione brought her honey gaze to Miriam's. So warm, Miriam thought.

"I can't see them like this." She gestured to the side of her face. "Maybe they're better off without me."

"No," Miriam said.

Ione looked at her.

"No, it's not better to be alone."

"I thought you liked to be by yourself. Why else would you live up here?"

"I don't mind being alone. But it's not better. It's never better than being with someone who loves you. You have sisters."

Ione straightened her back, adjusting her position.

"You're still in pain."

"Does it matter?"

"Yes, it does." Miriam stood and offered her hand.

Ione took a deep breath, steeling herself for the pain of movement, and rose with Miriam's help. "My sisters must be worried."

"Your sisters are fine."

Back in the bedroom, Miriam held the coverlet for Ione to climb back under.

"I'm so sorry for all your trouble," Ione said quietly. "I wish I could repay you..."

"All of life is trouble." Miriam shrugged. "It's just that sometimes, it's unanticipated. I can either be troubled with a hurt woman in my bed, or with the typical, everyday problems like rancid milk or a late newspaper. It doesn't matter. It's really all the same. But when someone else's trouble is more urgent, one's own troubles seem to fade. You could say that your being here gives me the rare opportunity not to be troubled by my own difficulties. Thank you."

After a moment of confusion at Miriam's backward logic, a small giggle escaped. Ione moaned and covered her bruised ribs with her arm. "Maybe someday, you can return the favor." She punctuated the absurdity with a pained, and unladylike, snort.

Miriam smiled. "You never know." She turned down the lamp and left her room.

Chapter 11

At the entrance to the alley, Jenny twisted her skirt between her sweaty palms. Her da had come, limping, back to the tavern. They needed money for next week, and he'd not worked in months. No one wanted a lame laborer. So instead, he drank until sending Jenny out was a sensible option. If she didn't work, then they'd both be on the streets anyway. She took a shallow breath and stepped into the circle of flickering light at the entrance to the alley. Her ribs still hurt.

Better to be working on the street for money to pay the rent than living on the street. She liked to think her da didn't consider what she did to get the money, but she knew better. She watched the other drunks curl their lips as she skittered out of the tavern under the cover of dark, while her da, bent over a decaying table, nursed another bottle of cheap something or other.

Jenny shivered in the damp breeze and pulled her shawl over her bare arms. Sometimes, she could still hear his smooth voice. Not hear, really, but feel. She could feel his voice as a pressure in her spine. She looked to the upper windows of the cathedral, wishing to see the deacon's window open.

A low whistle cantered through the branches on a wet breeze. Jenny stopped, her heart battering the inside of her ribcage. She listened for the clicking sound she'd forgotten about. He'd come to her with a clicking sound—a metal-tipped cane.

The whistle rose in pitch. Jenny swung into the shadows and huddled between the statue of the Virgin and the stone steps. She shouldn't have come. She rocked on her heels and thought of John, and how he'd been embarrassed when she thought he wanted her to work for him. Embarrassed...some men could still be embarrassed. He was in the church. He told her to come to him if she needed help. He said she'd be safe. Jenny pulled her shawl over her hair. She'd just had a bath, and she could smell the talcum powder she'd dried with. There was no clicking. She could go into the alley.

A sailor stumbled around the corner, with his friends close behind. They teased him, and even with alcohol fueled bravado, he paused at the entrance. Jenny watched from the shadows. He didn't look to be more than sixteen. He wiped his nose on his sleeve and pulled the navy blue shirt of his uniform taut before stepping out of the circle of the streetlamp and behind the overgrown hedge.

He'd be easy money. Jenny was tempted to follow, but her knees wouldn't let her stand. She probably wouldn't even have to do much. The boy was obviously skittish, obviously a boy, and obviously the evening's entertainment for the group that pushed and goaded from the circle of light. It was them she wouldn't trust. She wanted to go into the alley if only to help the boy create the ruse he'd need in order to survive the night.

John watched the young sailor pause once he hit the shadows, and his stomach sank. The boy was young—too young for the kind of guilt he was signing up for. Jenny was nowhere in sight, and for that, John was glad.

"Son," John whispered into the dark. The boy stopped abruptly and looked around.

"What are you doing here?" John stepped out of the heavier shadows, so the sailor could see his robes and know he was safe.

"I, uh…I…" He glanced back to the alley's entrance.

John could see he was considering a hasty retreat, but instead he dropped his head and stood there, resigned to his fate. John couldn't help but feel sorry for the uncomfortable situation.

"Are you Catholic?"

"Yes, Father."

"Should you be here?"

"No, Father."

"Why are you here?"

The boy shrugged, remaining silent, looking back toward the glowing lamppost.

John took a step closer. "It's no sin to let them think what they want. Don't lie, but you don't have to offer any information you are not comfortable offering."

He lifted his gaze to meet John's, slowly gathering his meaning. He nodded, appearing relieved.

"You can go back now." John placed his hand on the young man's shoulder and dismissed him with a half-smile.

The boy strolled back out with a smile on his face, and the members of the group, full of congratulations and jokes about his swift return, took turns slapping him on the back. Jenny heard them promise to buy him drinks at the next tavern they found.

When all was silent, she slipped from her hiding place and turned the corner into the alley, curiosity pushing her on. Still, she kept the wall of the cathedral to her back.

"There you are."

John stepped forward. Jenny coughed out in surprise. The boy, he'd been in the alley. "Did you...? I mean, have you...?" She stammered in confusion and turned to run. He was a priest. What was he even doing in the alley? She didn't even want to consider the boy.

John reached out and grabbed her arm before she could get away.

"Men are disgusting," she spat. "How could you?" She twisted out of his grip.

"What are you talking about? Stop. I just wanted to talk to you."

Jenny seethed—she didn't like to be held captive by a man.

"How could I what?"

"That boy. I saw that boy come out of here—" Her lip curled in disgust. "—with a smile on his face."

"No," John said, angry understanding etched across his face. "What?"

"No. I said no." John's hand found Jenny's arm in the dark again, and this time didn't let go until he'd dragged her into the light.

"Look at me," he said.

Jenny lifted her chin and met his gaze with her angry one. Her chest rose and fell in a fast staccato pattern. She couldn't believe she'd thought he might protect her just because he was somehow better than the other men. A man was a man. She knew it; she just didn't want to believe it.

John closed his eyes, hoping Father Ayers was not observing out of his office window. He knew he had to help Jenny see the truth. She was horribly mistaken. "I was waiting for you," he paced his words slowly. "I was in the alley, waiting for you, waiting to see if your attacker came back."

"But the boy..."

"His friends were pushing him to be something he was not. He found me instead of you. I talked to him and told him there's nothing wrong with him letting his friends think what they want to think."

Jenny's jaw dropped open, and her hand came up to cover her mouth. "Oh..."

"The young man is apparently a very good actor." The right corner of John's mouth dipped down in an attempt not to smile.

"Oh." Jenny covered her eyes with both hands. "I'm so sorry...I thought...I mean..."

"It's perfectly reasonable. Your conclusion, although admittedly not what I'd expected, was valid. I should have put more thought into the decision to catch you when you didn't expect to see me."

"Oh." Jenny pulled her shawl tighter around her shoulders. "I'm...oh."

"Don't worry about it. I've made a few mistakes myself." John looked down, considering her fading bruises and her stance. It did little to hide the fact that every step was still painful for her. "Come with me."

He took her arm and led her across the street to Miriam's warehouse. He knocked once, and Miriam pulled the door open just far enough to let them both through, locking it behind them.

A lamp burned bright enough to illuminate the stairs leading to her upstairs rooms. Jenny sent a questioning look to John. He motioned for her to follow Miriam up the stairs.

Ione sat at the table, waiting. Her hands rattled the cup on the saucer every time she picked it up to take a sip, so she decided to wait for it to cool so she could drink it without the noise. She knew that Miriam was sensitive to sound, not that the woman would have admitted it. She was entertainingly strange.

Jenny ducked in with the wide eyes of an abused pet in search of forgiveness. Only after she'd surveyed the visually abundant room did her eyes fall on Ione. Jenny reached her in three giant steps and, apparently forgetting Miriam and John, pulled her shawl down to show her the slash on her collar bone. Ione confirmed her similar injury without exposing her own shoulder.

Miriam and John watched the exchange. Jenny was a simple woman, but she would give a stranger anything they needed, or even wanted. That one quality made her an exceptionally rare specimen in a city where on one street the women walked with parasols, and a few blocks to the south, the citizens lost themselves in the opium dens. It was as if Jenny's father, and her profession, had matured part of her to the age of ancient, while preserving other parts of her personality in perpetual childhood.

"I wanted to warn you, but I was in bed for at least a week." Jenny pulled her shawl closed to cover herself, glancing back at John. She stood with her legs wide apart and her arms crossed. "He cut me with a knife. Why would someone do that?"

"Can I make you some tea?" Miriam offered.

Ione watched Jenny hesitate before agreeing, but the temptation to spend a minute or two out of the damp cold won.

"Yes, please. That would be nice."

Ione gestured to the seat across from herself, and Jenny plopped herself down. She pulled the bowl of sugar closer, and then folded her hands in her lap, striving to appear patient while waiting for the warm comfort Miriam promised.

With the three women crowding the small kitchen, John eased himself onto the approved chair in the sitting room. With anyone else, he might have been offended by the designation, and possibly even disturbed by his own acquiescence, but with Miriam the expected eccentricity, and his anticipated compliance, was a given.

Ione sat across from Jenny. John watched Jenny as she blindly followed Ione's subtle behavioral suggestions. In essence, through example only, Ione raised Jenny's etiquette to an acceptable level. It was a skill—Ione's steady presence had a civilizing effect even while treating Jenny as an equal. John looked down to his own feet, flat on the floor, and considered his own straight posture. He wondered if he would be slouching a bit more if Ione were not in the room.

Miriam pulled the kettle off the stove and poured the steaming liquid into cups. Her hair fell in unruly waves from the tight knot she'd most likely fastened that morning. Her forehead was clear of lines, and her shape fashionable, even without the tight stays that the women of means stuffed themselves into. Her neck was thin and straight, disappearing into her collar in graceful arches. The stunning gray—real gray—of her eyes made her memorable.

John stood and crossed to the window to watch the circle of light at the entrance to the alley. The women he fretted over were all safe with him, but the watching was a habit. A shadow moved beyond the light. John followed the movement with disinterest, leaning his elbows on the heavy wooden sill. The warehouse was so unlike the kind of environment a woman like Miriam should have graced.

She belonged in a ballroom at the Palmer, attending some gala, raising money for a suffragette cause. But Miriam's rejection of the life her father's money would have bought her was not due to an inability to adapt to a life for which she wasn't suited. John looked back to the room. Stacked canvases leaned against the wall underneath the huge clock. Pottery, decorated with colorful dragons, occupied the few empty spaces on her bookshelves. Jars with brushes sat next to the sugar bowl. Her hands were always stained. It was obvious that she was a painter. Miriam set the teacups on the table in front of the other women.

Unlike he'd assumed, her choice to be alone was exactly that—a choice. She'd rejected her scripted life because it simply didn't hold her interest like the strangers she watched every day from her windows above the street. She wasn't forced to be solitary due to an irrational fear of people, or anything else of that nature. Rather, she chose to sequester herself.

John studied Miriam as she sat at the end of the table, Ione to her right, Jenny to her left. Occasionally, her knee would bounce under her skirts, belying her discomfort with their proximity. Or she would drop her hands beneath the table and clench her fingers together until they were white, but she did so without the other women, at least Jenny, noticing. John doubted that Ione missed much of anything.

Miriam's lifestyle almost reminded him of...a monk, cloistered away in his monastery, finding solace in solitude. John smirked and turned back to the window, looking for the shadow he'd just seen.

"I'm sorry." A softer form of Jenny's voice sidled up next to him. She leaned her elbows on the sill and rested her chin in her palms. "I shouldn't've thought those things about you."

"I told you, I was just as wrong. Don't worry about it." John let a comfortable silence develop, both of them observing the wavering circle under the lamppost.

"I really need to go."

"No." Miriam came up behind them. "You don't. What you really need to do isstay."

"I couldn't. My da needs me."

"Does he?" John turned to her. "Do you think he'll not survive if you don't work?"

Jenny furrowed her brows, appearing to be deep in thought. Ione joined her at the window.

"What if I gave him some money?" Miriam said.

John and the women guests turned to ascertain if they'd heard her correctly.

"If I gave him some money, say what you might expect to make in a month's time, do you think he would accept it in exchange for your labor?"

John had never heard the word labor used to describe the services the women provided in the alley, but the offer was generous, and it made sense. After all, this was Chicago, and money spoke louder than anything else. Miriam was shrewd.

"Maybe I could still visit him?" Jenny chewed her lower lip. Ione pulled up Jenny's shawl where it had fallen off her shoulder.

"Of course. You can do whatever you like," Miriam added quickly.

"You might want to consider staying away for a while," John added.

Jenny nodded. "I don't have any of my things."

"Is there anything that can't be purchased again?" Miriam asked.

Jenny looked at the floor, rubbing her toe against the wood grain.

"Just a locket of my ma's. I keep it in a sock so he won't sell it."

"Jenny?" Ione took a step nearer and looked directly into her eyes. "I think you should do this."

"But he's all I got."

"But this isn't good. It's dangerous."

Jenny's hand moved up to touch the yellowed bruise over her eye. Outside, a slow, echoing tap was swelling. The sound of metal on concrete, timed to a man's gait. Ione's normally stoic face twitched in recognition. Both she and Jenny turned to the window, trying to discern the source of the noise.

"Do you remember that?" Jenny asked quietly.

"Yes." Ione's tone was flat.

John rushed to turn down the lamp behind them. The flame disappeared, and they were left in darkness, save the residual light from the streetlamp.

They stood in silence, hearing the slow tap of a gentleman's walking stick.

"Lots of men have those." Jenny didn't take her eyes off the street below.

Ione just nodded.

The steady click grew louder, closer, until Jenny took a reflexive step away from the window. Ione shook her head slowly, back and forth, and a man came into the light.

He stopped, turned, faced the warehouse, and touched the

tip of his hat with a gloved hand. His features were cloaked in shadows, but it was a greeting, an acknowledgement of their presence.

They all joined Jenny, a step away from the window.

"It's him," Jenny hissed.

"Are you sure?"

Ione nodded, watching as the man turned away, out of the light, before continuing down the street. His movements deliberate. His purpose calculated.

"I think I will spend the night here tonight," John heard himself say, long after the clicking had moved out of hearing and they'd all stood straining to hear through the remaining silence.

The three women nodded their agreement.

Ione shared her bed with Jenny. John reclined on the sofa in the front room. That left either her studio or her father's bedroom as places for Miriam to sleep. She would have to change his bedding, and air the room out before she could stay in there, but the decision to once again utilize the room seemed to be one that was made *for* her, rather than *by* her. Necessity was necessity, however, and not a one of them planned to step foot outside of the warehouse until the sun shone off the cathedral windows the next morning.

For now, she would sleep in her studio. There was a daybed, and it was sufficient.

The man under the light still had her blood racing. Miriam decided to sit at her desk before trying to convince herself to sleep in a house with three other people. She pulled a clean piece of paper, carrying the stamp of her father's business, from her drawer. She ran her thumb over the blue of his shipping symbol. What would he think of how she'd spent the time since his death?

He'd be disappointed.

After all, she'd done nothing to increase his fortune and nothing to provide for anyone, save herself. Her father had offered employment to a host of people. For the first time, Miriam wondered what all those men had done when she'd ended their jobs. Did she create any situations like Jenny's?

The machinery in the warehouse seemed to swell beneath the covering tarps, heaving under the floor. Miriam felt their presence under her chair, reminding her of her responsibility.

The errand boy would be stopping the next day. Miriam made a list with additional items and larger quantities. She opened the lower desk drawer and took out money for the items. Then she took out an extra coin. He was always punctual, always precise in his quantities. He could likely use the extra pay. Maybe he would buy his sister a candy.

Ione had sisters to care for.

Jenny had a father to hide from, whether she knew it or not. Tomorrow, Miriam would talk to John about meeting with Jenny's father and offering cash in exchange for Jenny's locket. There was no reason for her to return.

And now, they all had someone to fear, someone who knew where they were living.

Miriam said a short prayer. Again, she picked up a clean piece of paper and her pen. Again, her next decision would be one of necessity—a choice that circumstance had already decided for her.

> *Dear Mr. Michael Farling,*
>
> *Thank you for your continued service to my late father.*
>
> *I appreciate the discretion you have used in the handling of his accounts. I find, however, I need to make a few adjustments...*

Chapter 12

The townhouse was larger than Miriam remembered. She'd expected to look out the carriage window and feel as if her childhood had shrunken, that it would be easily contained in the tall box of a house. But the four-story stone façade loomed over the street, the concrete steps protruding from the first floor like a gaping jaw.

She'd had a while to become accustomed to the idea; it had been almost a week since she'd sent the message to Mr. Farling. Still, the sun cascaded through the trees, and the women promenading back and forth on the opposite side of the street did little to hide their curious gazes. They couldn't see into the dark carriage.

"Everything will be fine," John said from his seat across from hers. The carriage rolled to a stop.

Miriam still wasn't comfortable with his proximity, but it was preferable to meeting with her solicitor, in the day, alone.

"I know." Miriam ran her fingers across the sturdy gray fabric of her skirt. Her clothes were wholly unsuitable. The women across the street had ceased to disguise their interest.

"It is a fine carriage." John watched out the window.

"I instructed Mr. Farling to send a modest one."

Mr. Farling stood at the base of the steps, next to a giant carved lion head. It had been almost two years since Miriam had last seen him. He wore a narrowly tailored gray suit with a conservative tie. He adjusted his spectacles and smiled. As Miriam and John approached, he bent to take her hand in his.

John stepped forward, offering his own hand before Miriam had a chance to balk at the physical contact.

"It's a pleasure to meet with you. My name is John. I'm a deacon at the cathedral across the street from the warehouse."

"Of course, and it's a pleasure to see you again, Miri—" Mr. Farling cleared his throat. "Miss Beaumont."

"The pleasure is mine, Mr. Farling."

His height and size were deceiving. From the street, he held a bookish aura, but upon closer inspection, he still towered above Miriam, just like he had when she was younger. He was at least a few inches taller than John. Not for the first time, Miriam was grateful John had offered to accompany her.

"Should we go in? Perhaps you are looking for something specific?" Mr. Farling led the way up the stairs, key in hand. He'd asked if Miriam wanted someone to come in early and open the house for her, but she'd declined.

"Everything is as it was. The house hasn't been touched since..."

"September 12, 1881." Miriam glanced back to the women watching from the other side of the street. It was the day her mother died.

He opened the door and stepped to the side for Miriam to enter. "Please let me know what I can do."

"Would you please lock the door behind us?"

"Yes, of course." Mr. Farling turned the key in the lock, and the tumblers fell into place.

The parquet floor was exactly as she'd remembered it, with a worn spot to the left of the door, where guests had dropped dripping umbrellas before their butler intervened. Floor to ceiling mahogany paneling filled the entry and ran up the stairs to the floors above. Miriam brushed her shoes on the rose-colored Oriental rug before crossing to the closed pocket doors to the right.

The metal scrollwork released a small brass handle when Miriam pressed a hidden button. She pulled the first door over and then pushed the second one into the wall pocket, revealing a room of gold and mauve decadence. Narrow but long, the room contained four separate areas for visiting guests to sit in small groups, as well as a piano tucked into a rounded alcove. Draperies hung from ceiling to floor, shrouding the room.

"Would you open those at the side?" she asked John and Mr. Farling. "Not the front ones."

The windows she'd pointed to opened out over a gardened area, a hidden pocket of sun between the two otherwise connected homes. There were no windows on the neighbor's side. It had been a building specification of her father's. The men each pulled a cord on either side of the glass expanse.

Dusty light flooded the room, giving the covered furniture a less haunted aura.

"That's better." John brushed off his hands.

"Do you want us to uncover some of the furniture?" Mr. Farling gestured to the davenport.

A tall curio stood against the wall, near Miriam. She lifted the corner of the sheet, spotting the glass-cased treasures within. Music boxes of all shapes and sizes sat, untouched, on glass shelves. Even with the covers, a fine sheen of dust covered every surface. She looked at the men and nodded.

She helped, and they all began pulling sheets off the furniture. Dust floated in every direction, refusing to settle. Crystal and glass reflected the light. Bright upholstery defined the room's purpose. In hushed tones, John and Mr. Farling began to discuss the value of some of the more unique objects.

"Did you remember all of this?" John asked. He walked over to where Miriam sat after all of the covers had been removed.

"Yes." Miriam studied her fingernails. She remembered her mother's hands in the house, remembered how they would flit over the piano keys, and how her father would tease her. "I remember it all—every piece." Her old sketchbook was still on her writing desk in her room upstairs. She'd drawn a picture of her mother under the tree in the garden.

Mr. Farling sat on a nearby footstool, facing Miriam. He looked to John, and John nodded, essentially giving permission for him to speak with Miriam. She sent both of them a look she was sure they didn't understand.

He cleared his throat. "Miss Beaumont," he began, folding his hands in front of him. "Why are we here? Has something changed for you that I should know?"

She was dressed in her typical gray. In this setting, with the light showing off the gold in her hair, the gray looked like a ruse.

Her posture was perfect, her hands clasped benignly on her lap, her head tilted to show interest in what Mr. Farling said, without being too encouraging. But Mr. Farling didn't miss a thing. Every movement Miriam made, every expression, every smile, registered on the solicitor's face as if she were a long-lost friend.

The house was beyond compare. Gold-framed works of art hung from wires screwed into the moldings near the ceiling. Glass cabinets, filled with things of which John had never seen the match, dotted the room. The curio with the music boxes housed tiny filigree chests on jeweled legs topped with miniature renditions of impossible birds. He'd expected the upholstery to be deteriorating, but he was wrong. The furniture stood out, vibrant and ready to comfort the kind of people that wouldn't be overpowered by such opulence.

He stood in his black robe, his vow of poverty displayed in stark contrast.

The gardened area was overgrown, with dead branches and underbrush strangled by the new growth. Mr. Farling sat waiting for Miriam to explain. His eyes were on her face, and she didn't avert her gaze. A pang of jealousy reminded John he was still a man, and he concentrated on the lists of things that would need to be done if anyone were going to live in the home again. If that was what she'd planned. He only had suspicions.

"There are women in my house," Miriam began her explanation.

Mr. Farling blinked and, with the tip of his index finger, pushed his spectacles further up the bridge of his nose. He cleared his throat. "Are they your guests?"

"In a manner of speaking."

John, despite himself, enjoyed the handsome man's obvious discomfort.

"Maybe I should ask you why you wanted to meet me here."

Miriam stood and paced to the cold marble hearth that dominated the seating area. "I guess..." She traced the grains of the rose marble with a delicate finger while the men watched. "I guess I just wanted to assess the state of my home."

"What, in particular, are you looking for? Do you want to sell it? Or lease it out to someone? I would definitely suggest you remove some of the valuables if you are thinking of renting it."

"No. I just wanted to see it."

"Does this have to do with the women in your house?"

Miriam walked behind and to the left of a chaise. It was pushed into the corner of the room. Bending behind an urn that stood chest high, she flipped up the corner of the rug and retrieved a key. She let it dangle from the end of the attached sky-blue ribbon. "Do you know what this is for?" she asked without looking up.

Mr. Farling questioned John with his eyes, and John shrugged, enjoying the day and Miriam's eccentricities more with every moment that passed.

Hearing no response, she continued, "This was my mother's. She wore it around her wrist." Miriam pulled the curtain John had earlier opened further to the side, revealing a door that blended in with the wall. She put the key into a small hole, turned it, and pushed with her shoulder. The door tucked into the wall, and then popped out a few inches, exposing a brass ring.

Miriam turned and smiled at the men. "Are you going to follow me or just sit there?"

Miriam and John had left, leaving Ione alone with Jenny in the warehouse apartment.

Before the carriage that intended to pick them up had rattled to a stop outside on the street, Ione could see Miriam's anxiety build. But as Miriam heard the driver click softly to the horses, and after she watched him wrap the leather straps around the brake and drop to the road, she pulled her hands from her pockets, smiled back to Ione, and lightly walked down the stairs to disappear into the dark of the warehouse.

"I should be back by dinnertime," she'd called over her shoulder, appearing completely at ease. Ione suspected the anticipation of human interaction was, for Miriam, much worse than the practice of interacting.

"She's a strange lady," Jenny said from where she sat cross-legged on the sofa with a crochet hook in her right hand and a bouncing ball of yarn quickly disappearing into her scarf, or whatever it was she was making. "But I like her."

"Jenny." Ione sat down across from her. "Can you read?"

"Sure I can. I can do sums too...real fast," she added proudly.

"What have you read?"

"Ma taught me with the Bible. Mostly now I like to look at the dress advertisements—the ones from France are the best. Them ladies are beautiful, and I don't know how they get their hair to stay like that." Jenny didn't miss a knot, her wrist bending in a constant rhythm, tucking under and pulling through.

"Have you read any newspapers lately?" Ione almost stood and walked over to the window, before she remembered who had been waiting there the night before. Instead, she crossed her legs, attempting contentment with her confinement.

Jenny shook her head. "I don't like the papers. They just talk about what the society folk do with all their rich money, and what the poor folks do what's bad." Her wrist stopped its rhythmic dive in and out of the growing piece of fabric, and she looked up. "It ain't right, you know. The man what cut us was rich. Rich people ain't any better than us poor people. They just don't get caught, 'cause the poor people are too busy just trying to fill their stomachs to put up a fuss."

"It's just that I've been noticing some things in the papers." Ione folded over the paper in her hand. "I never used to read them, so I don't know if it's typical, or if something else is happening."

"Like what?" Jenny pinned the fabric to the ball of yarn with the crochet hook and leaned over to pick up that day's paper.

"Look on page four."

Jenny opened the paper. "What am I looking for?"

"Near the bottom. It says 'Girl washed up on shore. Second in a week.'"

Jenny leaned over the paper, squinting to read the tiny print. About the time Ione thought she might have forgotten why she was reading, Jenny set the paper down.

"I don't remember hearing about two in a week before. It says they's unidentified. Do you know anyone missing?"

"No. You?"

"Nope." Jenny folded the paper back the way she'd found it. "Do you think we should talk to the police?"

"John already did the day after I got hurt. They said they'd send someone to talk to me, but they never did."

Jenny nodded her understanding.

"Do you want some tea?" Ione stood and moved toward the kitchen. "In two days I get to see my sisters."

"Wish I had sisters."

"I left them," Ione confessed. Something about the young woman made her want to tell her everything. "I met a man and left them. I didn't even come back when he beat me." Ione set the pot of water on the small stove. "Then he brought his friends in. That's when I came back."

"I always thought you came back for your mama."

"No. I came back for me. When I returned, I found her sick. I ended up doing the exact same thing I ran from."

Jenny glanced around the room, obviously looking for a change of subject. "Miriam has some interesting things. What do you think those are?"

Ione looked to where Jenny pointed. It was a stack of canvases, leaning against the far wall. "I think those are some of her paintings."

"Have you seen any?"

"No."

"Do you think she would mind if we looked at them?"

"I'm not sure." Ione glanced at the still non-boiling pot of water. By the time she looked back, Jenny was standing, hunched over the canvases, flipping through them.

"Oh, my. These are beautiful." Jenny stopped. "Look."

"I'm not sure..."

"Just look." Jenny held the painting up to the light.

It was a rendition of the statue across the street—except Mary was colored as a real woman. But her face was different; it had lost its serenity. Her expression, even as she watched the babe in her arms, was wrecked with loss. It was as if, in her arms, the child she held had become the man she would watch die. Miriam painted her future experience to invade her young world, giving more truth to her face than any picture had a right to show. Ione took in a shaky breath. Jenny set it down and held up another.

This one was of the factory, but it took a while to place it. Again, the faces were the focus.

Women were lined up down the length of the building. Some were looking at their feet. Some studied the stained glass across the street. A few of the women exuded dreamy expressions of love, while others held their chins up in disappointed determination. One was hungry, another fat. And they were all different colors. Not different shades of brown or white, but different colors entirely. One woman's face was painted in red hues, the next in blue, and it was perfectly realistic. Ione could discern women of different races; she knew the woman with the blue face, as well as the woman in shades of orange, were both black women. Another blue woman was a white woman. Ione pulled the painting closer, trying to ascertain the details, but the closer she looked, the less she could see.

She tipped the painting away from her in order to take advantage of the outside light. Jenny, the side of her face illuminated yellow by the reflection off the cathedral's stained glass, watched the play of light on the picture. Ione moved it back and forth, picking up the different colors from the church window. The shifting shades changed the painted women's expressions. The picture was meant to be hung in a changing spectrum of light.

"When do you think this was?" Jenny whispered. "Who do you think these women are?"

"I don't think women ever worked here."

"So this is all in her mind?" Jenny sounded slightly scandalized.

Ione smiled at Jenny's completely sincere assessment. It wasn't an insult, not from Jenny. The kettle whistled on the stove, and both women jumped.

"I'll get it," Ione said. "You set them back, carefully."

Jenny followed Ione into the kitchen. "Four...no...three sugars, please."

Chapter 13

"Ione will be visiting today," Lucy said, again, to everyone seated at the breakfast table. Maggie tapped her under the table.

"Don't do that!" Lucy exaggerated her expression, making Maggie wish she would have kicked her instead.

Pastor Whitaker looked over the top of his open newspaper. "I bet you're excited." He winked at Lucy.

Lucy nodded and shoveled a spoonful of oatmeal into her mouth.

Mrs. Whitaker smiled at Lucy's messy face and wiped the corners of her own mouth. "I'm looking forward to meeting her."

"She's so pretty." Lucy picked up her napkin and wiped her own mouth.

Maggie had to agree with that statement.

"Maggie..." Mrs. Whitaker set her spoon down. "Do you want me to be here when she arrives or would you like to be alone with Ione?"

She hadn't thought of that. If she was alone, she might be able to ask what happened—if Ione would even tell her. But Maggie liked Mrs. Whitaker, and she wanted Ione to meet her, and like her, too.

"I think you would like her." Maggie looked up as the pastor's lips twitched up on one corner before he had the chance to stop his mouth from betraying his thoughts; he was glad she wanted his wife there.

Maggie took the last bite of her oatmeal, still tasting the sugar they'd sprinkled over the top. The thick, hot breakfast warmed her from the inside out. She stood to clear the dishes.

"You don't have to do that." Mrs. Whitaker joined her at the sink. "I want you to know, we don't expect you to work for us."

Maggie shrugged. "I don't mind. I like the dishes."

What Maggie wanted to say was that she knew there were only three kinds of people that stayed in other people's houses: family, guests, and servants. Maggie already had a family, so they couldn't be family. If she was a guest, that meant she needed to leave soon. That left servant. It was a job she could be proud to have.

Mrs. Angelene Whitaker watched the eldest of the two sisters gather the breakfast dishes. Her industrious expression clearly communicating that she was capable of handling the job she'd taken on herself. She was a good girl. She was the kind of girl Angelene always imagined God would give them.

But He hadn't.

Lucy enthusiastically stuffed her cheeks full of oatmeal, and Angelene's heart contracted a fraction tighter. She tried to think of other things, consider the community work she was able to do without the burden of motherhood, but sometimes, when she looked at the child next to her seated on a stack of newspapers, she had nowhere to put her arms.

Maggie was a hard worker, intent on earning her keep. Angelene gathered the few remaining dishes, trying to keep her mind off that afternoon's visit. She wanted Ione to let the girls stay. They had security, and enough food to go around, but she had no right to even ask.

"Would you like me to do your hair for your sister's visit?" Angelene asked Maggie as casually as she could. Maggie plunged her hands into the soapy water, scrubbing the breakfast evidence away. "I could use the hot iron, or we could put it up."

Maggie didn't stop her scrubbing. The girl needed so many things: clothes that fit, shoes without holes, new undergarments. But she was independent, and when an independent, almost-woman is challenged to grow up fast, she does so, and often admirably. The truth was, Angelene knew that Maggie would survive, and survive well, with or without her mothering.

Angelene was beginning to regret asking, afraid she'd pushed too hard, when Maggie slowly nodded. "Yes, please," she said, and then plunged a pot into the water.

Mr. Farling was the first to stand behind Miriam at the strange door in the wall. John wasn't far behind. Miriam pulled the brass ring. The door silently eased open.

She knew they were right behind her, and she didn't have to look at them to know what kind of expressions they shared.

Miriam ducked into the dim light and followed a narrow path. The walls were brick, and the floor angled up, so they essentially walked up a hill. She turned a corner and looked back to see how far behind they were.

"Pardon me." Mr. Farling brushed up against Miriam. He'd been looking toward the high ceiling.

"There are small glass block windows that run along the ceiling. If you stand on the outside of the building and look up, it looks like there are decorative tiles between the brick dental work that runs below the second floor. Those are actually small windows designed to light this hall."

John was smiling like a boy with a new toy. Miriam watched him gesture to Mr. Farling to move forward. Miriam held her skirt and took the few last inclining steps before stopping in front of another door. She opened it to a room stacked with papers and art and books. Large cushions lined one wall. They'd been left uncovered. A thin coat of dust dimmed their bright sheen. There were no windows, just a continuation of the glass block pattern.

"What was the purpose of this room?" John craned his neck to see around Mr. Farling.

"It was one of my mother's rooms. Only she and my father had a key, although she always let me join her here. These halls and rooms were places the servants didn't have access to...it was my father's concession to my mother."

"Rooms, plural?" Mr. Farling looked for another door.

"Concession?" John glanced down the hall they had just walked through.

"There's a network of small rooms that run along the perimeter of the house. And as far as the concession goes, my mother didn't want to move into the city. She preferred her privacy. But as my father's business grew, it became apparent they needed to be closer. She also needed to fulfill certain social expectations: dinner parties, charity events, and the like. These rooms were her compensation."

Mr. Farling craned his neck, examining the walls for the next hidden door. "Where do you go from here? And what was this room used for?"

"She liked to read and draw here, but she didn't paint here."

"She painted?" the men asked in unison.

"Yes. She was quite exceptional, actually."

"Have I ever seen any of her pieces in a gallery?" Mr. Farling met Miriam's gaze. "I wouldn't have known to look for her name."

"No." Miriam paused in front of a bookcase. "Here it is." She pushed an inlaid wooden oval and let go. It popped out, creating a handle. "I remembered it being higher."

Miriam pulled, and the heavy bookcase whispered open, revealing a narrow set of iron spiral steps that disappeared into blackness. "Do you mind?" Both men had squeezed themselves as close to the opening as possible. Appearing to assess each other's determination, they took a step back.

"I'll go up first and open the hatch. Then you can see where you're headed."

They crowded back in behind her as she took to the steps and disappeared into the blackness.

John was attempting to be patient with the man next to him, but he knew he would likely be stuck following the overly intrigued man up the narrow staircase.

Miriam's footfalls stopped, and they both waited to see what was next. The entire experience—meeting the strange little woman, bargaining with a drunkard for his daughter, getting lost in the bowels of a house designed by a woman with, at best, a tenuous grasp on reality—was like being dropped into someone else's life. And the man next to him couldn't seem to wipe the goofy sideways smile off his face. Of course, John couldn't promise he didn't look just as dimwitted. It was an unprecedented situation after all, and one never looked intelligent when faced with unexpected circumstances. The day was a compilation of the absurd.

"Found it." Miriam stood above them, shrouded by the dark. A crack of light appeared in the ceiling. She heaved the wooden hatch open. "You can come up now."

Mr. Farling—Michael, he'd told John to call him—gestured for John to go up first, making John regret his earlier thoughts about the man. John took the tiny stairs toward the dusty light and came out into a room without a ceiling.

Rather, it had a roof. John, standing at the top of the steps, looked up and stared, blinking in the blinding light.

"Um, excuse me," Michael called from underneath him.

John mumbled an apology and moved a step farther into the room without looking down.

The ceiling was a series of triangle glass panels, cloudy with urban soot, held together at their peak with a spider web of intricate metal framing. Pulleys were strategically placed around the round room, attached to ropes. John followed the ropes to where they were nautically wrapped in figure eights around wooden hooks.

The walls around the perimeter of the room were maybe six feet high.

"Watch this." Miriam unwound one of the ropes and tugged. It tightened and snapped against the pulley. She bent her knees, using her weight, and one of the dirty glass panels inched open. A rush of fresh air fell into the room.

"Every other one opens, all the way around." Miriam stared at the lazy clouds meandering through the open window. "Look at this." She secured the rope with the figure eight again and crossed to an oval mirror in a gilded frame. It hung from a bracket on the wall, directly over the spiral staircase. Miriam lined it up with another across the room, and with it, illuminated the dark entrance. "When my mother was in her rooms, she always left the doors open for me. It should be much brighter. These windows will have to be scrubbed."

"Is this the end?" Michael asked.

"It's the end of where I wanted to go today. Her studio is still through another passage, but what I came for is here in this room."

Miriam knelt next to the wall near a shelf of papers, took the key off her wrist, and pried up a short floorboard. Once loose, she set it to the side and, without hesitation, reached into the dark space. She removed a metal box from the depths of the floor, dropped it next to her, and unlatched the cover.

First out was a twine-bound stack of papers—stock certificates. She handed them over to Michael. He pushed his glasses further up the bridge of his nose and sat on the floor with his legs crossed. He set the stack in his lap and began to unknot the string.

"Father told me he hadn't said anything about those investments, because he thought you might advise against it. But he wanted to own part of a railroad." Miriam shrugged, as if the papers were likely frivolous. John could see Michael's pale expression—that they were the opposite of frivolous. "Now, I want to know where I stand—financially speaking, of course."

Next, she removed a blue velvet box about six inches square, and flat. "I'm sure this hasn't lost any value." Miriam cracked the lid open to reveal a necklace, liberally studded with large jewels. It was a confusion of wealth, dripping with cut gems in a multitude of colors. She lifted it to her smooth skin.

Michael stopped his sifting to watch, open-mouthed, as the stones settled around her neck. The weight flirted with her tendons, falling into the dips and hollow spaces of her body. She looked up and met John's eyes. John looked away from the flecks of color that suddenly seemed to glitter through the gray of her gaze. Miriam pulled it off her skin, and tucked it back in the box.

Michael cleared his throat. "Is there anything else I should know about?"

Miriam gestured to the piles of paper that now sat, temporarily categorized, on the floor next to Michael. "Do you think there is enough value there to pay to have the house opened back up?"

Michael coughed into his fist. "Miriam, there is enough in just this pile to purchase, furnish, and open every house on the next four blocks—with money left over. You have always been dreadfully rich, I'm not sure if you ever knew that." He piled the stack together. "This, though...this kind of rich is entirely different."

He glanced back to the papers in his lap. "But you have more than enough in your other accounts to open this house in any manner you please. You don't have to do anything with these certificates but keep them in a safe place." He paused. "And by safe place, I do not mean in the floorboards in a maze of museum-quality rooms. What I mean is in a safe-deposit box in the bank."

Miriam laughed. It was the sound of crystal falling against crystal. John had never heard it and knew instantly the danger. Miriam was wholly unaware of the effect it would have on men— Michael in particular. John watched.

Michael couldn't keep his eyes off her.

Chapter 14

Maggie paced in front of the window. She'd been waiting all morning, through lunch, and for most of the afternoon. Mrs. Whitaker had done her hair with the hot iron, so she didn't want to sit on the sofa and accidentally lean her head back. It had been nice, someone doing her hair. But Maggie tried not to think about that too much.

Lucy sat on the floor with a china doll in her lap. It had golden curls and blue eyes and the tiniest of painted freckles sprinkled across its nose.

Dr. Pierce's carriage rolled to a stop right outside the wooden gate. Ione sat next to him. He jumped down, hurried to the other side, and held his hand out for her. She accepted his assistance, and he slowly lowered her to the ground.

"They're here," Maggie called to Mrs. Whitaker.

Mrs. Whitaker set her needlepoint on the side table and stood, shaking out any creases in her dress. Lucy jumped up, racing to the door. She opened it and ran out before anyone could stop her. Dr. Pierce caught her before she reached Ione.

"You're sister is still sore," he cautioned.

Lucy's nose wrinkled. "What happened anyway?"

Maggie followed Mrs. Whitaker down the path. Now that she could see Ione was safe, Maggie wasn't sure if she wanted to run to her as Lucy had done, or if she wanted to turn around, walk into the house, and slam the door closed. She knew it wasn't fair, she shouldn't feel that way—Ione was the one who'd been hurt.

Mrs. Whitaker moved off the path, and Ione hobbled toward Maggie. She lifted her arms around Maggie's shoulders and drew her close.

"I am so sorry," Ione whispered in her ear. "I am so, so sorry.

You must have been so scared."

Maggie's bravado abandoned her. She pushed her face into Ione's chest and sobbed.

Michael kicked the apartment door closed behind him and sat on the small bench to untie his shoes. Railroad stock. Mr. Beaumont had bought railroad stock. He lined his shoes up against the edge of the carpet. And he'd bought a lot of it.

Dinner, as usual, was waiting in the oven. He'd hired Eliza after Miss Beaumont had made the decision to close the warehouse. She'd been one of the cleaning women employed by Mr. Beaumont. Michael knew she had children at home, and on a whole, he'd neglected his apartment, so he brought her on.

She was his first employee. Michael opened the oven and took out the still-warm chicken stew. Thyme and rosemary and something he could never place, but which was delicious nonetheless, rose with the steam as he removed the lid.

He had others employed now, primarily to work in the financial industry, but some to clean and maintain his buildings downtown. Miriam didn't know, but since Michael had begun working with her father, he'd taken the opportunity to learn, growing his own fortune in the process.

Michael ladled the stew into a bowl and sliced off a piece of bread. He knew she thought of him as her father's solicitor, and that was fine, but Michael hadn't been an active solicitor since her father had died. By that point in time, he'd made so much money investing his own small sums where her father had suggested, he hadn't needed to find a new position. In fact, after her father died, he'd never billed the estate for keeping track of her fortune. Instead he'd carried on with her father's investment strategies, watching both of their balance sheets grow.

He took a bite, letting the warm aroma seep into his day. The house had been astounding. And the stocks—he still couldn't get over the stocks. They were a sound investment. He knew, because he held a share almost as large as her father's. That man had been brilliant.

Michael reached behind his chair and slid the window open, letting the city noise into his space. He leaned back on two legs, trying to decide how best to proceed with Miss Beaumont.

She was pretty, even prettier than he'd remembered, not that that had to do with anything. She'd never had any idea of his feelings for her. She never knew how he waited for the invitations from her father, hoping he would get a chance to see her. He dropped all four legs of his chair back to the ground and carried his dishes to the basin. Her skin looked like silk.

The deacon was an interesting fellow. Michael liked him immediately. He was protective over Miriam, and, Michael could see, she was in much need of protection.

Not only from whatever she was dealing with—she never did say—but because she was considering re-entering society in a way she'd never done before. Her money alone would offer protection from some of the more benign dangers—society gossips and hungry reporters. She would not, however, be prepared for the men in the upper echelons. Miriam—Miss Beaumont, he reminded himself—with her gray eyes and honey brown hair, and a fortune so large it virtually couldn't be gambled away, would be in high demand.

He could show her, though. Michael had no idea what she was thinking, but if she intended to re-enter society, her deacon would not be of much assistance. And, Michael surmised, she could potentially be a significant donor for the hospital project he'd been considering. Michael decided to flip through his stack of invitations to discern what might be a simple beginning. Typically, he liked to avoid escorting anyone to most of the events, but Miss Beaumont would be an entertaining way to spend his evening. She might even make some of the more tedious of his invites a bit more attractive.

Her face and her slender figure as she'd disappeared into the dark kept revisiting Michael. He removed his glasses and rubbed his eyes. For now, he'd let her continue to think he still worked as a solicitor.

Ione could scarcely look the woman in the eye. She was a pastor's wife, she knew what Ione had been doing when she was attacked, and this woman had been the one who had picked up the pieces. All of that, and she was beautiful. Not just pretty—beautiful.

Lucy sat curled in Ione's lap.

"She missed you." Mrs. Whitaker picked up a piece of mending and set it in her lap.

Ione wasn't sure how Lucy could have missed her. The Whitakers' home was perfect with its white ceilings, lace curtains, and walls papered with the tiniest of yellow flowers.

Maggie darted in and out of the room, carrying a tea service from the kitchen. Ione hoped she wasn't treated like a servant. She was so responsible; it was easy to forget she was still young.

Maggie set the tray on the coffee table and headed back to the kitchen.

"We've been trying to get her to stop working ever since she arrived." Mrs. Whitaker leaned forward to confide quietly to Ione. "But she's determined to keep up with any chore she can think of."

Ione nodded and smiled. At least they noticed the work she did. And even from the short time Ione had been able to spend with Maggie after she'd returned home, she knew Maggie wouldn't accept anything from anyone without paying them back in some way. Even with no right to be, Ione was proud of her sister.

How she would compensate Miriam for her troubles, she didn't know. Miriam, or the doctor, or this beautiful woman who sat across from her.

"Thank you," Ione said, weakly. She brushed Lucy's hair back from her face.

"We missed you," Lucy said, looking up to meet Ione's gaze.

"I missed you too."

Mrs. Whitaker blinked rapidly and rose. "I'll go and see if Maggie needs any help in the kitchen."

"Will we go home now?" Lucy asked, twisting the doll's golden hair around her index finger.

"I'm afraid we can't just yet. I need to find a place for us."

"What about our old place?" Lucy sat up, her eyebrows drawn together in a frown.

"Someone else lives there now."

"How come?"

Ione took a deep breath and looked at the ceiling. It was so unfair for Lucy. "Well, we weren't there, and another family needed a place."

"It's nice here."

"I can see that."

"I like their food, and the bed, and they bought me this new dress." Lucy hopped off Ione's lap and twirled. The dress lifted in a bell.

"It's very pretty."

"Not as pretty as the ones you make."

Ione smiled. Everything was so wrong.

"Mr. Farling? Excuse me, Mr. Farling?"

Michael turned to see a man weave his way through the crowded financial district. He stepped closer to the building, out of the foot traffic, and waited for the man he didn't recognize.

"Thank you for waiting," the man said. He bent over for a second and took a breath before holding out his hand in greeting. "I'm Jacob Tenney."

Michael took his proffered hand. "I'm sorry, have we been introduced before? I'm afraid I can't place your name."

"No. We haven't. But I know who you are. I've been chasing all over town, tracking you down. I need to discuss some business, and I'm hoping you are the right person to speak with."

"My offices are right around the corner. Do you want to step in off the street?"

"That would be appreciated." The man brushed off his jacket and fell into step behind Michael. "I've been trying all day to ascertain the appropriate parties to speak with about an offer to purchase a piece of property. It's been a long day. A quiet office would be welcome."

Michael led the way around the building and through the heavy glass doors, down the main hallway, and into his office.

"Please, have a seat." He gestured to one of the open chairs on the other side of his desk.

He was young. He wore a smart brown suit and carried a leather attaché case. His shoes were shined, and although he looked like he'd worked that day, he was a man used to sitting at a desk. His black hair was slicked back, appearing as if it could withstand the force of a tornado.

"Would you like anything?"

"Really, I just need to ask if you are still the solicitor for the Beaumont estate."

Michael sat behind his desk and folded his hands on his ink blotter. "Yes, I am."

"Great," the man said, moving to the edge of his seat. "I have an offer that I was asked to bring to you."

"What kind of offer?" Despite the man's congenial demeanor, Michael had the uneasy sense that he wasn't about to tell him the details.

"Well, it's an offer to purchase the warehouse down by the docks. The red brick building."

"Yes, I'm familiar with the building."

"Anyway, my client wishes to purchase it. And for a fair sum, in my opinion."

The factory hadn't been on the market. It had never even been discussed. It had never needed to be. "It's not for sale."

"But will you take his offer to her? I can't imagine why a woman would want to hold on to a property like that anyway." The man sat back and crossed one ankle over his knee. "What's she going to do with it?"

Michael leaned back in his chair. The man was overconfident. "Who hired you?"

"He wants to remain anonymous."

"Why?"

"What do you mean?"

"Why does he want to remain anonymous?"

"I'm really not sure." Jacob raised a hand to the top of his head to smooth his already glassy hair.

Michael glanced out the window to the people passing on the street: women with handbags, rushing to their place of employment; men in business suits, muttering to themselves; boys squatting in the alley, throwing dice, waiting for the day to pass so they could sell the next morning's papers.

"Mr. Tenney." Michael took the tone of an advisor. "Do you know who your client is?"

"I said he wants to remain anonymous."

"I understand that, but anonymous to me and anonymous to you are two entirely different things."

Concern flashed across the younger man's face.

"Personally, I would feel uneasy about bringing an offer to a client without being able to discuss its origin. It would make me feel, well, as if I couldn't advise them appropriately."

Jacob shifted in his chair, leaning his elbows on his knees. Michael measured his body language as Jacob realized the fast sell he'd hoped for was not a probability.

Michael pressed to further discomfort the man, leaning forward again. "Do you feel you are serving your client to the best of your ability? How would you suggest I approach my client? Financial service involves more than making a quick buck. In the long term, you have to be careful about with whom your business is aligned."

Jacob Tenney's expression darkened at the unsolicited advice, and Michael knew that his need of money was a greater motivator than the potential business connection. Much of business was the ability to make the same decisions in times of need as one would make in times of plenty. This man hadn't yet learned that lesson.

Jacob pulled a folded paper from the leather case he carried and slid it across Michael's desk. "I'm sure you'll agree it's more than a fair price for a defunct warehouse."

Michael examined the paper, not for the price at the bottom, which he sensed would be exceedingly fair, but for a clue as to the identity of the person making the offer. Disappointed, he folded the paper back into thirds and set it on a short pile on the right side of his desk. Miriam would not sell, no matter how much the interested party offered, but he would bring the offer to her, more as her friend than her advisor.

Michael knocked on the warehouse door and then took a step back to look up toward the windows Miriam watched from. Her first response was to back out of sight and stand absolutely still, so she could pretend she wasn't there. But it was absurd, as her house was already invaded by two other women, and she needed to speak with him anyway.

"Would you like me to get it?" Ione asked. She and Jenny stood next to Miriam at the window. Ever since they'd seen the man with the cane watching them, the days had been a strange conglomeration of exterior world obsession and avoidance.

Miriam pushed away from the window. "I can go."

Ione and Jenny returned to their seat on the sofa. All day, they'd been discussing the future—how they would survive, how Ione could care for her sisters—and in a manner that was at least equal to the care they received from the pastor and his wife. If they should go to the morning mass across the street, where they might live, and how they might make a living.

Miriam brushed her skirts out and reached for the door latch. "It's Mr. Farling. He handles my father's accounts. I think he wants to follow up with some information after I met with him the other day."

Miriam walked down the dark stairs and opened the door to the blinding midday light.

After they'd discussed their futures, they focused on the questions regarding the man with the walking stick: what he wanted, why he cut them both in the same place, how he discovered where they were, why he even cared, and what they could do. They noted the increase in newspaper accounts of missing women and posited theories until they scared each other useless.

She motioned for Michael to follow her to the upper apartment.

"This is Ione, and this is Jenny," Miriam said by way of introduction. "And this is Mr. Michael Farling."

"Please," he said, removing his hat. "All of you, please call me Michael."

"It's nice to meet you." Jenny was the first to walk over, offering her hand for an exceedingly masculine handshake. Ione, meeting Miriam's eyes, stifled a grin.

"I have a number of things to discuss about your estate. Could we speak somewhere private?" Michael quietly directed the question to Miriam. She looked up and met his sincere blue gaze, and her fingers itched to paint him. She would paint him in the warm browns of security, because he filled the room. Her eyes slipped to study the shape of his lips, and stayed there until he cleared his throat.

"Of course. We can go into my studio."

Michael followed her down the hall and into a room that looked nothing like he'd expected. The women staying with Miriam were not who he'd expected either, and he was off balance.

Miriam made him feel like the young university man who would have done anything to impress her father, but now it was Miriam he needed to impress, and he didn't want to even begin to delve into the possible reasons. Michael had thought of little else after the young solicitor had brought the offer of purchase to his office.

"May I ask you a few questions?" Michael took the chair that Miriam offered. It was straight-backed, and splotched with dried paint in every color.

"I guess you can." Miriam pulled a striped dress off the back of another colorful chair and carried it over to where Michael waited. She placed it in front of him and sat, facing him, without the buffer of a desk.

Michael, further taken aback by her level of comfort, purposefully met her eyes to gauge if her ease was a façade, or if she was rewriting her approach. She met him with large, unblinking gray eyes, and he was the one to look away first.

"Who are the women in your front room?"

Miriam explained the situation. She told him about her walks, about finding Ione, about John, and finding Jenny. He interrupted when she told him about buying off Jenny's father.

"That was a generous thing for you to do," he said, carefully. "But men like that do not typically stop after they've found a source of funding for their addictions."

"That's why I had John take the money and the offer to him. I hope that he will have some sense that he can't chase down a man of the cloth." Miriam picked at the fabric of her skirt. "That's not the primary danger, though."

Michael waited for her to continue.

"The man who attacked Ione and Jenny might know they're staying with me."

"That's why you're considering opening the townhome."

"Yes."

"I can have it open in a matter of a couple of days. But what are you going to do with them once they're living with you in the townhome?"

"I'm not sure."

There were a number of things that didn't sit well. "What are your plans? Will you re-enter society?"

It was Miriam's turn to shift in her chair. "I'd considered it."

"What would hold you back?"

"I know no one," she said. "I've always followed the society pages, so I know the timelines of the families, but I've never met most of them."

"It won't matter. You have more money than most of them. You could start by getting involved in some charity organizations."

"That's something I will do." Miriam furrowed her brow and looked at Michael again. "How much money do I have?"

"I honestly don't know. But it's more than you could ever spend."

"How did that happen?"

"Your father made some incredibly wise investments. He also taught me, and over the past several years, I've continued his strategies." Michael drummed his fingers together. "You didn't really want to discuss it, so I thought it best to continue doing what I'd always done for your father."

"But have you paid yourself for your services?"

Michael glanced to the painting on the easel. It was Ione. There was no mistaking the determination invested in her wise eyes. In the painting, however, she wore a tailored business suit. Her shoulders were proud. High expectations exuded from her brown eyes, and Michael suddenly felt as if he might not measure up.

Miriam had been honest. It was time for him to be honest as well.

"There was no need to pay myself for my services." Miriam tipped her head to the side, indicating she was ready to hear the rest of his explanation. Michael took a deep breath. "Your father taught me enough to invest my own small sums. Those small sums have grown, and I now own a number of properties in the financial district, as well as the same stocks your father owns. In fact, with the additional stock certificates you pulled up from the floorboards." Michael raised one sardonic eyebrow. "I think, together, we may be majority stakeholders in at least one company."

"So I assume you are no longer a solicitor for hire?"

"No."

"Will you help me find another? I feel silly having you doing work that you no longer need to do."

"No. I will continue with your estate. It's the least I can do for your father."

Miriam nodded, pursing her lips together, avoiding emotion.

"There is one other reason I came over today."

She glanced up, her expression shifting to one of curiosity. Curiosity was her primary motivator, Michael decided. A strange finding in someone who'd lived for years as a recluse.

"There's been an offer to purchase the warehouse."

Chapter 15

"I have an idea." Miriam wrung her hands in her lap, nervous Ione or Jenny may not like the plans she'd been making with John and Michael.

"What is it?" Jenny asked, wiping her mouth on the back of her hand after swallowing a spoonful of soup.

Ione rolled a carrot around in the broth. Miriam knew she'd been worried about her sisters. Or more likely, worried about the decision she would need to make. They missed her, and she them, but they were also happy and well cared for. "What kind of idea?"

"I have another home. It was the home I lived in with my parents before my mother died." Miriam dropped her gaze to her untouched bowl of soup. "I think we should consider moving there."

"You want us to move with you?" Jenny said.

"If you would like." Miriam picked up her spoon and swirled the soup around the bowl.

"Is the house big enough for all of us?" Ione shifted in her chair. Miriam knew her real question.

"It's big enough to bring your sisters, if you decide you would like to do that."

"Why don't you live there now?" Jenny took another spoonful of soup.

"My father left when my mother died. We never returned. Everything is still there."

"You mean he just left?"

Miriam nodded. She never realized how strange abandoning a house was until she'd heard herself say it out loud. She stood and carried her uneaten dinner to the counter. She dumped the soup back into the pot and turned to face the two women.

"What will we do at your house?" Ione asked. "We can't be eternal guests." She dropped her spoon on the table and leaned back in the chair, crossing her arms. "Will you need to hire any help? We could work for you." She nodded toward Jenny. "I'm not sure about Jenny, but I'll never get a position in someone's household without a recommendation, and I've never worked for anyone other than a tavern owner."

Ione carried her bowl over to where Miriam stood. "Would you maybe consider hiring me? Do you need someone?"

Miriam took Ione's bowl from her and set it on the counter. "Sit back down for a minute, I'll be right back."

Ione sat as she'd been instructed. Miriam returned with her striped dress in tow.

"Did you make this?"

Ione nodded, obviously embarrassed by the brazen fabric and the garment's blatant use.

"That's real pretty." Jenny's spoon stopped in mid-air.

"The fabric is inexpensive. It's really not as nice as it looks." Ione's tone was apologetic.

"No." Miriam sat with the dress in her lap, turning the bodice inside out to demonstrate the stitching on the inside. "That's the magic of the dress. You took inferior fabric and created something that's better constructed than what most professional dressmakers make, even with the best of fabrics at their disposal."

Ione shrugged and Miriam set the dress aside. "The house is astounding. It's still furnished, decorated, and although maybe not in the most current fashion, it is entirely acceptable in any circle."

"So why have you never returned?" Jenny asked.

"Because returning to a house like that means returning to that kind of lifestyle. Before now, I've never felt the need, nor had the desire to change the way I'd been accustomed to living." Miriam rose and crossed to the window, looking down at the streetlamp as it sputtered to life. The fog would roll in thick that night, but instead of the excitement that used to thrum through her body with the thought of wandering unnoticed in the night, a sense of dread pooled in her limbs.

Miriam turned to face the women still at the table.

"I would feel better if you didn't stand by the window," Jenny said, quietly.

"That's the main reason we should move. I don't want him to know where we are." Miriam stepped away. She straightened a stack of newspapers before returning to the table. "But returning to society will be a challenge. You probably can both tell I'm not that comfortable around people I don't know."

"Yeah, we noticed," Jenny admitted. Ione sent her a subduing glare.

Miriam shrugged. "I don't think it's anything I can't get through, but there is one thing that nearly paralyzes me." She looked at Ione. "I don't want to work with a dressmaker. I don't want a stranger wrapping their arms around my waist to take my measurements. I don't want to invite people into my house until I am ready to entertain."

Ione sat stock still.

"And I think you could help me."

Ione ran her finger along the grain of the wooden table, following the grooves, avoiding eye contact.

"You would have the best of fabrics, and anything else you might need—all of the newest equipment."

"But all you have seen of my work is that." Ione gestured to the limp reminder of her sins.

"It tells me enough to know you have a rare talent. And I have a rare requirement, not to be touched by a dressmaker, nor have my business heralded from a dressmaker's lips to her next customer. I would pay you handsomely," Miriam added, concerned that she had somehow offended the woman at her table.

"You wouldn't need to give me anything."

"But I would. And I don't want to risk frightening you away, but not only will I need a wardrobe, but so will Jenny, and you as well. I also imagine your sisters need things. From what I can figure, there's more than a few months of work to be done, and you will likely need help."

Miriam dug into her apron pocket and pulled out a list. She smoothed it out on the table before reading some of the items. "I will need ball gowns, day gowns, even undergarments. And if you designed this dress, I would like to see some drawings for designs you think might work for me."

"Oh," Jenny added. "Can I help? I can cut the fabric, and I'll follow your directions, I promise."

"Jenny actually has a keen eye for design." Ione reached over and pulled a magazine from a nearby pile. "She likes the fashion pages, and she knows what will be desirable for the upcoming season."

Jenny did nothing to try to hide her smile.

"I think Jenny would look astounding in pink." Miriam smiled at the women at her table. "Most women with a light complexion have difficulty wearing the color, but I think Jenny would wear it well."

Ione nodded her agreement, and they both looked at Jenny, assessing her more critically.

"I never had a pink dress." Jenny bit her bottom lip with her gapped front teeth. "I wanted one, I remember, with my da, but he said no 'cause we had no money. But I wanted it bad. It had ruffles and lace on the bottom and a bow in the back. I saw it in a store window."

Miriam reached across the table to put her hand over Jenny's. It was still strange, the feel of another person's skin under hers, but she was trying to learn to like the sensation. "I think, after some sensible clothing is finished for all of us, a pink dress should be first on the list."

John watched the fog roll in thick and black. He sat on the edge of his twin bed and pulled on a pair of boots he hadn't taken out of the cabinet since he'd arrived in Chicago. His jacket was next, and a hat. John dragged a small trunk out from under his bed and flipped open the metal latch. At the bottom, under a bound stack of papers, under a quilt his mother had sewn, was a sheathed hunting knife. He wasn't what he'd considered skilled with the weapon—he'd used it primarily to cut fishing line when he was growing up—but it was at least something.

He tucked it into the back of his pants, under his jacket, and made his way out of the church.

The fog was thick. He avoided the illuminated circles of mist that hung in the air at regular intervals. The man with the cane hadn't been back to the alley. Neither had any other women. They were out somewhere else. The man would be out too; the fog was too convenient. There was no way John would be able to sleep knowing mere blocks away from the safe haven of the cathedral someone could be in danger.

John made his way past the warehouse, over line after line of rail tracks, and toward the rotting structures that had sprung up to serve the city after the great fire. Father Ayers had explained that the plan had been for the new city to be one of stone and brick, but temporary buildings were needed to house the workers. Consequently, some wooden structures were hastily assembled for short term use. They'd never been replaced, though, and now served as taverns. The kind with upstairs rooms for rental by the hour. The rooms typically came with a woman, or, if preferred, just about anything mainstream society would rather ignore.

Ironically, it was either the lawmakers or the enforcers in the city who owned and leased most of the dilapidated space. And for a price, any sin could be overlooked.

The knife was a heavy weight. John reached back to shift it to the right before he leaned against a stack of wooden pallets. He could smell the river snaking its way through the sewers.

The church bell chimed in the distance, three times. Water dripped from somewhere, landing in a puddle or a bucket. John shifted to sit in the shadows and listened for anything out of the ordinary.

When the bell chimed four, John made his way back to the church with the weight of his knife mocking his efforts.

Angelene pulled the afghan closer around Lucy. After church that morning, they'd returned home for lunch. Maggie sat on the davenport, reading a book with her legs curled underneath her. Lucy had climbed onto Angelene's lap, fitting her body perfectly into hers. After a pang of longing, Angelene put her arms around Lucy and hummed into her freshly washed hair. They rocked together like that until Lucy's breathing became deep and regular.

Maggie looked up occasionally, and Angelene didn't know if

she should apologize for holding her sister or offer to hold Maggie too.

"Mrs. Whitaker?" Lucy said in a tired voice.

Angelene thought she'd been sleeping. "What?"

"How come you don't gots no kids?"

She took a shaky breath and blinked quickly. Maggie looked up, waiting for her answer too.

Angelene answered the only way she knew how. "Because Jesus didn't give me any."

For a long time, Lucy was silent. Angelene held her breath until she sensed Maggie look away, then she quickly wiped away the tears that were threatening.

"He should," Lucy finally responded.

"Oh?" Angelene only trusted herself to the one syllable.

"You'd make a great mama. Tonight I'll pray he gives you a little girl."

Michael met the new housekeeper at the townhouse. He'd offered to do it, knowing that Miriam wouldn't ask after she'd discovered he wasn't being paid. They stood in the foyer. She was waiting for directions.

Mrs. Maloney, recently widowed, was unemployed due to her employer's move to New York. With grandchildren in the area, she didn't want to follow. Her professional reputation meant she didn't have to. Any number of families would have snatched her up, but Michael was the first to speak with her, and his offer was generous.

He had to be generous. Whoever took the position would not only have to know how to run a household of the highest caliber, but also how to squelch gossip, work in unusual circumstances, and, most of all, be motherly. All three women could use a mother.

"If you don't mind me asking, who owns the home?"

He also had not told her much about the job, yet.

"Miss Beaumont."

"Miss Beaumont? *The* Miss Beaumont? The one no one has seen since she was a little girl?"

"I see you've heard of the family."

"The family, or what is left of it, happens to be the default gossip. Rather than talking about weather when one runs out of things to say, the most common topic is the Beaumont family." Michael assisted Mrs. Maloney with her coat, and then shrugged out of his. They both paused, realizing they had no idea where to set them.

"How do you feel about working for her?" Michael hung the overcoats from the end of the banister. It seemed the least dusty place.

Mrs. Maloney shrugged at his temporary solution. "I don't see why it would be a problem. She wasn't burned in the factory was she? Poor thing. I've heard some people talk about an accident." Mrs. Maloney looked up thoughtfully, following the wallpaper pattern. "But," she corrected herself, "it really is of no consequence, is it?"

"No, it really isn't. But she has not been burned." That was a rumor Michael hadn't heard before. She was going to create quite a stir when she reappeared.

"Well." Mrs. Maloney set her bag down near the bottom of the curved staircase. "Where should we start?"

"I think the parlor would be a good choice, as we've already pulled the sheets off the furniture, and you can get an idea of what you are dealing with."

Michael gestured for Mrs. Maloney to precede him through the partially open wooden doors. She took a few steps into the room, stopped, and turned to face him. "This—" She gestured to the full room. "—has been here all this time?"

Michael nodded.

"How many rooms are in the house?"

"That's a tricky question. Maybe you should sit down."

Chapter 16

Ione knew Jenny couldn't help but watch over her shoulder as she sketched a design for a day gown for Miriam. They all needed sensible clothing, and soon, but Miriam was the one who would be under examination by nearly everyone. The house was in the process of being opened, and, although the housekeeper had promised discretion, the activity around the home was bound to attract attention. That meant callers. She certainly couldn't entertain visiting ladies in the shapeless things she typically wore.

Ione also knew that Jenny had all she could do not to make suggestions. And they were good suggestions, but Ione needed some space.

"Jenny?"

"I'm sorry, I'll sit down."

"No, I just thought of something." Ione looked at the pad of paper with her lists and lists of needed supplies. "There's a catalog on the table over there. Do you think you can look up the prices for the items and estimate the costs? You said you were good at sums, right?"

"Absolutely." Jenny smiled and grabbed the pad of paper. She rifled through the first few sheets, and her smile grew. "This'll be fun." She snatched up a pencil and tucked it into the loose bun at the nape of her neck.

Ione breathed a sigh of relief as Jenny found a seat on the sofa, curling her legs up underneath her skirts. She balanced the notepad on one knee, the catalog on the other, and began flipping the pages back and forth, searching for the items.

Ione examined her drawing. She was undecided on the bustle. They were still in fashion but had grown smaller, and Miriam had such an enviable shape. She slimmed the silhouette with a few light lines. A minimal bustle, she decided. One made of padding, not wire. Miriam's entrance into her social sphere would be a delicate balance.

"I don't think I will take much with us at first." Miriam walked into the room with a handful of paintbrushes. She looked around for somewhere to set them down but settled on stuffing them into her pocket. "I do want to take my paintings though. I'm just not sure how to move them."

"Do you have a studio at the other house?" Ione looked up from her drawing.

"My mother's studio." Miriam walked to the paintings leaning against the wall on the other side of the room. Ione watched her flip through, her critical expression changing with each one. "Maybe I should just leave some of them here."

"Not this one," Jenny said. She hurriedly cleared the notebook and catalog off her lap, walked over to Miriam, and flipped through to the one of the women standing outside of the factory. "You need to bring this."

Ione watched Miriam blink in surprise. She could see she hadn't been prepared for the intrusion.

Jenny, unnoticing, pulled the canvas from the pile and held it up. "This one makes me feel hope." She straightened her arms, examining it from different angles. "I don't know why, but I feel good when I see this one."

Miriam, having taken a step back, reached a shaky hand into the pocket with the paintbrushes. Ione could see her rolling them between her fingers, probably putting them in order from smallest to largest, or largest to smallest, or even counting them.

"Can you tell me what you think of this so far?" Ione rose from her seat at the table and crossed to where Miriam stood. "It's a bit different from some of the more popular styles, but I think it might suit you." She held the paper out for Miriam's critique. Normally, she would have never shown an unfinished plan, but Miriam needed a distraction.

Miriam held the pad of paper in her hands. The dress was

sleek, with a small bustle and short train. "You don't think this will be too low?" She said, pointing to the bodice.

"This is actually a bit higher than most of the designs being made right now."

"It's very pretty." Miriam handed the paper back. "I hope I will do it justice. I fear your talents might be wasted on me."

"Nonsense." Ione took the sketch back. She wrapped her arms around the pad of paper, holding it tightly to her chest. "You know, I am looking forward to this," Ione said, too quiet for Jenny to hear. "And I want you to know how much I appreciate what you're doing." She looked down at the floor. "I don't know where I would be if you hadn't found me when you did."

Miriam felt a pang of guilt at the number of times she'd returned to Ione's painting, trying to make her brush paint the truth she'd seen in the alley. But Miriam knew the truth was usually unhindered by factual fetters, and Ione's expression as she stood in front of her still wasn't right. Her posture was nothing like the confidence Miriam had painted for her. She watched the afternoon sun grazing the side of Ione's face, illuminating her hair, shifting the feel of the moment. Ione glanced up, her brown eyes meeting Miriam's, and Miriam understood.

Truth, real truth, was what you made it. Like all her other portraits, Miriam had painted Ione's future. But Ione's had a twist; her future required Miriam's involvement.

"No, Ione." Miriam began to formulate a plan. Ione would become the woman in the painting. "Without you, I wouldn't be able to do what I should have been doing all along. The dress is beautiful. It will be exactly what I need."

Ione nodded and returned to the table. Miriam walked back to her studio to gather the few supplies she would take with her the next week. *No, Ione*, she thought, *it will be exactly what we both need.*

John and Miriam watched from her windows for their carriages. Miriam would leave with Michael, and John would escort Ione and Jenny to the store to pick out fabric and other necessities. It was not the way John would have chosen to spend the day, but John didn't like the idea of the women going about unescorted. No one had been able to locate the man who'd attacked them, and the nausea of dealing with Jenny's father still lingered, so John resigned himself to the duty of escort. Together, they would make an unusual group.

Thankfully, Father Ayers had been patient with the demand on John's time. More than patient. He'd listened, offered advice, and fulfilled the duty of a Father perfectly. John rubbed his back where the weight of his knife had rested the other night, and was embarrassed.

"He's here," Miriam said, pushing away from the window. She'd lost the nervous twitches that used to accompany any changes in her environment. Miriam looked at Jenny and Ione and shrugged.

"When will you be back?" John asked, watching Michael jump down from his seat. Suddenly he felt like a father—and not the priestly kind.

Miriam smiled. "It will be before dinner. We'll have a lot of things to go through. I need to decide what I want done with my parents' rooms and where everyone should stay. I need to meet the housekeeper." Miriam shoved her hands into her pocket, concealing the sudden nervous movements of her fingers.

"I'm sure she's very competent." John opened the door and stood back.

"Michael said I would like her."

Miriam gathered her few things, waved, and disappeared into the warehouse.

Although closed in the back, Michael's carriage was open in the front. For a minute, after Miriam had paused before stepping out of her door, he wondered if it was too much too soon. But he saw her shoulders straighten and her chin lift a fraction, and he knew she'd adjusted.

He guided the horses slowly across the tracks and navigated the ruts in the city streets. Eventually the brick industrial towers, billowing soot into the sky, gave way to rows of identical stone houses, which then gave way to tree-lined streets and paved paths. A man on a bicycle tottered, slowing to a stop at the edge of a park.

"Have you ever climbed on one of those things?" Miriam nodded toward the man. He was dressed in a brown tailored vest with trousers tucked into boots.

"Of course I have. I take it you have yet to try?"

Miriam turned her gray gaze to meet his.

"It was quite a good time. I think you would like it. You know they're creating more and more paths all the time. Soon we will be able to get nearly anywhere in the city without a horse."

She said nothing as he slowed the carriage. Michael had to fight not to feel foolish under the pressure of her eyes. A breath later, he sensed her turn toward the house, and he allowed himself to steal a glimpse. The sun fell, fractured by the heavy foliage, coloring patches of her shoulders and hair. Her skin shone pink, as if she were blushing, but he knew it was only the anticipation of her meeting with Mrs. Maloney. Miriam on a bicycle, smiling, with the wind in her hair, was something he planned to see.

Michael closed the door softly. Mrs. Maloney stood in front of them. Miriam's eyes adjusted to the light cascading through the open doors into the entryway. The stairs, leading to the upper floors, disappeared into blackness.

"Mr. Farling asked me to wait for you to begin with the upper floors," Mrs. Maloney offered after Michael had introduced them. "In the meantime, I started in the kitchen. Tomorrow, we will begin hiring staff."

Miriam nodded to the older woman. She was what one might describe as heavily framed. A mound of silver hair was piled high on her head, doing nothing to conceal her considerable height. She stood nearly as tall as Michael, and almost as wide at the shoulders. She did not use her size to intimidate, though. Miriam relaxed under her careful scrutiny. Her color would be lavender. Her high cheekbones and large eyes advertised hard-won wisdom. Her steady hands commanded respect. Miriam felt dismantled under her gaze, but not in a harmful way. The woman watched only to discern needs.

"The word went out today." Michael took a few steps down the hall toward the kitchen, looking into a few of the newly opened rooms. "We didn't think it best to announce any vacancies in the papers. Rather, we discretely gathered some names and asked them to come here tomorrow morning."

"How many positions will this house create?" Miriam followed Michael deeper into the house.

Michael deferred to Mrs. Maloney with a nod.

"Once the house is open, we will need a butler, a cook, a kitchen maid, and two housekeepers. Temporarily, we will need more than that."

Miriam let her gaze wander up the carpeted staircase.

"Are you ready to begin?"

Miriam nodded and took a step forward.

"Would you like me to come with you?" Michael stood with his hands shoved awkwardly into his trouser pockets. The fabric of his jacket was pushed back under his arms. His spectacles had slid fractionally down his straight nose, and he met Miriam's eyes above the rim. His blue gaze penetrated without the filter of his lenses.

"I think..." Miriam touched the warm wood of the banister. The rumbling sound of her father's laugh filled her senses. "I think I want to be alone for a while."

"That's fine, dear." Mrs. Maloney nodded. "If you need me, I'll be in the kitchen." She turned to Michael. "I need to go over some budgets. Maybe you could help?"

Michael mumbled something, but Miriam didn't pay attention to his words. She was already halfway up the long, narrow stairs, the subtle wear patterns in the carpet pulling her along the habitual paths. Fresh air flowed from somewhere.

The upstairs hallway ran the length of the house, front to back. At the front of the house, double doors opened to a sitting room. It connected her parents' bedrooms. Mrs. Maloney must have opened the doors and the windows in anticipation for her visit, because it was from the windows over the uncovered red-velvet davenport that the breeze and light filtered into the hall.

Miriam passed the closed doors to her right and made her way to the open ones. The room smelled like her parents—not her mother, or her father, but her parents together. Dusty sunlight fell in ruined rectangles across the covered furniture. Miriam began pulling sheets off the other pieces.

Her mother's roll-top writing desk was first, followed by her father's reading chair, the bookshelves, and heavily framed portraits. She uncovered the game table where, much to her mother's dismay, her father had taught her to play cards. She whisked the sheets off the occasional chairs and finally, the heavy mantle.

Miriam knew the portrait that hung above—a self-portrait of her mother. Lifting a corner of the protective sheet, she exposed the silver details on the black frame. Her mother had insisted on the unusual frame. Her father had insisted on the portrait. Miriam let the sheet fall.

She sucked in a deep breath under the ageless assessment of her mother. The painting was created to mimic reality—her mother's soft skin and cascading hair the focus. It must have been her rebellion against her husband's demand for a painting, to create one that couldn't be hung in the main hall due to the intimacy of her subject. There was nothing objectionable, certainly no exposed skin. It was the casual pose, the satisfied lilt tucked into the corner of her mouth, the gray gaze, so much like Miriam's, that followed the admirer around the room.

Miriam ran her hand along the bottom edge of the canvas, feeling the gentle glide and individual strokes evidencing the investment of her mother's brush.

The light sounds of a lady's laughter rose through the open windows from the street below. Miriam brushed dust from her hands and moved to her mother's door. The knob turned easily, but the door squealed on its hinges. The room was dark. Mrs. Maloney hadn't entered here.

Miriam walked to the windows first, trying not to look at the individual pieces in the room until she could assess them in the light. The drapes opened in a dusty cloud. Miriam had to work to get the windows open, but their tight hinges finally gave, and she was able to push the sashes wide, letting in a burst of air.

The breeze rustled the curtains that closed off the canopy bed, and Miriam felt a moment's unease at pulling them wide. But it was for nothing. Her mother's bed had been made, her pillows lined up perfectly. Miriam lifted one to her face, breathing in, searching for a hint of the perfume she so easily forgot. Nothing lingered, and Miriam placed the pillow back in the exact same place. She would need to decide how to arrange the rooms, but for now, for the moment, she would keep it exactly as her mother had left it. Miriam brushed an imaginary wrinkle from the bedding.

She began pulling the sheets off the furniture, filling the air with illusive swirls of dust. She walked through the sunlit paths, back and forth, and deposited the sheets into the hallway outside of the main door to her mother's rooms. She worked faster as the pile grew, until sweat trickled down her spine.

Then she sat at her mother's dressing table. Yellowed perfume in crystal bottles, scented talcum powder in a silver case, and hair pins congregated together on a mirrored tray. Miriam pulled one long brown hair that was twisted around a hair pin. Freeing it, she stretched it across the wooden table, tucked it into the grain of the wood, and then tried to leave it there, but it clung to her fingers. She didn't want to drop it on the floor, or lose it, so she wrapped it around the teardrop stopper of the perfume bottle she'd decided not to open. Old perfume always had the same cloying odor—nothing like her mother.

Miriam crossed to her mother's armoire and slowly opened the doors wide. Her light scent rushed out and surrounded Miriam. She closed her eyes and stood, imagining herself as seven again, flirting with the thought that if she looked up, she would see her mother's hand reach for hers, the sun playing in her hair, her long lashes fluttering against her laughing cheeks. Miriam opened her eyes, glancing down at her own drab clothes, before examining the satins and silks, the brocades and linens filling her mother's closet. Her mother never hid her vibrancy, never wore a cape. If she hadn't died, Miriam might have worn things like these. She reached out and sunk her hands into the piles of luxurious fabric.

She opened the long drawer under the cabinet doors. Her mother's personal items were folded neatly. The translucent silk made Miriam blush. She closed the drawer, deciding instead to cross to her father's room.

His room smelled like him the moment she opened the door.

Miriam stopped at the threshold, unsure if she even wanted to go in. His presence hung in the air, and as she breathed in, it expanded her chest until tears stung her eyes. She ducked under the drapes and pushed against the window, swinging it open far enough to bang against the brick ledge outside. She took a deep breath, filling her lungs and her mind with any other scent she could.

She pushed the drapes off her back, opened them wide, and surveyed his room. Scattered papers lay strewn across the arm of his chair. His grandfather clock stood in the corner, stopped at the minute her mother died. Unlike her mother's bed, his remained unmade, with her mother's nightgown bunched up next to his pillow. Although they'd had separate rooms, Miriam knew her mother used her bed only for napping. As a child, when she woke in the night, it was to her father's room she would always go, because that was where she would find them both.

Miriam picked up a dusty newspaper from the bedside table. None of his furniture had been covered. She glanced over the headlines strewn in bold print across the yellowed paper. They spoke of the park, and of plans to reverse the river. She shook the paper out and found the date. It was dated for the week before he died.

He'd come back to the house without her. She touched the indent in the blanket where he'd lain. Where he'd obviously chosen to spend time inhaling what remained of her mother.

"Are you all right?" Michael's careful tones interrupted the progression of her thoughts. He took a step closer, and Miriam took a step back.

"Did you know he came back?"

Michael furrowed his brows, assessing the room. "No."

"He left me." Miriam sucked in her lips to try to keep her chin from quivering.

Michael stepped farther into the room, fast enough to require that she adjust to the change in space between them before she had time to back away.

"I thought he was fine." She looked at the bed. "That he could just give her up. He let me think I was enough."

Michael paused. "That was bad?"

"Yes." Miriam wiped the tears from her cheeks with the back of her sleeve. It was childish, she knew, but she didn't care.

"How?" he pressed, closing the distance until there was only a single step between them.

Miriam looked up and met his concerned gaze, wishing for the first time in her life that she knew what it was to be held. "Because I've spent my life feeling guilty that he wasn't enough for me."

Michael wanted to reach down and gather her into his arms as he would a child. Everything about her demeanor told him he should. But he knew he couldn't, wouldn't overwhelm her like that.

"Are you going to be able to open the house like you'd hoped?"

She looked around the room, at the dust-laden furniture. At the waste. Michael remained quiet, determined to give her as much time as she needed—which was characteristically short. She took a shuddering, cleansing breath before picking up a scattered newspaper, adding it to a stack nearby.

"Do you know why I save papers?" She looked up at Michael.

"No."

"Me either."

Michael pushed his spectacles further up the bridge of his nose. He raised one eyebrow, waiting for her next revelation. But she just smiled up at him, her full eyes all light and honesty, and his heart constricted in his chest. The undercurrent of the previous moment's pain was still there. She wasn't hiding it, she was working through it.

She turned and picked up the stack of papers and dropped them outside the door that exited to the hallway. "Voltaire says," she said, brushing dust off her hands and returning to face Michael, "'Let's work without theorizing. It's the only thing that makes life bearable.'"

Michael smiled down at her, hoping she could see his admiration. "I would agree, wholeheartedly." He picked up another stack of newspapers and dropped them on top of her stack in the hallway.

Miriam giggled from behind him, tossing more, and Michael

had to concentrate to breathe.

Mrs. Maloney took the noise upstairs as a cue it was permissible for her to join them with a tray of sandwiches. She called out from the sitting room that separated Miss Beaumont's parents' rooms, and turned to leave.

"Mrs. Maloney?" Miss Beaumont walked out of her father's room with a shallow copper bowl in her hands. Inside was a watch, a couple of pairs of cufflinks, and some other masculine jewelry. She set them on the desk next to the tray.

"I brought you some sandwiches. I thought you might be getting hungry. It's nearly one o'clock."

"Thank you." Miss Beaumont tilted her head to the side and looked her directly in her eyes. Miss Beaumont's eyes were gray, startlingly so, and Mrs. Maloney felt as if she were being unfolded and considered, like a bolt of fabric. Then Miss Beaumont smiled and looked down at the tray. "You only brought up two sandwiches?"

"Will you need more? How many would you like?"

"I think two will be fine. I'm fine with a half sandwich. Will you be satisfied with a half sandwich?"

"Oh..." Mrs. Maloney shook her head. "I'm still working in the kitchen. This was for you and Mr. Farling." She took a step backwards toward the door. She didn't want Miss Beaumont to feel obligated to include her. Mr. Farling had informed her that Miss Beaumont had never managed a household before, and maybe she didn't know it wasn't proper for her to eat with them. "I'll come to get the tray in about an hour."

"Nonsense," Miss Beaumont interrupted her progression to the doorway. "Surely you need to eat, and there is so much to discuss, it is a much better use of time for you to join us."

Mrs. Maloney glanced at Mr. Farling. He stood behind Miss Beaumont with a bemused but agreeable look on his face.

"All right, I would be happy to join you. Thank you."

Miss Beaumont walked to the other side of her father's desk and shuffled the papers around until she found a pencil. "I think we need to start with lists." She walked back around to the front of the desk where Mr. Farling had gathered a group of chairs. She sat down between them. "If it is agreeable to both of you, let's begin with what should be done with the rooms on this level."

Mrs. Maloney nodded, slicing the sandwich in half for the women to share. If anything, Miss Beaumont was efficient. She handed Mr. Farling his plate. Every move Miss Beaumont made garnered a bit of his attention. Mr. Farling liked her, and Miss Beaumont—with her busy pencil, scratching lines across the pad of paper balanced on her crossed knees—hadn't an inkling of his affection. Mrs. Maloney looked back to Mr. Farling, hoping he knew what he was in for. Oddly, Miss Beaumont was completely independent, but in serious need of protection.

Mrs. Maloney smiled and took a bite of her sandwich.

Chapter 17

Michael had certainly done his job, John had to concede.

The women sitting across from him in the hired carriage looked as if they'd just been on an impossible holiday to an impossible destination. And, for them, he knew that was what the day had been like.

Ione sat, her gloved hands folded demurely in her lap, looking out the window at the passing buildings. Jenny, next to her, crossed things off a list, and then wrote more whenever the carriage ceased rocking enough to allow her to hastily scribble another note.

And, John had to admit, the shopping had been an experience for him as well. He'd grown up in a comfortable household—they'd always had enough food on the table—but shopping in the stores Mr. Farling had suggested was to step into another world entirely. Furthermore, all of the owners had been expecting them, eliminating the possibility of awkward explanations for their atypical troupe.

The passing buildings were crowding together. The air was changing. John looked out the window. It was troublesome. A few blocks behind them was a world where boys, dressed in white suits, played with bats and balls on perfectly green lawns. In front of them, women squatted in the gutters to pick up what might be a dropped coin. The poor people thought the rich were rich because of luck, and the rich thought the poor were poor because they were lazy. The truth was, the only ones that truly found luck were the poor who didn't realize they were poor, and the rich who forgot they were rich.

Jenny stopped writing and scooted back against the cushion, away from the window, discretely watching the faces of the practically dressed passersby.

"Is there something you need?"

"No." Jenny sat back. "I'm just watching."

They were nearing where her father was living. He'd moved in the week after she left, using the money from Miriam in order to pay for a different room. He'd cried when John offered the money. He said he would miss his daughter. Of course, his sobriety had been in question.

"I miss him."

John listened.

"I know I shouldn't, but I do." Jenny tucked the pencil she'd used all day into her hair and looked up at John.

"It's perfectly fine for you to miss him. He's your father."

She nodded and looked at Ione before turning back to the window. "Sometimes I wish I could see him, but only if he couldn't see me. Like if I had a picture. Then I could see him, and only see the things I want to see."

"We have a lot of work to do now though." Ione placed her hand on Jenny's knee. "Most of the supplies will be delivered in the next couple of days to Miriam's house, and then we're going to be too busy for you to miss anything."

Jenny sniffed and scratched her nose, collecting herself with habitual gestures. "We didn't find those little pearl buttons you wanted."

"I think the clerk was going to try and order them from the catalog."

"It's hard to remember who's sending what, and to where."

Ione smiled and looked back to the window. "It was quite an afternoon, wasn't it?"

Michael thumbed through the correspondence that had piled up on his desk. He'd almost not even come in to the office, but he knew if he hadn't, his receptionist would spend the day chasing him down with messengers. Later in the morning, he would go and help Mrs. Maloney interview prospective employees. Miriam hadn't wanted to be there, which spoke highly of her trust in Mrs.

Maloney, but was worrisome, nonetheless. The only people she'd ever lived with were her father and a hired nurse. She had no idea what kind of involvement it would take to run a household. But Michael had seen glimmers of hope: the way she managed the tasks that needed to be completed, and the obvious respect her friends had for her. Still, she would need some guidance.

From Mr. Tenney there were two letters and a message. The first letter was cordial, the second, less, and the message reeked of desperation. The poor man had thought his generous offer would have resulted in a sale, and likely a sizeable commission for his own coffers.

The truth was, Miriam needed neither the money nor the hassle of a sale, and wouldn't have considered any offer, no matter the amount. When he'd brought up the possibility, she'd almost laughed it off. Later, seriously, she'd asked Michael to take care of it.

He had. He'd sent word in a timely manner, but the man didn't want to hear no and, Michael suspected, definitely didn't want to hear no from a woman who had no intention of considering the practical use of the space. Michael quickly scribbled a note asking the receptionist to send out a letter to Mr. Tenney, informing him, in no uncertain terms, that Miriam would not be selling. He also made a mental note, as long as he was interviewing people today, to be on the watch for someone who might make a suitable guard for the soon-to-be unoccupied warehouse. Mr. Tenney's insistence left the clinging impression that there might be more at work under the surface of the offer.

Michael sat and unfolded the morning paper, looking for any discussion of potential developments near the docks, seeking for a possible motive for buying the property. But the newspaper was filled with the typical: advertisements, social columns, discussion of the planning for the World's Fair—still a couple years off—and an article about a building fire. Fire in Chicago was always newsworthy. Other pages were filled with commentaries and letters to the editor on the topics of corruption and money laundering. Michael flipped to the last page. Near the bottom he saw a small article about a woman who was found murdered. Her neck had been slashed open. A bartender had found her not far from Miriam's warehouse.

Moving was the right decision for Miriam and the other women. He was glad they were only a short time away from being ready for the transition.

The newsboys were crying louder, vying for the attention of the walking businessmen. It was interesting, there could be a different boy at each corner, but most of the men Michael knew stayed loyal to the boy they'd chosen. In fact, they would walk a bit out of the way, or even wait for a few minutes, so they might buy the paper from the one they preferred.

He glanced out of his office window. It was growing lighter outside, and the traffic was picking up. A packed cable car rumbled by. At this time of the morning, the passengers were people in the service industries: many poor, many with dark skin, and some who traveled with small children. Soon it would be young, hungry entrepreneurs in cheap suits. It felt like decades ago when he, proud of his own cheap suit, had implored Mr. Beaumont for a job.

The last item on his desk was an invitation to speak at the ladies auxiliary for the Provident Hospital and Training School. It was a project he'd been working on in the background for some time, but it was now time to set budgets, and therefore time to raise funds and gather donations. The hospital would be dedicated to the black population of the city, serving to train doctors and nurses of color. He slit open the invitation to check the venue. Doctors of African descent were allowed to study in some schools, but finding a place to practice their skill, let alone a hospital that would allow surgical training, was another thing entirely. The new hospital was a solid and economical solution.

Nurses, Michael knew, faced the same problem. It had been an uphill battle. Nurses were on the verge of shifting the understanding of their job from that of an unskilled labor provided by a servant, to that of a service best provided by a trained professional. The shift in thinking was even slower on the part of the doctors and administrators when the nurses were dark-skinned. Michael left a note for his secretary to respond in the affirmative. It was short notice, but he was available.

Michael gathered the few things he needed, slung his jacket over his shoulder, and put on his hat. Nodding to the doorman, he jumped onto a slowing cable car, wondering if any of the people he would later interview shared the ride.

Miriam arrived back at the warehouse later than she'd expected and walked in to a scene she hadn't anticipated. Lamps had been brought down to the warehouse level, and a long table had been cleared of its industrial burden. Jenny and Ione stood on one side and John on the other.

"What are you doing?" Miriam approached the gathering. Michael had insisted on sharing her ride and seeing her home safely. Miriam wished he'd come in with her.

John turned to face her with an apologetic smile. "I hope you aren't angry, but we've pulled some of your newspapers out of your piles. We were searching for articles."

Ione and Jenny hadn't glanced up. Instead, they had their faces pressed close, both reading from the same column.

"What are you looking for?"

"News about other women who have fallen victim to a similar crime." John turned back to the table. "As you can see, we've gathered quite a few."

Miriam looped the strap of her bag around the post at the base of the stairs and walked over to join the group. Her papers were everywhere.

"We were careful not to tear them." As Miriam approached, Ione smoothed a new crease out with the palm of her hand. "And we can fold them back just like we found them."

Miriam clenched her hands in her pockets and forced her feet to move forward. She knew it was silly, but she wanted to fold the papers and stack them more than she wanted to know what they said. "What have you found?" Miriam did her best to sound casually indifferent.

The circles of lamplight shone on opened papers. In the middle setting on top—appearing to hold the papers down—was a man's walking stick. It was black, with a silver tip.

"Is that his?" Miriam pointed to it.

"We're not sure." Jenny's eyes shifted to the shining metal and back to the article that had her attention.

"We've found a number of small, related pieces," John said.

"How many?"

"At least one for every paper that's out."

The papers followed one after another, down the length of the table. "There have to be twenty papers here. And where did you get the walking stick?"

"It was leaning against the door when we arrived here," Ione said, flatly.

John frowned, shuffling through yet another stack.

Miriam backed away from the table and checked to make sure she'd securely locked the outside door. A supervisor's desk was pushed against the wall next to the exit. Miriam pulled on the middle drawer, forcing the wooden slides, swollen with complacency, to open. She grabbed a handful of pens, hoping a couple of them might still work, and two pairs of heavy steel scissors.

"Here," she said, dropping them onto the stack of papers. "If we're going to try to collect pieces of information, it will be much easier if we don't have to keep full papers."

"Are you sure?" Ione hesitated. Jenny was already cutting along the edges of the articles.

"Yes. It's just paper. And obviously," Miriam said, pointed to the walking stick she didn't even want to touch, "we need answers."

Sean tucked his red hair back under his cap, and then checked his jacket pocket to make sure that none of the coins the man had given him had fallen out. It was a lot of money.

He'd told him to watch until she came home. But it wasn't her that found the walking stick. It was the priest, and the other two women. And those women he knew. He'd seen them around town, and had heard the rumors they were staying in the warehouse. It was strange, the fog woman who never came out in the day, the one who'd paid him even to get her groceries, was now in and out of the warehouse. Not to mention, living with women even his mother wouldn't walk the same side of the street with.

The streetlamps flickered on. Sean moved farther into the

shadows, making his way around the building, trying to find a crate or something he could stand on in order to see through one of the lower windows. He could tell a lamp was on in the warehouse. The dusty windows glowed yellow. Usually, they were dark. Maybe the man would pay more if Sean could report what he'd seen.

He walked around the back of the building until he found a metal bucket. He lifted it carefully, trying to mute the clink of handle, and carried it back to the side with the windows. Still, he had to stretch on his toes in order to rub the dirt off the pane and peer into the room.

It was hard to see. He spit on the glass and rubbed again with his sleeve until he could make out four people at a long table. It looked like they were cutting shapes out of paper, but he couldn't be sure. And cutting shapes out of paper was a strange way for four adults to spend an evening.

The man might give him extra though, and Sean tried to memorize what details he could make out. But he didn't even know who the real man was. The man who'd given him the money was just another person who was probably paid to relay the message.

Sean would find out, though. He jumped off the bucket and fingered the coins in his pocket again. He'd ask around. He'd find out who wanted to know what the fog woman was busy with. The coins were warm and smooth, their weight reassuring.

She'd paid him for years. It wasn't wrong. Telling one person what another person did. Sean tripped over the storm sewer.

Just in case, he would try to find out why the man wanted to know.

Chapter 18

Maggie watched her from the partially open doorway. Her back arched in a perfect curve when she reached behind to pin up her hair. Lucy sat on the bed in her stocking feet, making the doll she held imitate Mrs. Whitaker's movements.

"Are you going to be gone long?" Lucy's tone was light, but the lines on her forehead grew deeper as she waited for her answer.

"No, just for the afternoon. I have to meet with the other ladies to discuss some details for the upcoming charity event."

Adults without children of their own always spoke to children as if they were small adults. Maggie watched Lucy nod as if she understood the concept of a charity event.

"What's a charity event?"

"It's where a bunch of people get together to try to collect money to help others." Maggie poked her head into the room, rescuing Mrs. Whitaker from the inevitable interrogation. Maggie reached for Lucy, and Lucy jumped into her arms. She was too big for that, but Maggie didn't mind.

"Are you sure you'll both be fine while I'm gone?"

"Yes, ma'am." Maggie nodded, carrying Lucy out of the room.

"Because if you want to join me, you know you can."

"I wanna go," Lucy said.

"We'll be fine. Lucy can help me make something sweet for after dinner...right, Lucy?"

"I guess so." Lucy wiggled out of Maggie's grasp and ran back to Mrs. Whitaker's side. "You'll hurry home." Lucy hugged her leg tightly, and then released it to run out of the room.

Maggie followed Lucy, wondering, not for the first time, how Lucy would feel about leaving the Whitakers' home. It was preferable to thinking about how she would feel to be back to worrying about where their next meal would come from. Ione hadn't told her what their plans would be. It was possible she didn't even have a plan yet, and truthfully, that was fine with Maggie.

She tied the apron string around her waist and reached into the largest canister. A cloud of flour rose when she poured it onto the board, shaping it into a bowl to hold the salt and eggs. Lucy had stopped asking when Ione was coming to get them for good. Maggie cracked an egg on the counter. And Maggie just never asked. Sometimes, if given enough time, difficult choices presented their own solutions.

It had taken days, but finally John took a step back and surveyed their work. Seventeen. There were seventeen separate articles about missing women, or found women, or floating women.

They'd tried to match up stories of missing women with the floating or found women, but it was difficult, and they'd only managed to put together two potential matches.

"How is it that they haven't figured out they have a problem?" Miriam asked anyone who was listening. Ione and Jenny also stood back, scanning the board they'd put together. Michael, having stopped by to discuss the date of the move, kept sending John silent looks over the rim of his spectacles.

"It's not anyone important." Jenny shrugged. "If it was someone important, then the articles wouldn't have been on the last page. No one reads the last page."

Michael turned toward John. "Did you find any articles about attacks that someone survived?"

"None that seemed similar to Ione's or Jenny's experience."

Michael walked over to the table and set his hat down by the walking stick. "Where did this come from? I don't remember your father using a walking stick." He picked it up, and Jenny took a step back. He looked at her from the corners of his eyes. "This is his, isn't it?"

"Maybe," Ione said.

"Where did it come from?" He turned it, examining it closer.

"It was here when they returned from shopping the other day." Miriam hadn't intended to offer that information. For some reason, she wanted to prove to Michael that they could make it without him.

"You mean, someone just left it?"

"That's how it would seem," John said.

Michael set it back on the table and turned to assess everyone. He pinned Ione with the next question. "Have you seen him since he hurt you?"

She nodded.

"Out by the light. He was watching us." Jenny pointed to the closed door.

"This is why you wanted to move back into your house? You'd said he *might* know where they were staying." He pointed to the other two women. "Not that he was making threatening overtures."

Miriam looked at the floor. A scrap of paper had fallen at her feet. She kicked at it and watched the dust rise and settle on her shoe. She'd taken care of herself for years. She didn't need Michael to question her judgment.

"I'm sorry," he said. "I'm just concerned."

Miriam punished him with a few long seconds of silence and then met his gaze with her own steady one. "Had you known, would you have done anything differently?"

"Probably not."

"Then what do you say we get on with our plans? It is why you stopped by, right?"

"Yes."

Miriam turned toward the stairs, and Michael stood back, waiting for the women to climb after her. Michael was the last to enter the small room at the top. Miriam felt his eyes measure her, and was satisfied with her ability to unsettle him. He was so confident in his skills with other people; it would do him good to have to wonder what she thought.

Which was convenient, because when she stole glances of him, she wasn't even sure what she thought.

The discussion had been day or night. Would it be better for them to vacate the house in the daytime, with witnesses, or at night, potentially under the eye of the attacker? At Michael's insistence, it was that night, or the next day. Ione folded her few things and stacked them in a box. It was one of the small conveniences of living above a warehouse; everything you could possibly need, like crates, or tarps, or pads of paper, could probably be found somewhere in the building. She didn't mind living above the warehouse—she liked it, actually.

"Did you pack up the catalogs?" Jenny stuck her head through the doorway on her way down the hall.

"They're in a stack on the kitchen table."

"We still haven't decided when," John said while passing by on the way to Miriam's studio.

"I've been considering how best to handle the move." Michael followed him down the hall. "We could have you escort one or two of the women, and I could escort the remaining later. That way, it would be less obvious that they were relocating."

Ione picked up the box and carried it to the kitchen table. Miriam had decided that most of the things would be staying. She said the other house was completely furnished.

"When we get there, we'll still have some work to do." Miriam dropped her box on the table next to Ione's. "I thought we would have a bit more time, but only the first and second floors have been cleaned and prepared for us."

Michael regarded her steadily. "Did you hear John and me? Maybe we should go separately; it would make it less obvious you were leaving. Also—" He lowered his voice. "—I arranged for a guard to be posted here on a permanent basis."

"Do you think that's necessary?"

"Yes."

Miriam played with the button on the cuff of her sleeve. "I guess that's prudent."

John and Jenny joined them in the kitchen. "Will you be taking your paintings?" John asked.

"No. I'll take some supplies, and maybe I'll come back later to retrieve them, but for now I think they're fine to stay here." Miriam buckled a carpet bag with some of her personal items and turned to Michael. "Maybe it would be best for me to go tonight and make sure everything is ready in the rooms we will need. John could bring Jenny and Ione tomorrow. If anyone is watching us, they'll think he's escorting them on another shopping trip, and they would likely wait here for them to return, rather than follow."

"That does sound reasonable," Michael agreed. "I'll just be glad when all of you are living in the other house."

"We'll make sure it's locked securely." Ione wanted to calm Miriam's growing agitation. She was good at hiding it, but Ione couldn't help but notice her shaking fingers, and her tendency to pick imaginary pieces of lint off her dress. Miriam was strong, but Ione knew her old world would be new territory for her. She met Michael's eyes. He saw the same things, he knew the risks. Miriam was in good hands.

John watched Michael and Miriam slip into the dark carriage under the cover of night. Ione and Jenny stood on either side of him. They were all a step back from the window, watching with the lamps turned down. They hadn't discussed it. It was an unspoken consensus of common sense. The lamps would stay off.

"What are we going to do with the articles we collected?" Jenny sat heavily on the davenport.

"I thought I might give one more try with the police." John sat on the chair across from her. He knew it was of little use, but he should make the attempt. It was better than chasing around in the dark with a knife. A knife—he was still embarrassed by the idea of someone finding out he'd gone on the hunt with a knife tucked into the back of his pants. What would he have done, anyway?

"If they see it all put together, maybe it'll make more sense to them."

"Maybe," Ione chimed in from the kitchen, "maybe not."

They regarded one another in silence.

"I wonder who all the women were," Jenny said.

"Women like us." Ione walked into the sitting room. "If they were people with families, or women of society, there would be more attention paid. We'd be hearing about the dangers of walking at night, and the police would be posting patrols at each street corner." She paused and looked up before finishing her thoughts. "Truthfully, the police probably think he's doing them a favor."

"Let's hope not." John drummed his fingers on his crossed knee. "I wouldn't be surprised if they've been paid to look the other way. Someone has to know what's been going on. You both said you thought he was wealthy. Money could have been exchanged to keep this under wraps."

"Wouldn't that mean you'd be in danger for bringing it to their attention?"

"Better me than another unsuspecting victim. If someone comes after me, it would be front page news." John shook his robes for effect and stood. He crossed to the window again, watching the muted shadow move around the streetlamp. It would be another foggy night. He should be out. But John wouldn't leave. He had two women to protect, and until they were out of harm's way, he wouldn't be able to continue his search.

Miriam felt the air press in around her. She took in a deep, wet breath, closed her eyes, and leaned back in the carriage.

"Do you want me to close the windows?" Michael asked.

"No," Miriam answered without opening her eyes.

Michael uncrossed and re-crossed his legs.

Miriam cracked her eyes open to glance at him. He didn't ride well, she could see that. He preferred to drive.

"The man driving is your new stable hand." Michael gazed out the window. Sometimes Miriam had the feeling he knew her thoughts. "Mrs. Maloney and I hired him the same day as the others. He's been busy fixing up the stables and stocking supplies."

"Where are our stables?"

"The other side of the park. They are within walking distance. They are very small, only a handful of stalls and room to park an open and a closed carriage. His name is Jonah."

"Jonah. I always liked that name. It must have been very dark in the whale." Miriam opened her eyes fully. In the dark she was free to let them roam over Michael. He shrugged uncomfortably in his suit jacket. Miriam hadn't thought what the moisture must feel like, gathering under the multiple masculine layers of tailored clothes.

"If you want to close the windows, I won't mind."

"We're almost there. Jonah will pull around back to the kitchen entrance."

Miriam hadn't explored the kitchen garden yet. Night was not the time. They skirted the overgrown raised beds, paying attention not to trip over the vines that obscured the paths. White miniature climbing roses grew in a tangled hedge and worked their way through the undergrowth and up the brick wall. They released a light perfume when Miriam, leading the way, brushed against them.

"I'm caught," Michael whispered loudly to Miriam's back.

"What do you mean?"

"I'm stuck in the thorns."

"Stuck?"

"Yes, stuck." He stopped pulling at the sound of tearing fabric.

Miriam stifled a giggle. Dropping her bag at the door to the kitchen, she made her way back to his shadow to set him free.

"Hold still." She ran her hands along the heavy fabric covering his arms and his shoulders. "I can't see anything. Ooh, ouch." She brought a finger to her mouth before continuing to look for the pestering thorns.

One vine wrapped across his left shoulder, attaching itself to his back, near his waist. Miriam squinted up into the overhanging tree branches, wondering where the vine had come from, before lifting his coat and running her hands along the underside of the fabric, searching for the thorns' penetrations. In the morning, she would take a look at the landscape, but the roses seemed entirely out of control. She tugged on the vine and it released.

"Got it," she said.

"There's still more. I can feel one up by my shoulder and another at my wrist. Maybe I can..." Michael unbuttoned his jacket with his left hand and tried to shrug it off his shoulders. "Never mind." He stopped mid-shrug with a groan. "You're going to have to find the others."

Miriam moved around to face him, working her small hands

141

under his jacket, searching for the next thorn. "Hold still," she said as he tried to twist out of the coat.

Michael stopped moving while Miriam concentrated on finding the thorn. Her hands stood out in contrast against his white shirt. She studied them for a moment, wondering at how clearly she could see on such a black night. Heat had collected under his jacket and radiated to warm her fingers. She hadn't realized they were cold. She had the urge to crawl in.

She flattened her palm against the warm muscle. His chest rose under the weight of her hand. His breathing was fast, nearly as fast as hers. His muscles rippled under the thin fabric of his shirt, responding to her touch.

"Oh." Miriam backed away.

She looked up. Shadows played along the side of his face. He watched her intently.

"I'm still stuck." The tenor of his voice had deepened, or maybe she just heard it differently, but it was a rich shade, deep and beckoning.

Miriam reached out again, this time her fingers fluttering in hesitation. She fisted her hands, took a shaky breath, and pushed them back under his jacket, determined to find the thorns, and quickly.

Michael grimaced.

"I'm sorry." Miriam found another barb, and then another. She worked her way down his arm until she had only a couple left.

"I've got it." Michael ripped the last few out of the fabric.

She didn't take a step away. Instead, to Michael's surprise, she stood staring up at him, openly curious. He watched her track the path his eyes took.

He tried to focus on her eyes, tried to keep his breathing under control, but failed. His gaze fell to her lips. On instinct, and without lowering her gaze, she parted them. The fog made her fearless. Michael took a step back. Her curiosity was a drug.

"We should get inside." The hitch in his voice said the opposite of his words.

Miriam blinked and backed up. Disappointment flashed briefly across her features before she turned. Michael let her lead the way to the kitchen door. He wanted to think of her walking away as a reprieve. It wasn't. Cool air slipped in behind her, leaving him instead to follow like puppy in her wake. Whether she even knew what passed between them was a question he couldn't answer. If she did, it changed everything.

A single candle burned on the counter in the kitchen. Michael locked the door behind them.

"It smells the same," she said.

Nostalgia changed her features. The curiosity was gone, replaced with warmth.

"You were cut." She pointed to a spot of blood on his white sleeve. "We should clean it."

"I'll be fine." Michael backed away before she could get any closer. "It's getting late. The scratches aren't deep. I'll come back in the morning."

"Nonsense." Miriam picked up a spoon that had been left on the counter and dropped it into the basin. "Jonah already took the carriage back to the stable. You would have to send for a hired carriage." Miriam twisted the excess water out of a dishrag and scrubbed the spot where the spoon had been. "There's more than enough room here. And no one would know. Mrs. Maloney stays here, so there's nothing improper—not that I care about that anyway. Well, not the improper. I care about it, you know. I..."

Michael covered her hand with his, stopping her from scrubbing. She didn't pull away.

"You don't want to stay here alone," he said.

Miriam bristled before dropping her shoulders. Her skin was soft and warm. Slowly, she turned her hand under his so that they rested, palm to palm. Michael wrapped his fingers around hers, understanding and reminding himself that her need was vastly different from his own.

"Where is Mrs. Maloney's room?" Miriam asked. She brushed her fingertips down the side of his hand. It was a movement not intended to entice. Michael knew she was merely familiarizing herself with the feel of another human. He reminded himself that she didn't mean it the way he experienced it. From anyone else, her question might have sounded like an invitation. But for her, it was a question of where people were situated in relation to her. She didn't know Mrs. Maloney well. She wouldn't want her near, but she wouldn't want to be alone in the huge house either. There was a reason she was content in the tiny rooms above the warehouse.

"Here on the first floor." Michael paused, weighing the risks of his next question. "Do you want me to stay on the second floor with you?"

A rush of air escaped from Miriam. She nodded, biting her bottom lip. "But I don't...I'm not..."

"I know." Michael let go of her hand and touched a loose strand of her hair, surprising himself with the intimacy of the gesture. He pulled his hand away, prepared to apologize, but she didn't seem to notice the impropriety. "The room between your parents' rooms has two sofas. What would you say to us spending the night in there?"

Miriam's look of gratitude almost made what was sure to be a tortuous night worth it.

Chapter 19

John held the door open for Ione and Jenny. They'd decided the kitchen entrance was the best option. The smiling woman stirring the pot on the stove confirmed their decision.

"I'm Mrs. Maloney." She rubbed her hands on her apron. "You must be Ione and Jenny."

The young women nodded at the matronly lady who stood at least a head taller than them both. She was nearly as tall as he was yet did not come off as formidable. Again, John thought, Michael had made a good choice.

"Have you eaten breakfast? Maybe you would like a little something before I show you around the house? Miss Beaumont is upstairs, boxing up some of her childhood things. I'm trying to give her a few moments to herself."

"Thank you," Ione answered first. "We would appreciate it."

They'd already eaten. John took note of Ione's skill with the woman. Ione had the rare ability to understand what people needed. This woman needed both to comfort them and to give Miriam some time to herself. Not only did Ione have the sense to understand, but also, she was quick enough to act on it with the perfect answer.

Mrs. Maloney smiled. "Well then, you three just take a seat, and I'll have something ready in no time. When Mr. Butler—and yes, he is the butler." She lifted her eyebrows up and smiled again. "When he comes down, I'll introduce you to him."

"How many other people work here?" Jenny asked.

"There are also two house maids and a stable lad. He spends most of his day with the horses though. The stables are on the other side of the park. Do either of you ride?"

Both women shook their heads.

"No matter."

Mrs. Maloney stacked cups and saucers on a silver platter. Next to them, she placed a plate of sweet breads and peeled apples. Biscuits were tucked into the last empty space, next to the teapot. Despite his breakfast, John's mouth began to water. Jenny poked Ione under the table. Ione sent her a censuring stare, which Jenny promptly ignored.

"This looks really good." Jenny grinned at Mrs. Maloney.

"Thank you, dear." Mrs. Maloney poured the tea and then sat to join them. "I daresay this is going to be quite the adventure, isn't it?"

John couldn't agree more.

Miriam and Michael met Jenny, Ione, and John in the front hall. They descended the staircase, trying hopelessly to brush at least some of the dust off their clothes.

"Oh good." Miriam rushed to greet them. "I'm so glad you made it. Do you think anyone noticed anything out of the ordinary?" She directed the question to John.

"No. We locked the door as we typically would, and climbed into the carriage when the street was busy. I think everything went as well as we could have hoped."

"This is beautiful." Ione looked directly into Miriam's eyes. "When you said you had a townhome, I thought you meant a townhome, not a mansion."

Miriam shrugged. She knew she'd downplayed the opulence of the home, and of her future life, but she hadn't wanted to make them uncomfortable. "I'm sorry."

"No," Ione said, her voice low and personal. "Please don't apologize." She glanced back at Jenny, who had not stopped talking with Mrs. Maloney. "I just hope we won't be a burden."

"You are not a burden." Michael glanced at Miriam before continuing. "Miriam needs people here. It's a large house."

Ione nodded her understanding.

Jenny's conversation with Mrs. Maloney paused, and the group stood for a moment in transitory silence.

"Well." Mrs. Maloney stepped forward. "Would you like to see where you will be staying?"

Everyone herded toward the stairs. Miriam watched Mrs. Maloney act as tour guide, appreciating her ability to simultaneously ask and answer questions. Michael, the last in line, gestured for Miriam to walk with him up the staircase.

It had been a long day. Jenny, standing in front of her—yes, *her*—window, stifled a yawn. She couldn't believe she'd be sleeping in a bed that looked like it was designed for sweet dreams. Sleeping would be an event in itself.

"Oh!" Jenny rushed over to meet Miriam at the bedroom door. "Are you sure you want me here?"

Miriam stepped in. "This was my room."

"But why am I staying here? Don't you want to be here?"

"No, I don't." Miriam crossed to the dressing table and met Jenny's eyes in the mirror. "I thought I would. I missed it when I was little, when we left." She ran her hand along the inlaid wood top, tucking her fingernail into a tiny gap. Jenny wondered if she remembered the flaw in the table from her childhood. "When I came back...it didn't feel like I had imagined it would."

"But the things here are so pretty." Jenny walked back to the windows. She couldn't keep from touching the lace details sewn into the draperies. Looking down, she could see the lush overgrowth of the kitchen gardens. She knew it was mostly weeds, but it was still prettier than any view she'd ever had.

"I'm glad you like it. I thought you might, after you described the pink dress you wished for when you were a girl."

Jenny paused, still looking out the window. That Miriam remembered the detail of the pink dress was both unsettling and comforting. Miriam was a woman who grew up with parents who'd considered her likes and dislikes. It was a relief to know that level of devotion existed. Jenny's childhood, spent learning how not to like something, or want it too much, was a drastic contrast to that kind of tenderness.

"I thought we would be another floor higher, or on the first floor, with Mrs. Maloney." Ione walked into the room. Jenny knew Ione appreciated everything Miriam had done, but she would have been more relaxed had Miriam assigned them rooms that shared the maid's floor. Ione had been disappointed when she was shown to her room. She'd told Jenny, in her words, their placement spoke of impermanence.

"We aren't one of your family, we didn't expect to be treated like this," she added carefully.

Jenny knew what Ione meant. Miriam didn't think like them. Miriam wouldn't know how heartbreaking it would be for Ione's sisters to live in opulence, and then lose it, as eventually they all would. Nothing lasted forever.

"I know." Miriam shrugged. "But you do like the rooms, right?"

"Of course," Ione and Jenny said at once.

"I know you didn't expect it." Miriam looked uncomfortable. Jenny sent Ione a look, hoping Ione would know what to say. "The rooms upstairs didn't feel right. They didn't feel like they should be yours. They were too far away."

Jenny pulled open an empty drawer. Mrs. Maloney said she and the newly hired girls had emptied all the personal items out of the rooms when they laundered the bedclothes and drapes. She had nothing to fill the drawers. Jenny tried to calculate the expense associated with buying enough for the drawers and the armoire in a room that size. Multiplied by how many rooms—it was astounding.

Ione faced Miriam. "I noticed my room is connected to another."

"That's so you can have your sisters with you if you like." Miriam hugged her arms to her chest before dropping to sit on the edge of the bed. Jenny sat down next to her. Ione was last. She swung her feet back and forth. The bed was so high, their legs dangled over the edge.

Jenny imitated her, swinging hers the opposite way.

Jenny watched Miriam, in the middle, hesitate. She could tell Miriam was unable to decide if she should match Ione's or Jenny's leg-swinging pattern. Whatever she did, it would be off balance.

Jenny giggled, covering her gapped-tooth grin with her hand.

"Well, we do have a lot of work to do." Ione changed the swing of her legs to match Jenny's.

"I'd say," Jenny hastily agreed. "I think we're expecting some deliveries tomorrow morning. And Ione has already cut one pattern for a dress for you."

"You both understand, don't you?" Miriam ignored the practical shift in the conversation. "I didn't want to be alone on this floor."

Ione and Jenny stopped talking about dresses. Their legs slowed. It was clear that Miriam wasn't finished explaining their living arrangements.

"What do you mean?" Ione gently prodded.

"That's why I gave you both these rooms," Miriam said. "I didn't want to be alone."

The three women studied their feet, and then lifted their gazes to look at each other. Jenny was the first to speak.

"Well, who would?" she said, resuming the kicking. "This place is huge."

Miriam blinked back tears and joined the kicking. Having spilled enough of their own, the other women pretended not to notice the tears.

John watched out of his window again. It was as if nothing had changed. But it had.

The collection of newspaper articles was stacked in a neat pile on his small desk. Tomorrow morning he would take them to the police. He didn't have high hopes.

The evening was breezy, and there was no fog. John looked across the street, watching for Miriam and her lamp. A soft disappointment settled after each forgetful glance. He would miss her. And he would miss Ione and Jenny. There was work to do at the cathedral, though. Work he'd been neglecting. Obligations Father Ayers had been more than patient in his willingness to overlook.

Soon he would complete his vows.

He'd pored over the articles that evening. Finally, he drew a rough map of the area and marked with a black dot where dead women had been found. The places where women were attacked, and lived to tell, were marked with a blue dot. Because the bodies of the dead were usually found in the river or washed up on the shore, the locations were scattered. On the other hand, the attacks spread out in a circle around the area of the city reserved for rich men that prided themselves on practicing their debauchery in style. Gambling houses with obscene minimum bets, gentlemen's clubs with richly appointed upstairs opium dens, and houses devoted to ruining women lined the respectable-looking streets.

The dates were next. John scratched the numbers next to each dot. They'd only gone back through the papers about six months, to the middle of winter. The reports slowed down by then. Whether due to the weather or if that was the beginning, no one could be sure. It wasn't necessary to go back any further, though. The information in front of him was disturbing enough.

John glanced out his window again. Cool, dry night air poured in through the opening. Somewhat relieved the women would have better chances without the fog—the man appeared to prefer foggy nights—John was still apprehensive. If the night had been misty, he would have gone out and possibly found the man.

Unlike the last time, though, he would start at the gambling houses and follow the men as they left in the wee hours.

John reached up and turned down his lamp. He would sleep, and then he would participate in the morning mass. He wouldn't see Miriam the next day.

She intrigued him. As a man, she aroused his desire to protect and cover. John stood and crossed to his bed. He lay on his back, his fingers locked behind his head, and stared into the darkness. If he were not dedicated to serving all people, she was someone he could lose himself caring for. The thought of her curled next to him with his arms around her, as her husband, charged with her protection, stirred him. He felt the absence keenly.

When he'd first considered the priesthood, the sacrifice had been a physical one—one he wanted to master out of devotion to God's service. But now, after the past few weeks, John understood the real forfeit. It was the decision to lose himself in service to all, above the service to an individual. Now he knew that caring for one person, one woman, was no less of a calling.

John rolled onto his side and punched his pillow into shape. He wasn't changing his mind. If anything, he was more determined to continue in his calling.

That didn't make it any less difficult to watch Michael watch her.

Chapter 20

Other than the guard that showed up, Sean hadn't seen movement in the warehouse for days. The man wasn't going to be happy.

Well, there had been one interesting development. The day before, a bum of an alcoholic stood outside the door, shouting something incoherent. Sean watched him stumble away. He didn't think that was the kind of information the man wanted to pay for though.

Sean had even spied into the dark warehouse windows again. It hadn't helped. Unless he was wrong, the women were gone.

He could ask that priest, maybe. He'd seen him in the warehouse, which was strange in itself. For years the fog woman hadn't spoken to anyone. She'd left money on the table so she didn't even have to talk to him. Then things changed. The priest was over there, and those women were over there. Sean couldn't begin to guess why.

He was supposed to meet with the man tonight. Sean craned his neck to see around the people mulling about the cathedral. He would have nothing new to report. He had also been unsuccessful in his attempt to find out who the man worked for. The entire situation was frustrating.

His ma was asking too, and he was running out of excuses. *Where'd you get the money? Why you gone so late? You runnin' round town ain't makin' me proud. Take your sister.* She'd shouted as he let the door slam behind him, without his sister. He was too old for her harpin'.

A low train whistle beckoned. When they'd first come to the city, he'd hated the sound. It shrieked and moaned day and night. Then he'd gotten used to it. Later, when the coal fell off the cars, the train whistles meant money. Now, they signaled life outside the soot-encrusted industrial district. Not the life of the meat packers. His ma had made him promise not to work there, and that was one promise he intended to keep.

"What's the news?" Sean jumped at the man's voice behind him.

He hadn't expected him to come from the direction of the alley. He turned to face the priest.

"Nothing," he squeaked out. The priest's arms were crossed over his chest. Sean tried to swallow past the lump in his throat, but only succeeded in a spastic cough.

"You've been watching the warehouse for days."

"No, I'm just standing here." He'd just lied to a priest. How was he going to confess that?

John looked down his nose at him. It was an intimidating, priestly glare.

"I'm sorry." Sean studied his shoes.

"What?"

"I'm sorry." He looked up, meeting the priest's eyes. They weren't so bad.

"That's all right. I probably surprised you. That still leaves the question unanswered though. What are you doing? Miriam isn't still paying you for something, is she?"

"No."

"Is someone else?"

Sean kicked at a weed that had sprouted through a crack in the cobbles. He wasn't going to lie again. But the remnant of the other man's payment to him still jingled in his pocket. Instead, he shrugged his answer.

"Someone is paying you to watch the warehouse?"

Sean looked down the street again, and then gave one curt nod.

"Do you know who it is?"

"No."

"Look at me. Do you know who it is?"

Sean looked up. "No, Father," he said with all the sincerity he could muster. He still couldn't believe he'd lied to a priest.

"Could you point him out if you see him?"

"Maybe. He said he would come after dark. I don't think he wants me to know who he is."

"Did you like working for the woman who lived above the warehouse?"

"Yes, sir."

"Was she fair to you?"

"Yes, sir. She was more than fair. She always paid me more than she'd agreed."

"Do you think this man who has asked you to spy on her has her best interest in mind?"

Sean looked down again, shaking his head. The inside of his lip was raw from chewing on it.

"If I told you that she asked me to pay you to watch the street for her, what would you say?"

Sean snapped to attention. "I'd say that man made me nervous, and I'd rather work for her."

"Are you sure?"

"Yes, Father."

"Then I think I have a job for you."

Maggie watched out the window as an expensive carriage rolled to a stop.

"Who do you think it is?" Mrs. Whitaker leaned over Maggie to share the view.

"I'm not sure."

A coachman dropped from the driver's seat and opened the door. A lady in a lavender dress climbed out onto the step the coachman had pulled out for her. She wore a summer weight cape and hood in white. The lake wind wrapped it around her body and pushed her to their door.

Mrs. Whitaker, abandoning her post at the window, walked to the door, brushing any possible wrinkles from her skirt. She waited for the woman to knock before she opened the door.

"May I come in?" Ione's voice called from the step.

"Please." Mrs. Whitaker moved to the side to let Ione in. The coachman waited in the street.

"I can't stay long," Ione apologized. "I just need to talk to Maggie."

"Your dress is beautiful." Mrs. Whitaker took a step back to examine it. "Please don't take it the wrong way if I ask you where you had it made. It's obviously not a standard design."

Maggie watched Ione try to hide her pride. It was one of hers, Maggie was sure. But it was created with a superior fabric, and with careful attention to detail. Where she got the money to do it was another thing entirely. And if she had that kind of money... Maggie let the thoughts die there. There must be some kind of explanation.

"Ione!" Lucy ran from the kitchen. "I missed you!"

Ione pulled Lucy up into her embrace. Maggie could hear her breathe in the scent of her little sister, and Maggie knew Ione had missed them too. "Oh, Lucy, I've missed you too!"

Lucy squirmed out of her embrace. "Do you want to see our room? I gots some new toys, and hair ribbons." Lucy shook her head for effect. Six braids danced around her neck, each tied with a ribbon that matched her dress.

"I would love to see your room, if Mrs. Whitaker doesn't mind?" She looked for permission.

"Please do." Mrs. Whitaker turned to lead the way.

Lucy ran ahead, pulled a box from under the bed, and hopped atop the bed with it in her lap. She opened the treasures slowly, drawing out the moment. Maggie looked at Ione, wondering if she remembered Lucy's penchant for drama. Ione met Maggie's gaze and nodded. She did.

"Oh, Lucy, that's wonderful." Ione watched each new ribbon color snake out of the box.

"And I gots jacks, and this." She held up a small wooden puzzle. "But I can't do it yet. I'm too little." Lucy gave Mrs. Whitaker a nod.

"Yes, but you're growing, and I'll bet you'll be able to do that before your next birthday." Mrs. Whitaker winked at Lucy.

"Uh, huh. Before my next birthday," she repeated, almost professionally.

"I sure miss you." Ione reached out. Lucy jumped into her arms for a quick hug. Then she wriggled out and hopped over to Mrs. Whitaker, tucking her arms around her legs and holding on.

"Mrs. Whitaker's real nice," Lucy said in her most serious little-girl voice. She looked up at her and smiled.

"I think you're real nice too." Mrs. Whitaker reached under Lucy's arms and lifted her. Then she looked to Maggie and Ione. "We'll leave you two alone to talk. Maggie, will you see Ione out when she's ready?"

Maggie nodded.

Mrs. Whitaker absentmindedly dropped a kiss on the top of Lucy's head. "And please, please"—she turned back to Ione—"please stop by any time you want." Lucy waved and tucked her head under Mrs. Whitaker's chin.

Ione watched them disappear. She turned to Maggie. "She really likes it here, doesn't she?"

"Yes."

"We have to talk."

Michael sat at his kitchen table eating dinner.

It took everything he had to come home from the office rather than run to Miriam's house. But he had no business to accomplish there. There was no reason to visit. No reason other than curiosity, and something else he didn't want to think about.

Thinking. He'd done little else all day. For the first time in a long time, he'd been generally unproductive. If he mapped the time he spent at his desk, it would come out to equal parts aimlessly shuffling through papers and listlessly staring out the window. Michael dropped a piece of leftover sandwich onto his plate and pushed back his chair.

He had accomplished one task. He'd hired an investigator.

Jacob Tenney hadn't ceased in his requests, and Michael wanted to know with whom he was dealing before he pressed the issue. The walking stick at the warehouse nagged at him too. He looked forward to hearing from John after he spoke with the police. Someone had to look into it. There were just too many women gone missing, too many in the river, too many with horrendous injuries.

The last time he'd been at Miriam's he'd spent the night sleeping—or, more accurately, not sleeping—on the couch across from the one she occupied. He watched her wake. He should have never watched her wake.

The private investigator was a friend. One of the few who'd served in the Chicago law enforcement who, Michael was confident, couldn't be bought. He'd retired years ago, and ironically, Michael just bought him.

He laughed out loud, the sound echoing in his quiet apartment.

He carried the dishes to the kitchen, slipped on his coat and shoes, grabbed his hat, and locked the door behind him.

The summer night was cool. He picked up his pace, passing by apartments lit by gaslight. Some buildings in the financial district glowed with steady incandescent eyes, revealing their inhabitants to strangers on the street. Michael watched, and the views changed.

Businesses gave way to residential townhomes packed together. Women and men, dressed for a night of symphonic bliss, tripped out of their homes. Children relegated to the upper floors with their caretakers watched their beautiful parents from their towering windows. Michael stepped aside for one woman dressed in velvet. She nearly stumbled, waving to the top story of her house. Her husband frowned and tucked her hand into the crook of his arm. He tipped his hat to Michael, and Michael returned the gesture. The man obviously would have preferred a night at the club.

And then he stood at Miriam's doorstep, ringing the door, and Mr. Butler was answering and ushering him into the parlor where Miriam sat sketching and Ione sat sketching, and Jenny crocheted.

"Oh." Miriam dropped her notepad into her lap. "How nice of you to stop by." She glanced at the dark window and stood to greet him.

Michael, already feeling foolish for his inability to explain his presence, was no worse off for his gaping jaw. The three women stood next to one another in a sea of soft pastels. Miriam, in the center, wore a simple dress of mossy green. Her hair was piled high on top of her head, and the neckline scooped to just acceptable. Ione, seeing the dress's effect, smiled and signaled for Jenny to follow her out of the room.

Chapter 21

John took a deep breath and stood in front of the police station with his collection of articles. He'd rung the officer earlier, so he was expected. He hoped it would make a difference.

He walked up the steps and pushed through the double doors. A matron sat behind the front desk.

"I have an appointment with Officer Wilke."

"Name." She neglected to look up from her ledger.

"Deacon John Kendall."

She peered up over the rim of her pince-nez at the inclusion of the title. "I'll let him know you're here." Pushing back from her desk, she sighed and then hollered through a small square window cut into the pea-green wall.

"He'll come get you in a minute." She waved John over to a row of chairs on the opposite wall. Only one chair remained, between a large woman with a squirming child on her lap and a heavily bearded man. Seeing him in his robes, they both attempted to move over without any real change in the actual space between them.

"Father Deacon?"

John hadn't anticipated being relieved by the sound of the officer's voice. He changed direction and followed the rotund officer to his desk.

It was the same desk, with the same half can full of ashes and the same soggy cigar. The man placed both hands on the surface of the desk and lowered himself onto a groaning chair. With the effort it took, he let out a rush of moist, onion air that hit John square in the face. John tried to hold his breath and smile as the man settled.

"So you've got something for me?"

"Yes." John set the folder on top of the other stacks of paper. There was no clear spot on the desk.

The officer dropped a meaty hand on the folder and slid it over to his side of the desk. The papers underneath slid off their stacks, mixing the piles. John resisted the urge to fix the mess while the officer scattered the clipped articles.

"You like to read about dead women?" His eyes rested on John's robes, then went back to the papers.

"Well, no." John fought the temptation to grind his teeth in frustration. "I don't like to read about dead women, but there seems to be a problem."

The officer at the next desk glanced over and joined the conversation. "Aren't you the priest with the, um, lady guest?" He sat back with his thick, hairy arms folded across his chest. There was no hair on his head.

"He was here before, and yes, it was about a...lady—" The officer in front of him rolled his eyes. "—who got herself roughed up."

"She was a fair bit more than roughed up," John argued, earning the attention of both men.

"If I remember, she was fine, right?" The officer glanced back down. "These women are dead." He closed the file.

"I know you're new to town, but these kind of women wash up all the time."

"Frank," the officer addressed the hairy one at the next desk, "did you ever go check it out after the Father here made his last complaint?"

"I'm not making a complaint. I'm trying to see if anyone is looking into this."

Officer Wilke's eyes darkened.

"Yeah, we checked it out." The other officer coughed, rubbed his nose, and then wiped his finger on his pants. "Seems like he's housing women in the warehouse across the street from the church, from what the neighborhood folks say."

"Did you find anything of concern?" Office Wilke asked in a flat voice.

"Nope." The other officer took the cue and, with a smirk, cut his answer short.

"Maybe." Officer Wilke slid the file back toward John. "Maybe you should concentrate on helping the people *in* your church, not the ones running away from it."

John gathered his file and stood. Clearly he was getting nowhere.

"She should just sell, you know," the officer added as John turned.

"What do you mean?"

"I heard she has an offer." Officer Wilke sneered. "She should just sell the place, then you wouldn't be faced with having a house of—shall we say, ill repute—across the street from your cathedral."

John cemented the smile on his face. "Thank you for your time," he gritted out as he turned once again to leave.

Michael had told him about the offer, but not that it was common knowledge. John hoped he hadn't made a serious error by voicing his concerns to the police. Evidently, there was something much larger at work down by the docks than some missing women.

He needed to talk to Michael.

Angelene entered at the rear of the room. As a minister's wife, she'd been invited to the ladies auxiliary meeting. Her husband had encouraged her to attend, although she wasn't sure she would know anyone.

She scanned the room. That was the unique pain of being a minister's wife, one she hadn't anticipated. She was a visible member of the community, but through no accomplishment of her own. She was expected to function socially, to be friendly, to make the other women in the community feel needed and included, but she couldn't develop deep friendships. She had to be comfortable with families who had significantly more resources than she did in order to raise funds for the church and their causes, but at the same time not alienate the members who might be less advantaged. She had to hold a standard, but not judge; dress nicely, but not too nicely; be vulnerable, but never let herself be offended. And, if this was not accomplished, her husband's professional and spiritual calling were at risk.

A beautifully appointed table of pastries stood to one wall. A maid—a young black girl—approached a group of women with a silver tray. Being the kind of women who never ate, they waved her away. She turned, almost running into a young white man who had just entered the room. He was tall, impeccably dressed, and wore spectacles.

"Mrs. Whitaker?"

Angelene smiled at the familiar voice, and turned and faced Dr. Pierce.

"Oh, Dr. Pierce, it's so nice to see you here." She didn't even try to hide her relief. If anyone understood her pressures, it was Dr. Pierce. Somehow, he'd managed to maintain his respected presence in the medical community while nurturing his alliances with both closed-minded colleagues and people who would normally be intimidated by his successes. He was a trained surgeon but practiced medicine out of his home. He never turned anyone away if they couldn't pay, and, like what he did for Maggie and Lucy, he always tried to heal more than the body.

"Would you consider gracing me with your presence, and take the seat next to mine? I think they will begin shortly." Dr. Pierce held out his arm to escort Angelene to the conference area.

Angelene accepted his arm, laughing lightly. Dr. Pierce was a unique human.

"Oh, look at these." He stopped at the passing tray of sweets. "Thank you, Bella." He nodded to the maid. She smiled up at him and moved on to the next group of people.

"She wants to be a nurse." Dr. Pierce bent to whisper to Angelene. "Very bright girl. No place to train. I really hope we can get the funding we need."

Angelene looked back toward Bella, imagining her in the long white nurse's dress. "We will." She patted Dr. Pierce's arm. "It's long past time."

They settled into seats near the rear of the room.

"Do you know him?" Dr. Pierce pointed to the young man with the spectacles. He walked onto the stage and sat in the row of chairs behind the podium.

"No. I don't think we've met."

"After he finishes speaking, I'll have to introduce the two of you. He is technically the solicitor for the woman, Miriam Beaumont, who has taken in Ione—Maggie and Lucy's sister."

Angelene's eyebrows shot up in surprise. "Maggie says she's a very different lady, but her house is unbelievable."

"Maggie is right on both counts. How is she doing, by the way?"

"Very well. Of course, I think her adjustment was difficult, not that she would have let anyone know. She's a strong girl. It's been good for her to visit and work with Ione, though."

Dr. Pierce nodded. "Have you had the opportunity to see what Ione's been working on lately?"

"Yes." Angelene turned to face him. "She stopped by the house a while ago, and her dress was nothing short of spectacular. In truth, I've not frequented the circles of women who typically pay to dress like that. But since she's stopped by, I've been trying to find an equal to her skill, and nothing compares."

"My wife said the same thing."

Angelene turned back to face the stage. Hotel employees were pouring water into glasses for the various speakers and placing them in the podium.

"How is little Lucy doing?" Dr. Pierce removed a small notebook from his jacket pocket and scratched something down.

"She's simply wonderful," Angelene said, studying her fingers. She looked up at Dr. Pierce. "Her mother must have been an amazing lady."

"I never really was able to know her before she was gravely ill. But if her daughters are any indication, she was a good woman."

Angelene watched Dr. Pierce from the corner of her eyes as he prepared to listen to the man at the podium. Very few men— very few women even—would consider the mother of a reformed prostitute to have been a woman of good character. But Dr. Pierce understood that sometimes circumstance dictated one's actions. Ione, although Angelene could never approve of what she did, provided for her sisters in the most immediate way she could. Looking around the room, she prayed that God would have different levels of punishment or reward based on the level of trial in one's life. Even as a prostitute, Ione had given more of herself for others than most were willing to give of their excess.

Miriam brought the last bite of pudding to her lips. Mrs.

Maloney was spoiling them.

"Do you wish you would have gone to the auxiliary meeting?" Jenny had already finished her dessert.

"No, I think we made the right decision. I haven't received any invitations addressed here yet, and there has been no mention of the house opening in the society pages, so I think, amazingly, we are still anonymous. Once I begin attending events, that luxury will be over."

"It's fine by me." Ione shifted on her chair. "It just gives us more time to make additions to your wardrobe." She pulled the napkin off her lap, folded it loosely, and placed it on the table. "Once people begin stopping by, you will need to have a variety of dresses. You wouldn't want them to see you in the same dress twice in the same week." Ione rolled her eyes at the silly truth.

Jenny pulled out a pad of paper.

"Where did you just pull that from?" Ione asked.

"From under me."

"You've been sitting on it all through dinner?"

"Yes." Jenny looked confused at the question. "What's wrong with that?"

Miriam smiled. "Nothing. Nothing is wrong with that."

Ione shook her head slowly back and forth.

Jenny shrugged and flipped open the cover. "From what I figure..." She pulled out a pencil that she had speared into the bun at the nape of her neck. "I figure Ione'll need about a week of time for your first ball gown. That's after we've ordered the fabric, and only if we can get Maggie here every day." Jenny stopped and looked at Ione. "Have you watched her work? That girl can sew fast."

"I know. If she were a little older, I'd make her my first hire."

"But she's got to finish school," Miriam interrupted.

"No doubt in that," Ione said. "Although with her kind of talent, she'll probably make a better income from the use of her needle."

"But unless she has a Jenny to do all her sums, she won't be able to tell if she's making money."

The three women nodded in unison.

"Speaking of sums." Jenny slid her pad of paper over to Miriam. "That's the final cost for your ball gown."

"That's obscene." Miriam scanned to the bottom of the sheet. "I could feed a hundred people for the cost of one dress. Sometimes I despise the world."

"Miriam," Ione chided.

"Oh, I know. In truth, that dress will probably allow me to raise a good deal more than its price for the hospital, but it still seems wrong."

"Part of me wishes I could be a fly on the wall at that event," Ione said. "I would love to see everyone's reaction to your ball gown." She paused. "Did that sound self-serving? I didn't mean it that way."

Miriam laughed. "Not at all. Why couldn't you go, though? Why couldn't we all go?" Miriam stopped playing with her spoon and set it on the table, lining it up perfectly with the bottom of the plate. "There's no reason Michael couldn't secure invitations for us all. He knows the hostess."

"I don't think that's a good idea." Jenny shook her head.

"That's not our world," Ione added. "But thank you for thinking of us."

"Why couldn't it be your world?" Miriam held up her hand. "No, don't answer. Let's just think about it for a while. In the meantime, I want you to design a dress that you would like to wear. Something that's not practical. Even if you never use it, it's good practice, and from the reactions I've seen from the few people who have seen your work, you are going to need to have a few ball gown examples for your portfolio."

Miriam's innocent smile earned a peppery glare from Ione.

Chapter 22

Ione and Jenny chattered away in the workroom off the kitchen. The mannequin displayed half of the ball gown. It was beginning to take shape. A filmy creation in cerulean navy, and lavender silk, it was stunningly unique. It made Miriam nervous just to look at it.

She ducked out of the room and pulled the key to her mother's rooms from her sleeve. Ione and Jenny were aware of the passageways scattered throughout the house, so they knew, if they couldn't find her, she hadn't disappeared. But they respected her solitude and never asked to see the rooms.

From the kitchen end of the house, the passageway opened immediately to a narrow staircase. Miriam walked up and slid open the pocket door at the top. The room here had no windows and no light, save the residual glow that echoed through a series of mirrors and tubes from the floors above. To work in the room, one would still need a lamp, but the contraption her father had thought up at least kept them from tripping in the dark.

If she would have followed the line of passageways from the front room to where she stood, there were a total of five rooms, this one being the fifth. The fourth was the studio. Miriam skipped lighting a lamp and took a second set of stairs to her mother's space, now hers.

A wall of windows provided a view overlooking the enclosed garden. The room did have its own entrance into the hallway on the third floor, but that door usually remained locked. It had only been added for the unlikely possibility that her mother would invite someone into her work space—wishful thinking on her father's part.

Miriam examined the painting on her easel. It was Jenny,

hunched over her desk in the sewing room while Ione circled a mannequin in the background. It was a very literal painting, one that she would not be covering or changing in any way. There was no future to predict. She wanted it for herself.

Miriam pulled tubes of gold out of the drawer that she never closed. The women in her painting worked by the yellow light of a flame. Miriam picked up her brushes and softened them in the palm of her hand before setting them on the tray of her easel. Twisting the tubes of paint open, she squeezed portions onto her palette, took her knife, and cut them together, watching the highlights and shadows inherent in the mixed colors disappear into the final, rich gold tone.

Her other paintings lined the wall under the windows. She thought she could leave them in the warehouse, but after only a few days, she'd missed them and asked for the man Michael hired to guard the warehouse to deliver them. Miriam rationalized that it was permissible for another person to see her paintings, because she'd never met him. Additionally, she gave Mrs. Maloney instructions where he should deliver them, so she wouldn't have to meet or speak with him. She did watch from the hidden door, though, as he stacked them against the wall of the studio.

He was a worker. He had a job to do. He carried them and delivered them without examination. Miriam was satisfied with the outcome and had Mrs. Maloney pay him twice what she'd offered.

She decided to mix her blues. She could have waited, but the Prussian blue, her current favorite, the color that would dominate the deep tones hidden in the shadows of the floorboards, wanted to be applied earlier rather than later.

A knock at the hallway door startled Miriam. She twisted the cap back on the metal tube of black she'd been squeezing onto the blue and dropped it on her tray.

"Miss Beaumont?" Mrs. Maloney tapped gently on the locked door.

Miriam hurried to turn the key and open it. "What is it?" She peered out through the small space.

"Mr. Farling is here to see you."

"Oh."

"Should I tell him you are busy?"

"No. Good heavens. I'll be right down."

Miriam wiped her hands off on a rag. Some colors never wanted to be removed. They clung to her skin and shadowed her nail beds until time finally wore them away. Miriam checked her reflection in her studio mirror, sighing in resigned dismay. She looked a mess. And not the kind of mess that could be cleaned up while someone waited.

She could hear—or more accurately, she could feel—the undertones of Michael's voice as she approached the top of the stairs. Mr. Butler stood in front of him, nodding in agreement to something.

John stood in the shadows outside the gambling house at the very center of the map he'd drawn.

The gaslights flickered, creating evenly spaced, damp halos of light. The thick fog required pedestrians to commit to walking out of the circle, into the dark, before the next light would appear. John felt for his knife that he'd again tucked into the back of his pants. Again feeling foolish, but again glad it was there.

He'd worn a dark overcoat, surprisingly similar to his robes, but falling only mid-calf.

It was late. The house was growing quiet, with only those remarkably determined to gamble remaining. The men closing the door behind them and descending the stone stairs did so alone. These were not men interested in spending time with the women of the house, or set on an evening of gaming with friends, these were the men who gambled as their profession. And the later it got, the graver their expressions.

Unfortunately, most of them wore overcoats. Hats and walking sticks were common. John sat back and waited. As they left, he made mental notes of any distinguishable characteristics. He planned to watch the papers.

The doorknob turned quietly, and a man stepped out. He was not wearing an overcoat.

John watched him take each step slowly. He paused at the wrought-iron gate at the base of the stairs and pulled on gloves, taking time to anchor them tightly around each narrow finger. Finally, he gave one last tug at each wrist, pulled out the walking stick he had tucked under his arm, and stepped into the fog.

John followed.

It was more difficult than he'd imagined it would be. The fog obscured the man's path, and John found himself stopping often to listen for footsteps or splashes or the click of a metal-tipped walking stick on pavement.

The man turned off the main street. John ducked into the alleys behind him.

Seedy taverns tucked into basement spaces advertised respite from the fog with their single yellow windows. They spat a few patrons into the streets and stumbling to the next square yellow beacon. John sidestepped into the shadows to avoid them.

He thought he heard a whimper. He stilled, waiting for the noise to die down and the street to empty. He'd lost the man anyway.

"Is someone there?" he whispered.

There was no response. John listened into the dark.

"I can help you," he offered. "Oh!" He jumped as he felt a tug at the hem of his coat. He couldn't see anything.

"Can you come into the light? I can't see you." John stooped to peer into the blackness. A child's pale face floated out of the night.

"Oh, Jesus." John dropped to his knees. He tenderly pulled the child up from the shadows.

The boy was not malnourished, John could feel that through the thin fabric of his shirt, but he was dirty, shaking, and feverish.

"Where's your mama?"

He felt the boy shrug and sway as if he would collapse. John scooped him up and wrapped his shivering body into the flaps of his coat.

"Hang on, son. I'm going to take you someplace warm. Then we'll find your mama."

The boy made no sound. He just hung on John like dead weight as John began the walk to Miriam's. It was only a few miles, certainly closer than the cathedral, and they would be able to call from her house for Dr. Pierce. John pressed his cool cheek against the little one's warm, dirty hair. The boy needed a doctor.

"Who is it?" Miriam stood in the dark at the top of the stairs, hurriedly fastening her robe, and waiting for Mr. Butler to answer the door.

"Who is it?" Mr. Butler called through the closed door.

"It's John. I need to come in."

"It's John." Mr. Butler slid the lock over.

John stepped in, shaking the fog off his shoulders and unbuttoning his overcoat. "Bring that lamp over." He nodded to Mrs. Maloney as he carried something bulky into the parlor. He shrugged off his coat, revealing a small boy curled in his arms.

Mrs. Maloney gasped and set the lamp on the table next to them. "Get some more lamps, and warm water, towels, and blankets," she ordered the maid who had wandered in behind her, blinking the sleep out of her eyes.

John sat with the boy in his lap and brushed the boy's blond hair back from his face.

"He can't be much more than three, maybe four." Mrs. Maloney dropped on her knees next to the davenport, removing the boy's dirty socks. "He's dirty, but he's not too thin." She ran her hands down his legs, feeling his knees. "I don't think anything is broken, but he's warm."

"I found him in an alley. I heard a whimper, and he reached out for me, but he hasn't said anything yet."

"Mr. Butler." Miriam touched the boy's limp hand. "Would you please send for Dr. Pierce? This shouldn't wait until morning."

Mr. Butler nodded and backed out of the room with the handful of dirty things he'd collected as Mrs. Maloney had taken them off the boy and dropped them on the carpet.

"What's going on?" Jenny stepped into the lamplight. Ione followed behind, tying her robe tightly about her waist.

Jenny stopped, staring at the limp boy in John's lap. She pulled Ione by her sleeve. "Look." She pointed.

Ione's eyes grew wide. She glanced at Jenny and back to the boy. "You don't think..."

"What?" Miriam asked, looking between the two women. "What?"

"It certainly looks like him." Jenny paused, biting her bottom lip.

"For heaven's sake." Mrs. Maloney planted her hands on her hips. "If you know something, just say it."

"That looks like Millie's boy." Ione knelt next to John and touched the boy's cheek. "I'm sure it's him. Where'd you find him?"

Mrs. Maloney shook out an extra blanket and placed it over the sleeping child's feet.

"He'll be fine." Dr. Pierce met her eyes.

Mrs. Maloney nodded her shallow agreement and followed the doctor out of the room, quietly closing the door behind her. Everyone, except Jenny, waited in the connecting sitting room. She stayed to watch over little Theo. Earlier, he'd woken up long enough to tell them his name, and that he didn't know where his mama was.

"We need to find his mother." Mrs. Maloney picked up a forgotten teacup. She looked around for a tray to set it on so one of the maids would find it but gave up after a minute and set it back down on the side table.

"I hope she's findable," John said. He stood at the window that let the morning light in and stared out at the park. "Look at all those people." He rested his forehead against the glass. "They have no idea that last night a child was crying in a gutter, looking for his mother."

"Where shall we begin?" Mrs. Maloney sat down next to Ione.

One of the young maids backed into the room, balancing a tray loaded with pastries and tea. John cleared a space on the desk and the maid set the tray down.

"Thank you, Nettie." Mrs. Maloney picked the stray teacup back up and handed it to her to take to the kitchen. The girl was doing admirably, she noted. She would talk to her later that day. The other maid cradled a cup of warm broth in her hands. "That goes to Theo." Mrs. Maloney nodded her through the door. The second maid, Stella, was younger. Patience would be the key.

"Mr. Farling is here to see you." Mr. Butler stepped into the room.

"Me?" Miriam asked.

Mrs. Maloney didn't know why she was always surprised when he visited. If she were the kind of woman who placed bets, she'd put money on it that he thought of little else but Miriam when he was gone. His excuses for visiting had grown more suspect as the days waned on.

Miriam glanced at herself in the mirror. She tucked a few strands of hair behind her ears and brushed the wrinkles out of her skirt. John, leaning his back against the window sill, watched her fuss.

At least they'd all dressed for the day.

"Did you read the papers yet this—" Michael halted his entrance into the room. The paper was folded and tucked under his arm. "What happened?"

"John found a little boy last night," Miriam said.

"What do you mean, found?"

John stood up and walked to the tray of food. "She means that I literally found him in the gutter." Disdain dripped from his voice. He picked up a small pastry with an enormous glob of frosting and stuffed it into his mouth in one bite.

Michael, eyebrows up, looked to Dr. Pierce for answers.

"Ione and Jenny think they know his mother." He waited to finish his explanation until the two young maids walked back out of the room. "She is a woman who sometimes..." He cleared his throat and looked at Ione apologetically. "Who sometimes shared their, um, previous profession."

"Is he the boy?" Michael asked Ione, the sick feeling in his stomach expanding with each second.

She nodded.

"You're sure?"

"As sure as we can be, but there's not too many boys that look like him around."

Michael dropped the paper he'd been holding onto the desk

with a thump. "This is why I'm here." He'd had it folded open to an article that was, once again, buried between advertisements for hair curlers and the standard disorderly conduct police reports. "Another woman was found."

He looked to John. "How'd you come across him, anyway?"

"I was watching the gambling houses. I followed a man into an alley. I lost him in the fog, but stumbled on the little boy."

"Was it the man?" Miriam, obviously not having heard that part of his story, listened intently.

"I don't know. Something about him was wrong. But that could be anything from having plans to kill someone to having to explain to his wife that he'd just gambled away her jewelry. Who knows?"

"Where is the woman now?" Jenny picked up the paper with the tips of her fingers, as if she were afraid of it.

Michael took it from her before she could read it and, meeting her eyes, flipped the paper over on the desk.

Ione looked down to the floor. "Did they give a description of her?"

"Not much of one. She was blond and tall in stature."

"Curly blond hair?" Jenny partially closed the door Michael had entered through. "She looks just like her boy. Curly blond hair, gold really, and round cheeks with dimples. She has brown eyes, but not the dark kind. She has light brown eyes."

"The paper didn't have a name, did it?" Mrs. Maloney asked.

"No. They don't know who she is."

"What do they do if they don't know who she is?" Miriam picked at the tassels on the pillow next to her.

"They will keep her for a couple of days, and then if no one claims her, they will bury her."

"In a pauper's grave," Ione finished bitterly.

"What's the boy's mother's name?" Michael asked.

"Millie," they all answered in unison.

Michael watched John's back at the window until he turned to face him. John nodded, knowing what had to be done. Jenny sat in a chair next to the desk.

John scooted a footstool closer to her and bent to sit in front of her, meeting her eyes. "Do you know what we need to do?" he asked, holding his hand out for her.

She looked up at him and placed her small hand in his. "Yes."

"Are you the one we can ask to do it?"

Jenny took a deep breath. "I'll do it. Theo needs to know if he has a mama." She looked at Mrs. Maloney, who sent her a sad, supporting smile. "When should we leave?"

"We're never going to find him like this," John said to Michael. They were leaving together in one of Miriam's coaches after dropping Jenny back at the house. She'd been confident it was Millie. But it was a brutalized Millie.

Jenny had been stoic. They pulled the sheet back from her battered face, and Jenny nodded. John knew she was observant though. He knew she'd seen the jagged cuts around Millie's neck.

"What have you seen at the warehouse?" Michael asked.

"There is the boy, Sean, I told you about."

"Anything new with him?"

"Not really. He failed to give them the information they wanted, so they've left him alone. I've paid him, though—enough to make him come to me if anyone starts looking again." John shifted in the small seat. "Have you heard anything from the investigator?"

"No. Except that the anonymous client has money, and the investigator thinks he's holding something over Jacob Tenney. Tenney is being far too discrete for a typical solicitor relationship."

"There is something that's bothered me." John leaned forward, placing his elbows on his knees and lowering his voice even though he knew no one could hear him over the rattling of the wheels on the cobbled streets. As if on cue, their carriage clattered over multiple sets of rail tracks.

"What is it?" Michael asked, reminding John where they were in the discussion.

"I told you the police were fairly hostile at my last visit."

Michael nodded.

"What I didn't think to tell you right away was that they either inadvertently, or maybe even purposely, linked the offer on the warehouse to the women."

"How's that?"

John shifted, wishing the carriage would stop rocking long

enough to think. "As I was leaving, after I'd shown them the newspaper articles, they said that she, speaking of Miriam, should consider the offer."

Michael's eyebrows furrowed over his glasses. "Had you mentioned the offer?"

"No, of course not, that's why it surprised me."

Michael sat back and looked out the window. The landscape and air change as they neared the cathedral. "In essence," he said, still facing the window, "they linked the missing women to someone with money."

John nodded, frowning. "If it was new information, it wouldn't concern me so much, but it's not. It confirms what Jenny and Ione have said."

"And it means someone paid them off first." Michael looked back at John. "With Tenney holding his cards so close to his chest, there's no way he leaked that information. Someone is feeding information to the police, and paying them to overlook the things they're inclined to overlook anyway."

"Which makes their other assumptions even more disturbing."

"What other assumptions?"

"They insinuated Miriam may have ulterior motives for housing Ione and Jenny."

Michael muttered something John didn't ask him to clarify. "We're going to have to do something. This is only going to intensify."

"I know. Not to mention that women are still dying."

"You said you followed someone when you found the boy. Did you have any sense that it might be the man who had watched you outside the warehouse?"

John paused, thinking. "I can't be sure. When I think about it, he did have the same type of build, the same quality of clothes, and the deliberate mannerisms. But quite frankly, so do most of the upper crust."

"Nevertheless, it might be prudent to watch that establishment. You could do your best at a description, and I will have the investigator try to put names with frequent patrons. It's a start."

"That's not enough."

"I agree," Michael said.

"The longer we wait, the more women will die."

"And the more danger Miriam, Ione, and Jenny are in."

"We have to come up with a plan. We need to draw him out."

Michael nodded. He had an idea. And he knew, unfortunately, Miriam would be a willing participant. He was beginning to think he preferred her alone, isolated, and living safely in the warehouse.

The carriage rocked to a halt in front of the cathedral.

"I'll speak with Miriam tomorrow morning," Michael said to John as he jumped out of the carriage. "Will you be available in the afternoon? I can fill you in."

"How about if I meet you there in the morning?"

"Good enough. Nine?"

"Nine." John slapped the side of the carriage, and Michael watched him take the cathedral steps two at a time.

Chapter 23

Michael had sent a message requesting to visit at nine in the morning. Jenny and Ione were in the workroom. Miriam pulled her father's watch from her deep pocket. Eight fifty-five.

Theo sat on the kitchen counter next to Mrs. Maloney. She fed him sweets—bite-sized pastries dusted with powdered sugar. His golden curls were tipped in white, and his fingers were sticky with jelly. His fever had broken after his first night. Ever since, he hadn't stopped asking for his mama. God had placed him in the right home for that. Last night he'd slept in Jenny's bed. Ione was sewing him clothes. Who better to mother than three women who'd lost their mothers, supervised by one grandmother?

"May I come in?" Michael knocked on the doorframe.

Miriam smiled.

"We need to discuss some things." Michael joined her at the window.

"Yes, I think we do." Miriam unlatched the garden door. "Do you want to go outside? We've started to clear some of the overgrowth."

"Sure. But John will be joining us any minute."

"We'll leave the doors open."

The sun shone on half the garden, and up one brick wall. Miriam stepped into what felt like a tower with no ceiling and looked up. Everyone did, every time they took the gravel path that led to the bench under the trees. Before they'd begun tearing out the weeds, the bench was almost completely obscured. Miriam turned toward Michael, watching him as he looked up into the vertical tunnel.

"It's a little unsettling," he said, bringing his gaze down.

"Why?"

"I don't know. I guess because there's no way out."

Miriam smiled.

"There is a way out, isn't there."

Miriam led the way to the stone bench. It was green with age. Lichens had grown up the legs, and a carpet of moss covered most of what used to be a crushed granite path.

Michael settled next to her on the bench. His proximity to her was not improper due to the circumstance of there being only one bench. He looked uncomfortable though, and when Miriam's leg brushed against his, he fractionally twisted away, giving her more space.

"John spoke with the police." Michael slapped some dirt off his pant leg. "They're no help."

Miriam listened while Michael explained everything she'd already known. They—Miriam, Jenny, and Ione—had discussed it at some length. They'd thought of, and dismissed, any number of plans to find the man. There was the new element, however. Michael shared how he and John were considering a link between the offer on the warehouse and the attacks.

"It's time for me to reappear," Miriam interrupted Michael.

He stopped mid-sentence.

"I know you won't like it, but if he doesn't know where we've gone, and he's looking for me, we might as well make it easy for him."

"I don't particularly relish the idea of making you an easy target."

"Unless I plan never to leave the house, he'll eventually find me anyway. I'd rather be prepared and watching."

"You're right." Michael stood and leaned against a twisted tree. "I don't like it. But I'd already come to the same conclusion."

"I'm waiting to hear it." John walked out and looked up. He let out a low whistle. "This is an interesting place."

"Miriam is going to be re-entering society."

John nodded. "I don't see many more options. We need to find this guy."

Michael plucked a leaf from an overhead branch. Methodically, he peeled it down each vein. "I have a number of invitations for upcoming events. Why don't I contact a few of the hostesses and secure invitations for you? That should start the ball rolling."

"I was thinking of something rather faster." Miriam stood and crossed to the tree. Michael let the leaf flutter to the ground. John took a step nearer.

"Do you like my dress?" Miriam asked.

John's eyebrows bunched together, and he looked toward Michael, confused.

"Well." Michael cleared his throat. "It's very nice."

"It's a bit more formal than a typical morning dress, wouldn't you say?"

"I suppose." It was Michael's turn to send John a questioning look.

"Follow me."

Miriam led the men back into the house, leaving the doors wide in her wake. She crossed to the front windows and pulled the floor-to-ceiling drapes wide. "Now," she said, "just watch."

A cluster of young women, grouped together and clucking under lace parasols, turned as one of their delicate hands pointed to the exposed window of the house. Soon, five pairs of eyes turned, blinking, at the mansion.

"Mr. Farling," Miriam said, in her best mock-formal voice. "Would you be so kind, sir, as to escort me for my morning constitutional?"

John chuckled, a half-smile spreading across his face.

Michael tilted his head to the side, assessing her.

Not very long ago, she wouldn't allow anyone to even open the curtains. Now, she was the one asking to go for the walk—and with an audience.

It was on her terms.

Her hair was pulled up and piled on top of her head in a mass of curls that must have taken not a small amount of effort. Thin tendrils hung down, flirting with the skin on her neck. Her dress was a pale copper, silvering the cool gray of her eyes. She wore no jewelry, but the absence had the opposite of the expected result. Instead of making her appear plain, it highlighted the phenomena that she needed no ornamentation.

What she needed was predictability; that was her key. She was used to knowing what was going to happen. And, when her foresight failed her, she turned inward—like when her father died.

"I'll go to the kitchen," John said. "I assume everyone is down there?"

Miriam nodded, watching Michael put on his hat. He held out his arm, and she took it to walk down the steps to the street level.

They strode together down the sidewalk, waiting for the carriages to pass. When the street cleared, they crossed to the park, Michael tipping his hat toward the group of women. They stood with their mouths gaping open.

"By tomorrow morning," Miriam stretched up to whisper, "I'll have half a dozen invites on the hall table."

Michael controlled his breathing. She had no idea.

Jacob Tenney decided to watch for himself. He'd tried to pay the redheaded boy, but that hadn't worked out. For the first week, he said he hadn't seen anything. After that, he was just hard to find. There was too much at risk to trust it to a kid anyway.

It was evening, and the traffic had slowed. The priest, who seemed to watch so carefully, had left in a carriage that was far too fine for someone who'd taken a vow of poverty. He watched the warehouse for a lamp to turn on, or some other sign of life, but there was nothing. Where could she have gone? He'd asked around, casually, and everyone said the same thing—that she was a hermit, a witch, or some other name which meant she never left and had no contact with the outside world.

But she wasn't there now.

Jacob stood in the shadows against the cathedral to the side of the stairs. Possibly the priest was involved, but that would be unlikely. Her solicitor, Mr. Farling—Jacob inwardly sneered—said he'd spoken with her. Jacob had done some research, and Farling had some of his own assets. For all Jacob knew, he never asked the woman, because he was considering his own future use for the space.

If Jacob only knew, really knew, the identity of the man who wanted to purchase. But he didn't. The man was beyond careful, and transactions happened anonymously all the time anyway. There was no reason for Jacob to press the issue. Besides the fact that if he didn't deliver, he would have no recourse to force his secretive client to pay him for his time. Jacob fisted his hands and shoved them deep into his pants pockets. The night was turning out to be a waste. Worse, the night was telling him that the entire endeavor was a waste.

A light splashing began outside of the streetlamp's circle. The small puddles in the cracks of the cobbles hadn't evaporated yet. Jacob examined his own wet boots. They were wearing thin on the bottom. He'd promised himself a new pair after his next payday. That was getting further and further off. Soon, he would have to pick up side jobs doing accounting again. He'd thought he was past that. Jacob bent to brush some of the beaded water from his toes.

The splashing grew louder, more like a stumble, and Jacob moved fully into the shadows to wait.

A drunken bum nearly fell off the curb, catching his fall with a counter balancing swing of his arms. The move was almost graceful if it hadn't been so pathetic. He was large, very large, and balding. The kind of man who smelled like yesterday's drunk. His pants hung low on his waist, held up by a tortured leather belt. His boots were remarkably shined.

"I know what you're doing with her," he slurred out, pointing to the warehouse.

Jacob furrowed his brows, listening to the unexpected statement.

The man rubbed his face with the palm of his hand, then proceeded to cough and blow his nose onto the street—without the luxury of a handkerchief. Jacob took note where not to step.

"I know what you're up to, you sneaky whore," he yelled louder, emboldened by the lack of an audience. He tripped up to the warehouse door and pounded on it with indecipherable threats.

"Don't you think I don't know what's going on," he said, dropping his chin into his chest. He slumped to a sitting position with his back against the door. "I'm gonna wait for you to get back, then you're gonna pay me for stealing her." The man pulled a flask from his voluminous pants pocket, twisted off the cap, and took a swig. He tried to stand up but slumped back down as Jacob stepped out of the shadows.

"My name is Ned," Jacob lied. "You know the woman who lives here?"

"She's a witch, she is. She stole my Jenny."

"You don't say." Jacob moved closer to lean against the wall.

The man took another swig and held the bottle out to Jacob. Jacob took it and pretended to drink when he turned away. He handed the bottle back.

"How'd she do that?" Jacob asked.

"N...none of your bi...bid...business."

"You see, it's a secret, but I'm looking for the woman who used to live here. Do you know where she went?"

"No." He coughed. Spittle clung from his fleshy lips. "Know what though, it were that priest that's involved. I bet he knows what's happened to her."

Jacob slid down the wall to sit next to the man who smelled precisely how he'd imagined. "If you can help me find her, it would be worth something to me."

The man's breathing slowed, and he turned to face Jacob. "I'll tell you how to find her, all right. Her papa was rich, and he owned more'n one building in this town."

Jacob nodded. He took the opportunity to remind the drunkard why he was angry. "But why did she steal your Jenny? Was she your wife? Sister?"

"She's my daughter. And she knew how to get a man's money outta his pockets, tha' she did. That witch is taking a cut."

Jacob had to fight not to recoil. The man was disgusting in every way. His bare ankles stuck out between his pants and new shoes. He covered his nose with his handkerchief for a moment of reprieve. But even disgusting people had their value. "So, how do I find her?"

"I'd follow the priest." He took another swig. "He's the one."

Chapter 24

Miriam turned around, checking the back of the dress in the mirror.

"Oh." Jenny walked in with Theo on her hip. Ione was on her knees on the floor with a needle between her teeth. She was making some final adjustments. "That's the prettiest dress I've ever seen." Theo squirmed out of Jenny's arms. She snagged him back before he reached the dress with his perpetually sticky fingers.

It was the one Ione had been working on whenever she had a day that threatened to be wasted due to a wait on a special order fabric, or some buttons that hadn't shipped properly. The last minute ball was that night, and the dress would be done just in time.

Miriam glanced in the mirror again. The back cascaded off her shoulders, angling down to gather just below the small of her back. The fabric had been a splurge. It was unlike anything any of them had seen before: silk, almost translucent, with the melting colors of twilight. It began with navy, almost black, balancing wide on her shoulders. The silk twisted in folds from there, like long fingers running at an angle around her ribcage. It was blue-green by the time it dipped into her waist. It turned almost green at the flare of her hips, and by the time it trailed behind her, it did so in a ruched cloud of lavender.

Miriam twisted in the mirror, watching the colors shift against her skin. The thin fabric did little to hide her figure. She could see the shape of her legs unsuccessfully hidden by the flat front of the dress.

"Hold still, please." Ione still clenched the needle in her teeth. "I think fitting Theo is easier than fitting you."

"I've never worn anything like this before."

"Well, if you don't let me finish, that won't change."

Jenny lit a lamp, and the dress shimmered with even more color. She sat at the dressing table with Theo on her lap and opened Miriam's jewelry box. Theo reached in, carefully examining the glimmering contents.

Miriam watched the top of Ione's head. "Are you sure there shouldn't be more of a bustle?"

"Yes, I'm sure."

"But I haven't seen too many dresses like this one."

"I think that's the purpose, isn't it?" Jenny held a gold broach up to her throat and examined herself in the mirror. "What jewelry are you going to wear?"

"I wasn't sure until I saw it with the lamplight, but I think my mother's emeralds will pick up the green."

"Ooh, where are those?" Jenny started digging in earnest.

"In the drawer to the right. They're in a velvet case." Miriam turned back to Ione. "And you're sure there shouldn't be more sleeve?"

Ione sat back on her heels and looked up at Miriam. "Every eye in the ballroom will be on you, but you won't pull it off unless you're confident about it. Are you going to be able to do it?"

Miriam examined her reflection again and tried to imagine what it would be like to be the kind of woman who would wear such a thing.

"There it is," Ione whispered. "If you look at people like that, you'll do just fine."

"Here." Jenny stepped up behind her and laid the cool metal of the necklace against her skin. It was out of fashion, with a heavy silver chain, rather than gold. One large green stone set smoothly in a bed of cascading circles. The lines weren't the typical, busy, layered look. Instead, it was clean. The heavy jewel at the center rested on her pale skin just above her neckline, appearing to have grown there like it was a part of her.

Miriam took in a shaky breath, hardly recognizing herself.

Theo just stared.

"Don't worry," Ione said. "I made you a matching cape to wear until you get there."

"Oh, good." Miriam let out a rush of air. The night would be a challenge. But the emerald was on her chest, taking the heat from her skin, in return offering its calming green luminescence.

"But will Michael like it?" She would be on his arm for the entire night, after all. "I won't look like the other ladies."

Jenny raised her eyebrows and snorted, earning all of their attentions. "You got nothing to worry about." She laughed, scooping Theo back into her arms and swinging out of the room. "He ain't gonna be able to look away." Jenny disappeared down the wide hallway.

"Is that good?" Miriam bent to ask Ione.

"Yes. It's good. And would you please, please hold still?"

It was growing dark. Watching the cathedral for most of the day was tedious. Jacob was just about to lose hope when the priest stepped out of the alley and quickly made his way down the street. Jacob tucked in behind him and followed.

He wore his robes. He could be on his way to visit a sick parishioner. Jacob resented the way he felt, having to stalk a priest. But he could be on his way to visit Miss Beaumont. He wasn't going to miss that opportunity.

He'd tried to get the information by more traditional methods, but no one knew much, or they weren't talking. Her father had owned a number of buildings and, rumor had it, had a large stock in some railroads, but no one knew the status of his estate. The buildings, all of them, stood empty, as far as anyone knew.

The priest hailed a hack and jumped in. Jacob cursed under his breath. If he hailed his own hack, it would not only cost him money, but there would be a witness to the fact he was following the priest. He raised his arm and jumped in the first one that slowed down.

"See the hack up there?" he shouted to the driver.

"Yes, sir."

"Follow it."

Jacob sat back. His finances were a mess. His rent was past due, and he would have to sneak past the landlady again. He picked at a hangnail until a small bead of blood bubbled to the surface. He cursed again and rubbed the blood on his jacket. He'd find out tonight. He'd definitely find out tonight.

Michael called at the agreed upon time. He couldn't believe she'd received an invitation to the Penns' ball. He'd not even received an invitation. He suspected it had something to do with the rumors of her mother's artistry, or of her fortune, or of the potential for scandal. It could be anything, but Mrs. Penn had an insatiable thirst for art, and not just the typical things the rich of Chicago felt privileged to procure. Michael straightened the white cuffs of his shirt, lining the seams up with the seams of his jacket before pulling the jacket sleeves down to cover his wrists. He adjusted his pristine white gloves. Mr. Butler answered the door.

"Good evening, Mr. Farling." He motioned for Michael to enter.

"Good evening to you too."

"Would you like me to take your hat?"

"No." Michael glanced toward the stairs. "We'll need to leave as soon as Miriam is ready."

"I'm ready now." Miriam walked into the foyer. Jenny and Ione followed, Ione holding her cape.

Miriam turned to say something to them both, and then Ione helped Miriam cover herself, fastening the gauzy cape across her bare shoulders and arms with a silver rope. It allowed her astounding emerald to show against her pale skin like a medallion.

"Are you ready?" Miriam asked, evidently confused by his silence and the fact that he still stood but two feet from the door.

"Yes, of course."

There wasn't a hint of nervousness in her demeanor. Her dress caressed her like it loved her. It clung to every curve, every dent he tried not to think about. Was it possible to be jealous of fabric? He held out his elbow. She wrapped her gloved hand around his arm, holding the muscle in the loose grip of her tiny fingers rather than rest her wrist in the crook of his arm. Michael took a deep breath, relieved when they reached the open carriage door so she could climb in.

The gaslight shone on her side of the vehicle. He watched her settle herself against the dark velvet. Whether it was his imagination or something lacking in the dress, he couldn't tell. His hands itched to touch the fabric, to feel it drag against his own skin. The carriage lurched ahead.

Miriam watched him, a smile flirting with the corner of her mouth. He'd been discovered. Michael cleared his throat and looked out the window, waiting until he could feel her gaze drop so he could look at her again.

Her gaze didn't drop. Michael shifted, crossed one leg over his knee, and tried to think of something else, of the real reason why they were there together, anything to get his mind off of the night's torments.

"You like my dress."

Michael's eyes darted to hers, then down her frame. The cape, which concealed nothing, was pushed away from one shoulder. Her creamy skin glowed. Her dress had the effect of making her look like a pearl ready to be plucked from an iridescent, unsuspecting oyster.

Her honesty was refreshing, and a bit disconcerting.

He looked her in the eyes, knowing, God help him, he was going to be just as honest. Being with her was like a game. But rather than a game of dodging and ducking and slinging around half-truths, it was a contest to see who would be the most honest. A contest of bravery. It was a contest she wouldn't be winning tonight.

"Miriam." He leaned forward and whispered, "I've never seen a woman who could even be close to your equal."

Miriam blinked and finally dropped her gaze to her gloved hands.

"And." Michael paused. "Your dress is beautiful too."

The mansion on the lake was nothing short of spectacular... and a little gaudy. Turrets rose above the landscape, supported by stone masonry. Miriam had all she could do not to stare up at the building. She hadn't been to this area of the lake since they'd begun developing it.

She and Michael walked up the stairs into the mansion

together. A three-story glass ceilinged entrance, with views to the floors above, overcame Miriam's aloof façade, and she stood in the center, looking up. Mrs. Penn had said it would be a quieter affair, with music and a few local artists. They relinquished their outerwear to the team of attendants, not even realizing they'd done so until they were ushered past the glimmering dining room and into the parlor.

"There must be forty chairs around that table," Miriam whispered to Michael as they traversed the foyer.

They were announced in the parlor to a hushed silence, quick whispers, and finally a rush of people attempting to appear casual.

"Miss Beaumont, so nice to finally meet you." One young man took Miriam's hand in his, brushing his mustache across her gloved knuckles. "I've heard so much."

"Really?" Miriam negotiated a few more introductions before continuing the conversation. "What is it that you've heard?"

The man flushed over his white starched collar and stuttered out an excuse to leave. Miriam watched Michael smile possessively at the man's retreating figure.

A man in white livery offered small glasses of wine; a nod and a complement to the dinner they would be served. Miriam took the crystal glass filled with scarlet wine and thanked him. Appropriately, he nodded without making eye contact.

A group of women made their way through the throng, and Miriam began to tremble. She folded her hands together and smiled. The room was so close. There were too many people. She felt Michael's hand brush against the small of her back and stay there. In the crush of people, no one would see the liberty. She stood a little taller and smiled at the approaching women.

"It's nice to meet you," one girl interjected into the multitude of conversations. Instead of vying for the coveted spot directly in front of Miriam, she'd swung over to stand by her side.

"You too. I'm sorry, would you please tell me your name again?"

"Miss Vaughn." The woman's rose-colored dress hung in layers of lace, almost fish-scale like, but beautiful. Her dark hair was piled high on her head. A tiara of rose-colored stones glinted from the mass of curls. She was at least a head taller than Miriam, and by the looks of it, she did nothing to hide the fact.

"I hope I'm not being too forward, but your dress is astounding."

She leaned in to speak in a volume that was understandable, but only for Miriam.

"Thank you." Miriam looked up at her after making some excuses to a few of the others. She turned to face the beauty, realizing she was not as young as she'd first thought.

"I hope I'm not being too forward, but would you mind if I called on you tomorrow?"

Michael stepped forward, preparing to intervene. Miriam touched his sleeve before answering. "I would be delighted for you to stop by. Would ten-thirty work well for you?"

"Yes." Miss Vaughn smiled brilliantly. "Thank you."

In a second's reprieve from the crowd, Michael sent her a questioning glance. Miriam ignored it.

Miriam shrugged her perfect shoulders, and the emerald, resting low on her chest, shifted and caught the chandelier's fractured light, drawing his eyes down. It was an evil trick. The worst part was Michael wasn't even sure she was aware of her effect on him.

He felt like growling at each approaching man, and unfortunately, the opportunities to fight the instinct abounded. Every time he looked up, it was to see another man working his way across the ballroom, necessitating Michael's preemptive shuffle toward an imposing group of women. He knew she would do better speaking with the men, she seemed most comfortable with men. It was, after all, the purpose of the night. He was watching, however, and taking note. She didn't have to talk to them.

After a few tense moments, she'd adjusted admirably, and now she was smiling and flirting as if she hadn't hidden herself for years in a warehouse. The men negotiated the crowd, trying to catch a glimpse of her in the dress. It revealed everything and nothing. Try as he might, Michael couldn't find a single thing that was in the least bit improper, but the fact that he was trying so hard was a testament to Ione's skill. If his and everyone else's reactions were any indication, Ione was a genius.

At the dinner gong, Miriam slid into the crook of Michael's arm without even looking his way. It was as if her instincts told her he was there, waiting. They crossed to the dining room together, somewhere in the middle, about ten couples behind the guest of honor.

"Fifty," Miriam said.

"What?" Michael asked. They found their place holders, and he held the chair out for her.

"There are fifty chairs around this table."

Miriam sat, allowing Michael a glimpse of her back, courtesy of the few inches where the fabric dipped in precarious-looking folds. He'd thought the night would be a challenge for her. He hadn't anticipated Ione's wickedness.

The other women knew of his interest in Miriam. He was sure. It was Miriam who likely had no idea. But that meant she also had no idea about the other men, and their triumphant looks as they learned they were to sit in close proximity to her, and the evil glares of the women they'd escorted. More than anything, his duty was to protect her. He owed it to her father.

The waiter reached in, pulling his napkin off the table and dropping it into Michael's lap. Mrs. Penn stood next to her husband at the head of the table, welcoming her guests. It was an interesting mix of people, and an unusual choice—serving dinner seated in the dining room, rather than buffet style in the ballroom. But Mrs. Penn was unconventional, and Michael was positive there was a theme, and a purpose, to the evening.

Musicians, artists, and real estate moguls were interspersed down the length of the table. There was a concentration of high-powered women present, ladies who'd championed and won the site selection for the World's Fair. Like most big decisions in Chicago, the site was won in the parlors and dining rooms of the homes of the elite—not in the board rooms as one might expect. Mrs. Penn was a brilliant businesswoman who knew how to manage Chicago's magnates to her own end. She was also a social magician who knew how to work a crowd.

Michael hoped for a light menu—either a light menu or minimal dancing. To do both a dinner party and a formal ball in one evening would be a huge undertaking for the constitutions of even the most un-corseted women present. If Miriam wore a corset under the filmy gown, it was unlike any he'd ever seen. Michael flushed and began counting the candlesticks on the table. He couldn't believe his mind had wandered to the structure of her undergarments. Heaven help him.

"Thank you all for coming." Mr. Penn stood, placing both hands on the table as if he were going to shout orders to the officers of his corporation. "We appreciate you joining us for this occasion, and at this time, I hope my fine wife will take over, because I would be hopeless to describe the events she's planned for this evening." He winked at Mrs. Penn.

"I also thank you for gracing our home with your presence. I hope you enjoy what will be a light but pleasant dinner, followed by dessert and dancing on the rooftop. I also have a special surprise, an unveiling, really, to take place after the dancing. Please enjoy your time, and enjoy the company."

She picked up her champagne glass and held it out over the table. The rest of the guests followed suit, standing for her first toast. It was a break in tradition, to offer the first toast before the main course, but Michael had the impression that little that happened there that night would follow strict tradition.

"To friends, to beauty, to success. To great conversation, sublime music, and art. To a wonderful night."

The room resounded with a "hear, hear," and they all sipped together. Fifty power brokers making strategic eye contact from over the edge of their crystal glasses.

The priest knocked on the door of a townhouse. Jacob watched from the park across the street. A man answered, admitting the priest without hesitation.

Lights shone from the front windows, but they were too high off the street level for him to walk by and look into. The park bench facing the home was already growing damp with evening dew, so Jacob leaned against the jagged bark of an old oak, watching, waiting, and thinking of how he could get a view of the interior.

If that disgusting man had been right, his daughter—Jacob shuddered at the thought—his daughter was working for the priest. It didn't seem right.

Jacob knew that sort of thing did happen, but, looking at the clergyman, he just didn't get the sense that he was that kind of man. After all, why would he be so bold as to walk up to the front door of a brothel he owned, in his robes nonetheless, and walk right in? It wasn't adding up.

No light seeped from the upper floor windows. They couldn't have a large staff, nor did it seem there could be many people living there.

But there was an accusation. An accusation could always be used, even if it might be false. Jacob drew a line with the toe of his shoe in the gravel path. There were advantages to be leveraged, pressures to introduce. He just needed to decide how best to handle it.

He shoved his cold fingers into his trouser pockets and watched the house for movement. If he were to get the police involved—it would be rather easy—he could pressure Miss Beaumont to sell. But there was a missing element. An advantage not leveraged. Jacob could see the priest had not kidnapped that man's daughter and taken her to work in a high-priced brothel. Any man willing to look deeper than the surface could see that. But not everyone was willing to look beyond the obvious. There was the key.

The police, already on his employer's payroll, were willing to do anything he asked. He could threaten, more like hint, at the potential for trouble. If Miriam was planning to re-enter society, a public investigation would significantly hamper her chances for success. The man's daughter was a prostitute. Jacob guessed Miriam would not want that knowledge to be public.

Leverage. Jacob kicked up from his leaning stance and started on the long trek toward his rented room. It would be late by the time he reached his building, but it saved him from paying for transportation. The added bonus was his landlady would be asleep by the time he tiptoed past her door.

Chapter 25

Miriam pulled on her gloves. The dinner, supposedly a simple affair, had been grand. Five courses—she supposed this was the part that earned the "simple" description—of every delicacy she could have imagined. Growing up with her father, they'd eaten simply. She remembered parties, but she'd been too young to be included. Each of the five courses had multiple selections: consommé or cream soup, cold salmon and lake trout served hot, salads unlike anything she'd ever seen, jellies piled high with fresh fruit. Even a small taste of each plate made her grateful for a moment of respite before the dancing began.

Everyone around the table stood as the women exited toward the parlor to allow the men to smoke in the dining room. Michael nodded to her as she left, his expression gauging her readiness to visit with the women of the group. She discretely nodded back, trailing her gloved fingers across the back of his hand, reassuring him.

The women spoke in hushed tones, crossing to the parlor. A string quartet played softly in one corner.

"Miss Beaumont." Mrs. Penn approached Miriam from behind. "I just wanted to thank you for coming tonight. I realize it was short notice."

"Thank you for inviting me." Miriam smiled. "Your home surpasses any compliments I've heard. It is exquisite."

Miriam knew each of her words were weighed by the brilliant woman standing in front of her, and her success as an active member of Chicago society relied on the Penns' endorsement.

"The artwork you've taken such pains to collect is beyond any collection I've seen. I have the feeling I could spend days lost in your home, just wandering from masterpiece to masterpiece."

Mrs. Penn's eyebrows hitched up in a barely perceptible arch. "I've heard your mother was quite a painter, but I've yet had the opportunity to see any evidence of her work."

Miriam hid her surprise. The woman was testing her, feigning ignorance, and touching on subjects that she knew might be sensitive.

Miriam was determined to rise to the challenge. "She was unparalleled. During her lifetime, much to my father's disappointment, she never exhibited her talents, but I have her paintings and would be honored if you were the first to view them."

Mrs. Penn's eyes widened fractionally, betraying her delighted shock at Miriam's offer. She quickly recovered. "I would relish the opportunity. Let's speak about it later, when there's not such a crowd."

Mrs. Penn smiled and took a step to the side before she paused, appearing to change her mind. She turned back to Miriam.

"I'm not going to pretend that I do not know you paint as well, my dear. I hope you enjoy the unveiling tonight. And if you are inclined, I would love to see some of your work as well. And, your dress is unlike anything I've ever seen. I hope at some point you will share that secret too."

Michael watched for Miriam to step from the parlor. An overflow of color spilled out in refined fashion. Miriam was at the center of a flock of young women, nodding and smiling but pale. Something had happened.

She looked up from the group, directly into his eyes. Michael did his best to discretely rush to her. The crowd was milling around, slowly making their way up the stairs to the ballroom. Michael put his hand at her waist and guided her down a dark hallway. The conservancy was at the end. She needed to sit, and he waited to find out what had happened to cause such a reaction.

"I'm fine, really." Miriam waved his concern aside.

"You're pale. You can sit for a few minutes and tell me what happened." Michael opened the door and ushered Miriam forward into the dark. He held his finger to his lips, signaling for Miriam to keep quiet while he walked the perimeter of the room, insuring they were the only ones there. He returned to her side and locked the door before escorting her through the cool, damp air to a settee.

She sat on one end of the cushion. Michael stood across from her.

"Sit down." Miriam patted the seat next to her. "I can't talk to you while craning my neck up to see your face."

Michael smiled at the dropping of her adopted formal voice. He felt privileged to hear her genuine inflections, even if they did make her sound a bit like a testy school mistress.

He gave in and lowered himself to the other end of the cushion. It was not as long as he would have liked. A little air between their bodies would have made sitting next to her, hidden in a dark room, much easier.

"What happened?" No sense beating around the bush.

"I spoke with Mrs. Penn."

"Good."

"She brought up my mother's paintings."

"I wonder what her reasoning was. She's typically very discrete. I'm sure she knows of your voluntary withdrawal from society."

"She was testing me." Miriam looked up into the glass square ceiling pattern. Michael followed her lead. The stars were out. The black iron frames that held the windows in place disappeared against the dark sky. Michael felt as if they were sitting in a forest. He gave himself the liberty to examine her profile. He wanted to pull the pins out of her hair and watch it shimmer in the moonlight.

"How did you respond?" Michael asked, trying to distract himself with their conversation.

"I invited her to come and see them." Miriam turned her silver eyes to Michael. She cocked one eyebrow up, displaying her affinity for challenges.

"But something else must have happened."

Miriam dropped her gaze to her gloved hands. With the thumb and forefinger of her left hand, she pulled on the middle finger of her right, drawing the glove down her arm, revealing the soft skin beneath. She mimicked the action with her other hand.

"She also asked to see my art," she said softly, smoothing her long gloves across her knees.

Michael was entranced by the vision of her skin in the moonlight. He leaned his elbows on his knees and clasped his hands together. He looked for a pattern in the clay floor tiles; he counted the leaves on a vine that had overgrown its confinement. Finally, he closed his eyes, summoning the will to stand and return to the group. Miriam's hand closed softly over his.

He turned his head and looked directly into her large eyes.

"It was fine. She succeeded in shaking me a little. I don't think I gave her any reason to question my constitution."

Michael's mouth went dry, and he berated himself for his reaction to her. He wasn't a youth by any means. He should be able to watch out for her best interest. Miriam didn't draw her gaze away. Instead her eyes dropped to his lips...and stayed there.

Her lips were small, pink, and perfectly shaped. They would be soft, and she would taste of candied fruit. Her hand on his shifted. He felt her examine the texture of his skin with her small fingers, opening her hand against his palm and lacing her fingers between his.

"Do you think I'm pretty?" she whispered.

Michael's mind struggled to register the question that had escaped when she opened her lips. "I've never met anyone more beautiful."

She dropped her eyes to where their hands were joined. "Then why have you never kissed me?"

Despite his best efforts, Michael couldn't think of a single reason.

He let go of her hand and reached for her chin, once more lifting her gaze to his. He held her like that for a moment, savoring the play of the moon on her luminescent skin. He knew she watched for changes in his expression, and he knew his face was set like stone, revealing nothing to her. It would have revealed everything to a woman of experience.

Her eyes fluttered closed as Michael hovered over her, feeling her breath puff against his skin, savoring the throb of her pulse as he slid his hand down to cradle her jaw. Her lips parted slightly, and with only a hint of pressure at the back of her neck, she came to him.

The ballroom was magnificent. Miriam floated in, her arm in Michael's. The casual atmosphere meant couples were not announced, and the rooftop venue encouraged attendees to wander. Some danced, a number perused the sumptuous dessert table, and a few wandered the rooftop gardens.

Mrs. Penn danced a waltz with her husband. He led her around the room. Miriam had a difficult time reconciling the hard-driving woman she'd earlier glimpsed with the woman who was being tossed about. She appeared to be enjoying herself, while not losing an ounce of dignity.

"Would you like a glass of punch?" Michael leaned in, speaking over the music.

"Yes, please."

Miriam watched Michael leave. Soon he was caught up in conversation with a group of men he appeared to know. He glanced back to Miriam. She nodded. She didn't mind wandering alone for a minute.

"Excuse me." A man's voice rang from behind. "In the parlor, they announced you as Miss Beaumont. Are you she of the Beaumont, Beaumonts?"

"I'm afraid so, sir." Miriam turned to face him. "I'm sorry. I didn't catch your name."

The man was taller than average, with a slender build and a scrupulously clean affect. He had small, black eyes, and black hair brushed and pomaded to stay off his face. Miriam took a step back. She didn't like him.

"Edward Tate." He gave a slight bow. Miriam took the opportunity to glance back to the table. Michael wasn't there.

"I'm looking forward to viewing Mrs. Penn's newest acquisition."

"Yes," Miriam agreed. "As well as am I."

"Is that what brings you here today?" He took a step nearer, backing Miriam up to a towering planter.

"I suppose it is." She couldn't see Michael.

"I thought I'd heard the Beaumonts were art connoisseurs as well?" He leaned closer.

"Aren't we all?" Miriam said lightly, hoping her tone would

break the intensity of his stare and she could excuse herself.

No, she didn't like him. He had the black eyes of a snake. But the only color that flashed for this man was red. He would be impossible to recreate on canvas, because the canvas would be layer upon layer of scarlet. He shuffled nearer, bent toward her. "Would you care to dance?" He smelled of cologne and something else she couldn't place. It was almost like a cleaning, vinegary smell, but different.

"I'm sorry, she's already promised this dance to me," Michael announced.

Miriam nearly sagged in relief. Michael couldn't see the dead flash in the man's eyes when he heard Michael's answer to the question clearly meant for her.

"Oh, yes. I did." Miriam held her hand out for Michael to take, leading her to the floor. "Maybe later?" she called over her shoulder, with the intention of doing nothing of the sort.

Michael settled her, facing him on the dance floor. "Who was that? I'm afraid I've never seen him before."

"I think he's relatively new. He appears well dressed, but there's a hungry and angry look about him. I can't imagine Mrs. Penn would have knowingly invited someone like that to her gathering."

"Nor I."

Michael placed his hand on Miriam's waist and led her into a waltz. Not every couple danced, but there were enough for them to lose sight of the disturbing man.

"I'm afraid I'm not a very good dancer."

Michael looked down at her with his eyebrows furrowed. "You happen to be a fine dancer." He turned and she followed, her gown gathering around her legs and then swaying the opposite way.

"It's just that I learned the steps from my tutor, who was a woman. Ione helped me too, but she's also a woman. The truth is I've never danced with a man."

"You do admirably." Michael's eyes focused on hers. "You've done admirably, and you will continue to do admirably, and I'm honored to be the first man to share this dance with you."

Miriam felt his arms tense under her gloved hand. He brought her closer, until their bodies brushed with every turn, every crescendo in the music. Miriam looked up. He watched her intently until the music died off.

"Would you like that punch now?" Michael whispered in her ear.

"Yes, but this time I think I'll come with you." Miriam scanned the room, searching for Mr. Tate, but he was nowhere to be found.

Chapter 26

The doors to the gallery were opened by two men in white uniforms, one at each door, pulling on the handles in synchronized precision. It was a presentation.

The room was then lit to glittering. Five crystal, electric chandeliers hung high in the ceiling. Wall sconces blazed with their gas flames burning hot. Every available inch of wall space was covered with priceless masterpieces. Mrs. Penn entered the room on her husband's arm. A painting, covered by a blue and gold silk sheet, was on display on an easel in the center of the room. Miriam crowded in behind the others, as anxious as they were to see the new artwork. Anticipation temporarily overshadowed the real reason she and Michael were there.

"She may display my painting next," Mr. Tate whispered in Miriam's ear.

Miriam's heart clattered against her ribs. For once, she wished for the hard shell of a corset. He was close enough to touch her, and no one in the crowd would see. They all stood too close.

"Tonight?" Miriam weakly replied. She grasped at the sleeve of Michael's jacket.

"No. Not tonight. Tonight is not my night." A bitter warning skirted Mr. Tate's words, and Miriam tugged at Michael.

He turned, but by the time he asked what was wrong, Tate had slid back into the crowd.

"What happened?" Michael's breath brushed against Miriam's ear.

"It was Tate. He's an artist. There's something drastically wrong with him."

"I know. Tomorrow I'm going to start digging into who he is."

Their attention was drawn back to the statuesque Mrs. Penn

standing in front of her collection. Miriam could spend days in the gallery. The paintings were frame to frame, sometimes stacked up the wall three high. With the help of her husband, Mrs. Penn drew the sheet off the painting. It slithered to pool on the floor, and an impressionist masterpiece glowed under the lamps.

"Renoir," she announced. "*Near the Lake.*"

People surged in a distinguished crush around them. Michael, pushed to stand behind Miriam, grabbed her waist with both hands and pulled her out of the crowd.

"We can look at it when the guests are less enthusiastic."

"Agreed. Thank you."

They fought their way to the edge of the room where a closet, disguised by a paneled door, was left open. Miriam glanced inside. It wasn't a closet; rather, it was a room. Miriam stepped into the dark and felt for the knob on the lamp. She turned up the flame. Here, too, paintings were hung to fill the walls. One sat on the floor, awaiting its turn.

It was an abstract work: a dark-skinned woman, exquisite in her delicacy. Miriam stooped down to gain a better look. Michael stood behind her.

"Do you think we are supposed to be in here?" he asked.

"The door was open." Miriam picked up the small painting and carried it over to the light. The expression on the woman's face changed to one of horror. Miriam could feel the blood drain from her limbs. "Michael."

"What?" He stood watch at the door.

"Michael."

He turned in time to grasp the picture out of Miriam's loosening grip.

"Do you see it?"

"See what?" He closely examined the painting.

Miriam pointed to her face.

It was also in the style of the impressionists. A painting where close examination revealed more about the painter and his interpretation of the subject than it did about the subject itself.

"She's beautiful?" Michael asked.

Miriam backed toward the door. "Look again. It's Ione." She pointed to the red and browns across the collar bone that could be explained as misplaced shadows. "Hold the painting farther from your face. Look at her expression."

Michael's mouth dropped open. He set the painting against the nearest wall and began to usher Miriam out of the room. "We need to go."

"Wait." She stopped, pulling him back.

"No."

"Who's the artist?"

Michael stopped and turned. He brought the painting back into the light. "It's Tate."

Miriam felt the color drain from her face. "You're right. We need to get home, now."

Little Theo, curled up next to John, snored softly.

"Don't you think we should put him to bed?" It was late, and the women still insisted on waiting up for Miriam to return. It was all well though, because he had no intention of leaving until he found out if they learned any new information about either the killings, or the offer on the warehouse.

"He won't stay there unless one of us sleeps with him," Jenny explained.

"We've tried, but he always wakes just about the time we're closing the door, and he comes running out in a panic. We don't have the heart to leave him in the dark," Ione said, her pencil still scratching away on her pad of paper.

John knew this type of fear was to be expected. It was tragic. More tragic was that the women before him took it so matter-of-factly. As if it were normal to grow up fearing you would wake alone, or in the dark, or without the care of an adult.

"Does he sleep well when you are in the bed with him?" John asked. He let one of the boy's tight blond ringlets slide through his fingers.

"He sleeps like the dead," Jenny said. Ione stared at her.

"Sorry, that was a bad choice of words."

Ione nodded, turning back to her page.

"What do you think?" She held it up for Jenny to see, then John.

It was a sketch of a small boy's suit.

"Doesn't he have enough clothes?" Jenny asked.

"It's not for him." Ione set the pad of paper on her lap and sat back in the chair.

"Then who's it for?"

"What would you think about a line of children's clothes? Ones that could be made simply, with heavy fabrics, but made well enough to stand up to hand-me-downs? Also," Ione continued, "ones that could be sewn on a machine."

"Why?"

Ione stood and crossed to the hearth. "Have you ever noticed," she said as she paced to the garden doors, crossing her arms in front of her, "that poor children are often wearing little more than rags?"

"Well, yes," Jenny said.

"If they are poor, and their mother has neither the talent with a needle nor the time in her day, finding suitable clothes is either very expensive, or it simply isn't done. Did the kids in school tease you because of your clothes?" Ione asked Jenny.

Jenny examined her new shoes.

"Do you think you might have stayed in school longer had that pressure been somewhat removed?"

"One year I didn't go to school because I didn't have shoes," Jenny admitted.

"I want you to start working on numbers. You might need help, I don't know. It will be complex, but I'm sure businesses have to do it all the time."

Ione sat back down and flipped her pad open to a page with a pair of trousers drawn out.

"On the next page, I've drawn the layout for the pattern. That way I know how many pairs will come out of each yard of fabric. What I can't figure, however—" She flipped to the next page. "—is how to most efficiently organize labor. If we purchased five sewing machines and paid five women to use them, would it cost us more or less money than it would if we had six women on six machines?"

John watched Jenny's eyes light up. "I'll work on it. I might have to ask Mr. Farling for some help, but I'm sure we can figure it out." Jenny picked up her yarn and hook and began chaining.

John could hear her count under her breath, but he knew she was thinking about her next task. Theo coughed and then settled deeper into sleep. The fire in the hearth hissed and sputtered, and no one bothered to stoke it back to life. The grandfather clock in the hall struck midnight.

Miriam watched the black night rush by the carriage window. Michael sat across from her, holding her gloved hand in his, staring straight ahead, the pleasures of the night forgotten.

The painting was Ione. Miriam knew it. The shock in her face, the artistic lies of the brush, the exposed violence in full sight, yet hidden and apparent to only those who knew.

"What I don't understand is, why would he give that painting to Mrs. Penn?" Michael said to the ceiling of the carriage. He rested his head back on the cushion.

"He needs attention, notoriety. He needs to extend the torture." His soul was black, and he'd left the party before they'd had the chance to offer their appreciation for the invite. Once they had realized he'd left, they made their excuses, connected with the guests actively seeking Miriam, and thanked their hostess. Over an hour had passed by the time Michael had lifted her into the carriage.

"At least the fog isn't coming in off the lake tonight," Michael muttered.

It was him, there was no doubt. But how to prove it was another matter entirely. "No one else will see the painting like we do."

"I wonder if John is still here." They slowed in front of the townhome.

"John was adamant about staying until you were home. He didn't like the idea of the man figuring out where everyone is before we could at least discern who he was."

"I guess we did that."

Miriam held her skirt as Michael escorted her up the stairs. John, having apparently been watching for them, opened the door.

"We're all in the parlor. Is there any new news?"

Michael hung his hat and coat on the tree. They collapsed together on the davenport in the parlor. "We've had an unexpected encounter, and I think our timeline has been advanced beyond what we'd thought was possible." Michael stretched out his long legs. "This house is going to get a lot busier, very quickly. And the man responsible for the attacks isn't satisfied yet."

Chapter 27

Maggie dreamt of her mother and Ione and Lucy, lost in the dark. Someone chased her. Then she was alone, floating face down in the river with the garbage that washed up on shore. Disintegrating newspapers dissolved between her fingers. Then it was hair, and she was tangled. She stood dripping on shore, and Ione was still lost. She dragged Ione out of the black water. The weight of her soaking costume dress pulled her back, and Maggie couldn't hold on. She cried and yelled angry words at Ione for not getting up, but Ione stared back with dead, open eyes that shimmered in the dark. Maggie was about to kick her when another, smaller form hovered under the water. It was Lucy. She was tied with rope to Ione's ankle.

Maggie ran into the water, splashing through the garbage, searching in the thick dark by feel for her little sister, remembering her warm body against hers in their bed before her mother died. She reached her cold, bare foot inches below the surface, and Maggie woke.

She was alone in the room. Lucy's place in their bed was cold.

Maggie's bare feet hit the floor. She stumbled to the door, bursting into the hall. Her sweaty nightgown clung to her back. She stopped at Pastor and Mrs. Whitaker's bedroom door, breathing hard. She paused for a second, wondering if she should disturb them. They didn't deserve it. They weren't her parents. But Lucy was gone, and she didn't know where to look. She knocked lightly.

"Mrs. Whitaker?" She listened with her ear to the door, relieved when she heard a murmur and shuffling on the other side.

The door eased open a few inches. "Maggie? What's wrong?"

"I can't find Lucy, and something's wrong with Ione."

Mrs. Whitaker tied her robe around her waist and stepped into the hallway. "I'm sorry. I didn't want to wake you," Mrs. Whitaker whispered. "Lucy came into our room. She's sleeping with us."

Maggie blinked, processing the needlessness of her panic. "Oh, I...I'm sorry." She looked at the floor, waiting for the relief she should feel. "I...I guess I'll go back to bed." Maggie slowly turned.

"What did you mean, that Ione's in trouble?"

Maggie stopped, thinking. "I don't know. I think she needs me."

"Now?"

Maggie considered the difficulty she was causing. "I'm sorry. I think so. She's lost. I had a dream. She was lost in the water, and it was dark."

Angelene shook her husband, trying not to wake Lucy, who'd been snuggled between them.

"What is it?"

"It's Ione."

He sat up slowly, smiling at the snoring child facing his wife's side of the bed. He reached out and stroked her hair. "She's sure sweet, isn't she?"

Angelene nodded. She didn't even try to keep the longing from her eyes anymore. But it wasn't Lucy who needed them, it was Maggie.

"Maggie had a dream, and she came to the door thinking she'd lost Lucy."

He pursed his lips. "We should have woken her when Lucy crawled in with us."

"That's not the problem. She was relieved to find out that Lucy isn't missing, but her dream disturbed her, and she thinks there's something wrong with Ione."

"Does she want to go there tomorrow?"

"I think she needs to go there tonight. Even if it's only to reassure herself that Ione is fine."

Pastor Whitaker slid his feet out from under the blankets. He grabbed his trousers from where they hung over the back of a chair. He was buttoning them up when Angelene left the room to tell Maggie he would take her over to see Ione.

The clock struck a single chime.

Ione had heard what Michael said, but she couldn't process it. She crossed her legs, scooting to the upholstered corner of the chair, tucking herself in as closely as possible. They could talk about it, but she was the one who remembered. She remembered every achingly long second.

Part of her knew he wouldn't have whispered as he had, he wouldn't have caressed her neck, wouldn't have pinned her to the ground unless he'd somehow enjoyed her terror. The clock on the mantle ticked away, and Ione concentrated on the rhythmic reassurance. The confirmation that he enjoyed it enough to relive it by painting her, that he was not horrified the next morning by what he'd done, made Ione want to shrivel up into herself. The proof of no shame, of his revelry in subjecting innocent others to his depravity was debilitating. Even more debilitating was the probability that the innocent would be entertained by the strokes of his brush.

Jenny slid into the chair with Ione, placed her head on Ione's chest, curling up to her like a child. They sat with arms around each other, staring into the dying fire.

Across the room, the others whispered plans and potential solutions. She knew they wanted to fix the situation. But who could fix a situation like this? And why would anyone want to? To what end? They didn't understand the hopelessness.

She'd made her way through the dimly lit alleys, not them. They'd had money and parents. Ione had wandered the gutters, faced the beatings, the loss, and the backlit, double-edged blessings. She'd felt evil lurking behind her in the shadows. But she'd mistakenly thought evil's penchant for dark, for concealment, was due to its shame. This, this was different. It was strategy. An undoing, a blatant intention to harm for the sheer enjoyment of it. There was no shame. There was no remnant of good. It was distilled depravity, left free to roam.

Jenny shifted closer. They, the two of them, were pathetic.

Thinking they could just step out of their sin and the clinging talons would release. They were naïve, naïve to think of evil as something to be managed, something that could be overcome. They were dead wrong. It would always be hiding, luxuriating in their fear. It nourished itself, grew, expanding in the city's fog and soot. The city owned it. The evil, so integral to their surroundings, the portrait of her terror was art, appreciated by the ones who fed the monster with their apathy. It was a circle with no end.

What they planned made no difference. She would always be a whore. The job fed her, and she didn't have to wear a veil of ignorance. She didn't have to pretend the depravity didn't exist. She could watch for it, and if it struck, she would strike back. Or not. But the pretense—the slugging along; the pretending she was not what she knew she was; that she somehow had a right to live without fear of what they all could see lurking in the fog—she couldn't do it.

A knock on the door stopped the incessant, pointless conversation. John looked at Michael. Michael rose first, picking up a fireplace poker on his way to the door. John followed, not reprimanding him for the apparent lack of faith. After all, if they'd learned anything that night, it was that there were two kinds of evil: one you corrected, and the other you chased with a fireplace poker.

Maggie could see the lights were on. She looked worriedly at Pastor Whitaker. His expression echoed her concern.

When he stopped the carriage, Maggie jumped down and ran to the door, knocking before she could catch her breath. A man in a tuxedo opened the door a crack. Seeing her, he pulled it wide. Deacon John stood behind him.

"Come in." The man fairly pulled Maggie and Pastor Whitaker into the dark but familiar entryway. Maggie had visited before, when Ione needed help with the sewing.

"I'm Michael Farling." Mr. Farling, passing the fireplace poker to his left hand, held out his right hand to Pastor Whitaker. "I assume this is Maggie, and that would make you Pastor Whitaker?"

"You assume correctly."

"Ione is in the parlor," Deacon John bent to tell Maggie. Maggie looked at Pastor Whitaker, and he nodded. She ducked out of the continuing conversation and into the parlor.

Ione and Jenny were curled up together in a chair. Maggie dropped, kneeling next to them. She rested her head in Ione's lap. "I thought you were lost," she whispered into Ione's skirt. "I had a dream, and I thought you were going to leave me again."

A single tear slid down Ione's face, making it all the way to her neck.

"What happened?" Maggie listened to Ione's steady breathing.

Jenny lifted her head and looked down at Maggie. "Does she know?"

"No," Ione said.

"Do you think she should?"

"I knew," Maggie corrected without lifting her head off Ione's lap. "I knew how you fed us when Mama was sick. I told myself different things, because I didn't want to think about what you had to do for us, but I knew. I'm sorry you had to do those things."

"Maggie," Ione said, her voice tired. "What I did was my choice. It wasn't your fault."

"But it was. If Mama hadn't left two of us for you to care for, you wouldn't have had to do it. You could have kept singing. You could have made enough mending and washing. But you had three people to feed." Maggie looked into Ione's eyes. "I was so scared for you."

Jenny shifted and stood up. Ione followed her, holding Maggie's hands and bringing her up to stand next to them. She was growing. She was nearly as tall as Ione.

The clock chimed twice. "Why are you here?" Ione asked again.

"God gave me a dream," Maggie answered, looking down.

"God?" Miriam walked over to stand next to the other women. Maggie was silent.

"God wouldn't waste his time sending you a dream about me," Ione said.

"How'd you know it was God?" Jenny gently asked.

Maggie looked back to Ione. "I know because you were in a dark place, and I was angry because you stopped trying to get out, and I lost you, and then I lost Lucy. I know it was God, because I couldn't feel better until I found you were all right."

"Does God always give you dreams?" Miriam asked.

"No."

"Then how do you really know?" Ione challenged.

"Am I wrong?" Maggie looked at Ione.

"No." It was Ione's turn to look at the floor.

"Come with me," Miriam said. "All of you. I have something I'd like you to see."

Miriam lit a candelabrum in the front hall and carried it up the stairs. She still wore her ball gown, although the small train had been buttoned up prior to the dancing, and she hadn't bothered to let it out again.

She could feel Maggie's eyes on her, regarding the dress with pride. She knew it was her sister's creation.

Miriam led them to the third floor and to the door of her mother's studio. It was her studio now. She unlocked it and stepped inside, the light filling the room, reflecting off the mirror in the corner. After lighting the gas lamps, Miriam turned to the other women.

"You all know I paint. But there is something you don't know. I've never wanted to think about it, because I really can't explain it, other than it's the way I work."

The three other women looked confused but listened with rapt attention.

"Maybe I should just show you."

Ione's painting leaned against the brick exterior wall. Miriam picked it up and carried it into the light. "I liked living in the warehouse. There were so many faces. People walked by, especially the children, and I would paint them."

Miriam paused and took a breath. Her hands were shaking. It could be the late night; it could be the people in her studio. More likely, it was the knowledge that what she was doing was right.

"I paint the children, and then I see a color. It's hard to explain. I guess you could say I feel a color." Miriam shook her head, trying to think of a way to put her thoughts into words. "Whatever it is, it begins when I paint over the child's face. I paint who the child will become. Ione..." Miriam looked up at her. "...it changed with you."

"Can I see it? Is that of me?"

"Yes. It's of you." Miriam rushed to explain. "I painted you years ago, when we were both children. Then I saw you in the alley, and I was confused because you didn't match the future I painted. I tried to paint it over, to get it right, but every time I returned, I chose the same colors, followed the same lines. I couldn't do it.

"Then I realized, for the first time, I painted who you were meant to be, and God told me..." She nodded toward Maggie. "...that I was to help you. You see, He always knew who you were, even when I tried to make you into who I saw."

Miriam turned the picture into light. Ione brought her hand to her chest and stared. Jenny covered her mouth, and tears filled her eyes. Maggie smiled brilliantly.

"That's her," Maggie said. "That's you. It's the you I know." She laced her fingers through Ione's.

"Don't you see it?" Jenny asked. "Do you see where you're at? You're back at the warehouse, upstairs. You're in the office." She pointed to two squares of light. "Those are the windows."

Jenny stepped closer. "The stripes of colors behind you— they're bolts of fabric. And you have your pad of paper, and you're wearing a suit. Oh, Ione. It's you."

"You painted this before you knew Ione?" Maggie asked.

"Long before I knew her. Sometimes..." Miriam looked at Maggie. "Sometimes, I think God has plans for us we can't even imagine. Maybe, though, when we don't have enough faith to see us how He sees us—through His grace—then He lets us borrow it from someone else."

Jacob Tenney answered the insistent knocking on his door, his mind racing for any excuse that might buy off his landlady for the next few days.

"Mrs.—" He stopped, looking down at a young, dirty youth.

"I've got a message for you, sir."

Jacob took the paper from the boy's outstretched hand and slammed the door in his face. He peeled the seal open and read the handwritten scrawl. The person wanting to purchase the warehouse had decided to cancel his offer. Jacob slammed the paper on his small kitchen table and kicked the door. The family living on the floor below pounded on their ceiling. Jacob stomped loudly on his way to what served as a makeshift kitchen and sat on his one chair.

He'd put a lot of time into that transaction. The man owed him something. But he didn't even know where to find him. Jacob dropped his head on the table in front of him, crumpling the message in his fist. If that woman hadn't been such trouble, he'd have had the transaction complete, and he'd be in a much different situation.

Chapter 28

Miriam woke the next morning, remembering the appointment she'd made with the woman at the ball. She threw off her blankets and stumbled to the window. It was already light. She never slept late. She grabbed the watch on her dressing table and checked the time, sitting heavily when she realized she wasn't in any danger of descending the staircase looking a wreck.

The night before had been a confusion of impossibilities and realities she both wanted to relive and didn't want to face. She'd shown Ione her painting. Ione had run out of the room, followed closely by Maggie. Still later, they'd all talked with the men. Pastor Whitaker spoke privately with Ione and Maggie.

Another decision was made. Maggie would be staying. She worried about Ione, and she wanted to be available in case Ione needed her. Of course, she was intelligent enough to connive with Jenny. Together, they convinced Ione she needed more help to get their wardrobes complete.

Miriam crossed to the armoire. She chose a morning dress with a lightly flowered pattern. It had almost no bustle but buttoned nearly to her neck. The sleeves were padded in the new style. Miriam liked the dress but wasn't sure about the padded sleeves. It seemed that there was always something to be pushed out. First it was the hips, with wire hoops, then the rear, with the bustle, and now the shoulders. The shoulders made the least amount of sense, but Miriam deferred to Jenny and Ione and their fashion sense. They were certainly right last night.

Michael had liked her dress. He'd touched her. He'd kissed her. It was much different than she'd anticipated. She touched her lips, remembering, staring at her reflection in the mirror.

She'd expected the kiss to feel nice, but not much more. But it was much more. When he'd held her, she'd forgotten to breathe. After that, every time he was near, she felt him before she could see him. It was as if the kiss connected them even after they'd rejoined the party. She wondered if he felt the same way.

He'd made no mention of it after they'd returned home. Of course, there was nothing close to an appropriate time to talk. She hoped he would stop by. She wanted to see if she still felt that connection when he was near. If a kiss under her roof would have the same magic as one in a dark conservatory while the stars floated overhead.

He probably had things to do.

Miriam slipped the dress over her head and made her way down the stairs to the dining room. She hoped Ione and Jenny were awake. That woman would be coming to visit, and Miriam couldn't remember if she'd even told either of them.

She found them in the workroom. Maggie sat at the table under the lamp sewing on buttons. A tedious but necessary task. Theo sat on the table next to Jenny, sorting buttons into piles according to color.

"He needs a toy," Miriam said. "I would suspect there are a number to choose from in the attic. I'll have to ask Mrs. Maloney if she remembers seeing them. I know I played with blocks and balls and dolls. They must be around somewhere."

"That would be wonderful," Jenny said. "Keeping him busy can be taxing."

"Are you sure Millie had no one?" Miriam walked over to Theo and held out her arms. He climbed up, eager for the attention.

"Yes. I remember talking to her about it. That was her biggest fear, that something would happen to her, and no one would know to come looking for him."

They silently stared at the boy.

"I bet you're hungry." Miriam bounced him on her hip. "I'm sure Mrs. Maloney has something in the kitchen we can try." Theo scrambled out of Miriam's arms and out the door toward the kitchen.

"Does anyone in here want anything?" Miriam offered.

"No, we've just had our breakfast. We rose somewhat later than planned," Ione said.

"Oh, I forgot to tell you last night. A woman will be stopping by this morning. I think she wants to discuss the dress. Her own dress was magnificent. I may ask you to join us."

Ione looked up, surprised.

"I didn't get a chance to say it, but thank you. The dress was perfect. It drew the right amount of attention, and, just to let you know, you've now set a precedence. I don't know what you're going to do for the hospital benefit."

"Did it draw the right kind of attention from Michael?" Jenny said, slyly.

"Jenny!" Ione chided at Miriam's blush.

Jenny smiled smugly and went back to her figures.

"Thank you for having me." Miss Vaughn sat on the chair across from Miriam. Her hair, in a more casual style than the previous night, was still piled high on her head. Tendrils, curled to perfection, hung down around her ears. She wore a lavender suit with a white shirt, gathered at her chin. The skirt was just above floor length, making it suitable for accomplishing city tasks, and the jacket was tailored to flare slightly at the hips. It was gathered in pleats at the back, giving the impression of a bustle, but without one.

"It's my pleasure. I'm sorry, I've been out of society for quite some time, has your family been in the area for long?"

"We moved here last year from New York."

Miriam wanted to ask what industry brought them to Chicago but couldn't think of a polite way to do so. She would ask Michael next time she saw him. "Are you involved in any charity work?"

"Yes. I work closely with Mrs. Penn. We're trying to encourage the dairy industry and the city to work together to create ways to get quality milk for families at a reasonable price. The milk available, especially to those who work for the meat packers, is of dismal quality, with little nutritional value."

A pang of guilt stabbed at Miriam. She'd never considered that there might be a difference in the quality of milk available in different areas of the city. "If you have need of additional hands, I would like to learn how I can be involved." Miriam leaned forward. "I realize, however, that it's likely that's not the reason for your visit."

"Yes." She sent Miriam a self-depreciating smirk. "What brings me here today is much more self-centered."

Mrs. Maloney backed into the room with a tea tray. Nestled in the center was a small plate of petit fours, the delicate frosting echoing the red and yellow rose-pattern on the china. Miriam thanked her and poured the tea, handing one cup and saucer to her guest. Without hesitation, Miss Vaughn also reached for a sweet. Miriam liked her lack of pretention.

"So, how can I help you?" Miriam took a sip, waiting for her answer.

"I've never seen anything like the dress you wore last night, and it might be selfish, but I wanted to ask if I could find out who designed it before anyone else asks. I have the feeling it's no one from around here."

"You might be surprised. Do you mind if I ask what it is you're thinking of having made?"

"I wondered if I might discuss my spring wardrobe with her. Unfortunately, I really have no need for anything yet this season. I have my ball gowns planned, and my autumn and winter wardrobes are complete, but before I start on spring, I'd like to speak with her."

Miriam bought herself a few seconds to weigh the situation by taking another sip. Miss Beatrice Vaughn seemed, above all, practical. If she were to discover some of the peculiarities of their living situation, Miriam couldn't imagine her causing trouble, let alone descending on the rest of society with loose lips.

"To be completely honest, I've brought her on full time for now. She's staying here as one of my staff."

Miss Vaughn's mouth dropped open. "If she's here full time, does that mean she wouldn't have time to work on other designs?" Suspended disappointment edged into her tone.

"If you are looking for next spring, she might be able to fit you in. Would you like to speak with her?" Without waiting for her answer, Miriam stood and walked to the front hall where she knew Mr. Butler waited. Mrs. Maloney always placed a bell on the tea tray, but Miriam hadn't been able to bring herself to ring for another human. It seemed ridiculous. She asked him to see if

Ione was free to visit.

"I'm sorry," Miss Vaughn said smiling, "but did you just call your butler Mr. Butler?"

"Yes." Miriam smiled. "Sometimes I can hardly call him without laughing. If I could find a gardener named Mr. Gardener, or a cook named Mrs. Cook, it wouldn't matter one bit if they had any skill whatsoever. I'd hire them purely for entertainment purposes."

Miss Vaughn laughed out loud, covering her open mouth with her hand. She wiped a tear from her eyes before turning to watch Ione walk into the room.

"Did you need to see me?" Ione asked Miriam.

"Please come in, Ione. Ione, allow me to introduce Miss Vaughn. Miss Vaughn, this is Ione. She's the one who designed and made my dress."

Miss Vaughn hurriedly stood and walked over, holding her hand out to shake Ione's. It was a decidedly masculine gesture. Ione handled it well, shaking hands with the woman as if she'd been party to any number of formal business transactions.

"Please." Miss Vaughn turned to look at both Miriam and Ione. "Call me Beatrice."

"Truly, Ione is a friend. She calls me Miriam, and I would be honored if you would do so too." Miriam looked at Ione. "Do you have time to sit with us? Beatrice is interested in your opinion on a spring wardrobe, and if you think you might have time to take her on as a client."

Ione's eyebrows lifted. "I would be grateful to have the opportunity to design for you." Ione pulled over an occasional chair to sit near Miriam and Beatrice. Ione tucked an imagined loose strand of hair behind her ear. "What is it that you have in mind, exactly?"

"I will need a full wardrobe update: a couple of morning dresses, a few working suits, and ball gowns for the season." She ticked off the list on the tips of her fingers. "Probably eight, maybe ten dresses."

Ione glanced at Miriam, and Miriam shrugged. "I think you will be largely done with mine by that point. Do you think you'll want to commit the time it takes to create another entire wardrobe?"

Miriam could see Ione calculating in her head before she

answered. "I think I would like to design your wardrobe. I have someone who helps me—her name is Jenny. She does all the figures, and she'll be able to estimate the time involved." Ione paused for a minute, shifting in her chair. "Before I give a definitive answer, I'll want to speak with her."

Ione glanced at Miriam, and back to Beatrice. She crossed and uncrossed her ankles uncomfortably.

"As you get to know me," Beatrice began, "you'll learn that I tend to be quite direct. If you are debating how to broach the subject of my budget, you don't need to be afraid to ask."

"Thank you," Ione said. "I'm afraid my inexperience is exposed."

"Maybe a little," Beatrice agreed. "However, I do not for a minute question your ability. Miriam's gown was exquisite, and her dress this morning"—she gestured to Miriam—"is outstanding. You do not need to ever be shy about demanding a fair price for your time."

Miriam could see why this woman knew and worked next to Mrs. Penn. If Miriam had owned a milk parlor, the children of the city would be getting their milk for free, and she would have been happy to do it.

"Have you heard about the Provident Hospital project?" Miriam asked.

"Yes, I have. Are you involved?"

"Not yet, really. I'll be joining the women's auxiliary in the next few weeks. Funding for a down payment on a building has just been committed, so we'll begin raising money for their first annual budget as well as seeking donated items from the community. Would you like me to send you an invitation?"

"Yes, please do. It does go hand in hand with milk distribution. I suppose the hospital will need to raise funds for nearly everything, including healthy food." Beatrice paused. "They will also need uniforms." She looked meaningfully at Ione, and then toward the garden doors. "Is that a courtyard? I didn't see it from the street. Is it completely enclosed?"

"Yes. My father planned it that way for my mother." Miriam didn't know why she so easily offered personal information to this woman. "Would you like to see it?"

Ione stood to leave. "If you'll excuse me, I think I'll go speak with Jenny about Miss Vaughn's gowns."

"Beatrice," she corrected.

Ione smiled at her. "Beatrice," she said.

Michael's office was huge. John had approached the building, thinking he might have been wrong, but he wasn't. Michael's name was lettered in white on the glass door. A secretary made sure John was who he said he was. Even the robe didn't buy sway with that formidable creature—she should have been a nun. John glanced back at the door as she closed it softly behind her.

Michael had stacks of paper on his desk: correspondence, newspapers, important-looking documents. John, although he knew Michael must be well established in the city, hadn't anticipated the level of influence now obviously possessed by the man across from him.

"What's the plan?" Michael waved John in and got right to the point.

"We know a lot more than we did yesterday."

"I've been thinking about it all night. Although Miriam is sure it's him, the painting is not proof in itself. No one else would see what Miriam saw. I wouldn't have seen it had I not been there and had I not met the man myself."

"Well, we have a suspect." John sat forward. "We also know he prefers the cover of fog."

"We know he's an artist. And, more importantly, he's not afraid of being caught. It was bold of him to approach Miriam." Michael stood up behind his desk and walked to the window. He crossed his arms over his chest and looked out onto the street.

"Did you ever hear any more about the purchase of the warehouse?"

"No. And that troubles me too. I think we can deduce that the one who wanted to buy the warehouse was the same one who attacked the women. Things just line up too nicely. But why stop? His solicitor, a Jacob Tenney, was tenacious in his pursuit, and then nothing. I'm beginning to think it might be because there's another plan of action brewing."

"Plan of action to what end though?"

"That's the part that troubles me. For now, I have the investigator I hired watching the townhouse instead of tracking Edward Tate." Michael sat back down and picked up a pencil.

"But that won't stop him from killing anyone else."

"I know." Michael leaned back and looked up at the ceiling.

The two of them were not enough. They both knew it.

"It was disturbing," Michael confessed, still staring at the ceiling. "The painting made me uneasy, but after Miriam pointed out what she saw..." He paused. "Well, it almost made me ill. I don't know where that kind of evil comes from."

John did. The pits of hell, that's where. There were two different kinds of depravity—the kind that grew slowly through victimization or poor choices, and then the kind that satisfied itself by hurting others. And that's what this man wanted; he wanted to extend the pain, to enjoy it more. He wanted to relive it every time he watched someone squirm as they walked by his demented art.

"How does he think he won't be caught? That's what troubles me most."

"That's what I don't understand either. Do you think he isn't thinking coherently?"

"No. He's too smart for that."

"Then he has a plan." John stood and paced to the window. "That means we need one too, and fast."

Michael waited in Mrs. Penn's parlor. He hoped she'd forgive his intrusion, almost as much as he hoped she could spare the few minutes to meet with him.

"It's so good to see you." She floated into the room in her typically regal fashion. She was an accomplished hostess.

"Thank you for agreeing to talk with me on such short notice. I know your schedule must be tight."

"Nonsense. Have a seat." She gestured to the chairs in front of the cold fireplace. "How have you been?"

"I've been well. I do need your help with something, however."

"Is it about the lovely lady you were with the other evening?"

Michael always underestimated her perception, and her penchant for direct discourse. "In a way, it is."

"If I recall, when her father was alive, you served as his solicitor."

"Yes."

"Are you still working in that capacity?" Mrs. Penn sat back. She crossed her legs, settling in to listen. Michael relaxed. She appeared to be ready to spend several minutes.

"I am," Michael admitted. "Mr. Beaumont taught me everything I know about the financial world. I owe him a great deal. Managing what is now Miss Beaumont's fortune is the least I can do."

"It's substantial, then?"

"Yes." Michael met her piercing gaze.

"I'm glad to see she's moving back into society. I did worry about the child when her father died. But we had seen so little of them both. I guess I thought she was happy where she was."

"To be honest, I think she was. Miriam—Miss Beaumont—is an interesting creature. She's stubbornly independent in her approach. She's fearless when she should be afraid, but uncertain in situations you or I might easily handle."

Mrs. Penn held up a long finger, stopping Michael. "You said 'fearless when she should be afraid.' What does that mean?"

"That's why I'm here."

Chapter 29

The summer evening was heavy. The fog rolled in even before the lamps were lit, the low clouds trapping the industrial soot. John used to like the fog. Not anymore. Not when he knew it meant another woman would die. He quickened his pace to the steps of the gambling house Michael had learned the man frequented. Every step was louder than the last. The clicking of his heels on the wet cobbles echoed back to him off the brick and stone buildings. John tried to quiet his steps, but it was of no use. The thick air held everything in, even the sound of his overcoat brushing against his pants. The smell of expensive tobacco permeated the air.

"Over here," Michael whispered from behind. John had walked past him and hadn't even noticed.

"Is he here?" John followed Michael's voice to where he waited next to an iron gate to yet another building obstructed by the fog.

"I haven't seen him yet. But that doesn't mean anything. I've only just arrived, and I'm not sure we'll be able to see anything anyway."

"I know."

"I spoke with Mrs. Penn today. She'll help us."

"Good," John said. "But how?"

"She had Tate's painting because he'd had it dropped off via a messenger. She hadn't even looked at it. One of her staff placed it in the room where Miriam and I saw it."

"That's good news. The idea of displaying Ione's terror as art..." John let the sentence die off.

"Exactly. When I told her about Miriam and the women, and what Miriam thought the painting was, she insisted that we look at it together. She saw it immediately. She also said she would have never displayed such a thing."

"Did you link Ione to the other deaths in the city?" John asked. Michael held up his hand. Someone was approaching. Lighter footfalls, those of a woman, rushed past them. She never knew they were within only a few feet of her path.

"It would be distressingly easy to kill someone on a night like tonight."

"I know."

"I wasn't going to tell Mrs. Penn about the rash of deaths relegated to the last pages of the newspapers, but I found it was necessary in order to help her understand the scope of the problem."

"Does she know this Tate well?"

"Not at all. She sent him an invitation because he'd contacted her regarding his artwork, and she thought he might appreciate the Renoir. They'd only corresponded through mail, so she'd never actually spoken with him before."

"Where is he from?"

"That's what Mrs. Penn is looking into. She's going to talk to her husband tonight to see if he can dig up any information on him. Other than the fact that he paints, he has what seems to be a substantial fortune, and he's remarkably unconnected to the community, we have no information about him."

"Where does he live?"

"We don't even know that. I would assume he's renting a home somewhere here in town."

A hired hack slowed in front of the building, its lantern swinging on the pole next to the driver. Tate stepped out and tossed a coin to the man with the reins before climbing the stairs toward the waiting doorman.

Michael watched the door close behind them. "I'll talk to the driver?"

John nodded, and Michael ducked out of the shadows.

"Excuse me." Michael approached the driver. "Can you take me to where that man got into your hack?"

"Yes, sir."

Michael climbed in. John would wait outside the club, ready to follow Tate into the fog if need be.

Michael watched the orange streetlamps fade in and out from his seat in the carriage. They'd gone some distance when the horses slowed to a stop.

"Here we are, sir," the man called down.

Michael handed up a coin. "Are you sure this is the place?"

"Yep. He came out of that house." The man pointed to a small townhome. "He's a strange one."

Michael stopped. "What makes you say that?"

"Don't know. I just don't like him, is all. Picked him up a couple of times now, but there's something not right about him."

Michael tossed the man another coin. "You'll keep this conversation between us?"

"Yes, sir." The man tipped his hat. He snapped the reins lightly; the fidgeting horses didn't need much in the way of encouragement. The small hairs on the back of Michael's neck bristled as he took in the three-story brick home. He agreed with the horses.

She hadn't seen Michael all day. Miriam paced in her studio, trying to convince herself it was normal. That he hadn't breached any etiquette by not visiting. Just because he'd kissed her, it didn't mean anything had changed.

But she couldn't paint. She stared at the canvas on her easel, and for the first time in a long time, nothing entered her mind except the glow of the lantern in the black night.

It made a circle on the table and stretched out to press down on the varnished, wide plank floor, where countless drips of paint had fallen—some noticed, others forgotten until they were stepped on and smeared. Miriam sat on one of the wooden chairs and stared at nothing.

"Miriam?" Ione knocked on the partially open door, stepping in without waiting for her to answer.

"Hi, Ione. Have a seat." Miriam gestured to the chair on the other side of the table.

"What are you doing?"

"Not painting. What are you doing?"

"Not sewing." Both women smiled. Ione leaned her elbows on the table and put her chin in her hands. "What do you think about me making that woman's wardrobe?"

"I think if it's something you'd like to do, then you should do it. You couldn't ask for better exposure for your skills if you want to grow a business."

"That's the thing. I would love to be able to make things like the dresses Miss Vaughn will want, but I'm not sure it's what I should do."

"What do you mean?"

"Jenny's been doing some figures for me. For a long time, I've had an idea that we could make sturdy clothes for children that are affordable for parents who don't have much money." Ione dropped her hands into her lap and sat back, looking at the black windows. "You've probably never thought of it. One year Jenny didn't go to school because she didn't have shoes. For poor kids even when they do have a warm enough coat or shoes, sometimes they don't want to go because their clothes are so ugly, the other kids tease them."

"You're right. I haven't thought a lot about that. I didn't spend much time with other children." Miriam wanted to apologize, but there was nothing to say. She'd never done anything wrong. Her only guilt was being born with privilege.

"I wasn't trying to make you feel bad," Ione corrected. Miriam always forgot how easily Ione could read her. "It's just that, well, I have a second chance, and I feel like I could be successful making wardrobes for patrons like Miss Vaughn, but I wonder if that's what I *should* do."

"You said Jenny was running figures?"

"I made some clothes for Theo, and I thought, if I cut out only trousers from a long piece of fabric, and controlled how much scrap there was, how many more pieces of clothing I could make for the same price."

Miriam watched Ione's face relax into her subject. She was excited about the prospect.

"So I drew patterns, and Jenny figured out the costs. The

interesting thing is, the more we make, the more profit there is. I know that must be how stores work, but I hadn't thought of it before. I always thought of income based on how much one person could produce, not on how efficiently a number of things could be produced at once."

"It does make sense." Miriam shrugged.

"Can I show you something?" Ione asked.

"Sure."

Ione stood and crossed to one of the stacks of paintings that leaned on the wall. "You showed me the painting you'd done of me. Later that night, Maggie pointed something out—it's amazing how much she's grown—she said we all have the same responsibility. Even if the world is bad, all we need to do is be strong where we can be strong, and trust God to put the right people into our lives to help us when we can't be strong. That way we can still accomplish what we need to accomplish."

"What are you going to show me?"

Ione pulled out a painting. Miriam knew the one. It was the one where women were lined up outside the warehouse, waiting to get in.

"How many women do you think need jobs?" Ione asked, bringing the painting into the light.

Miriam stood and examined the brush strokes, the faces that had been painted with a sheen of expectation. "Probably more than are on this painting."

"If we could train women to sew, maybe teach them to read and figure, that man wouldn't have so many victims to choose from." Ione set it on the easel, on top of Miriam's empty canvas. "Maybe it's our turn, mine and Jenny's, to help this vision"—she pointed to the painting—"become reality."

The cathedral bell struck twice. John was beginning to wonder if there was another exit the man might have used when he heard the door open. The light from inside illuminated the mist, making it difficult to see his face, but John could tell it was him by the way he tapped his walking stick lightly against the steps, as if it were a toy rather than a tool. When he reached the bottom, he peered down the street, pulled his hat further onto his head, and dragged the metal tip across the cobbles. John shivered at the predatory sound of metal on brick.

John stepped in behind him, timing his footsteps to fall with Tate's. He turned at the alley, the same one as before, and John's heart doubled its rhythm. He ducked in, praying he'd not lose the man this time, that he'd be able to keep another woman from his knife. Moving silently in the shadows, avoiding the seeping orange tavern light, listening through the muffled laughter, John stayed with him until he heard seductive tones resonate in the alley ahead. The incessant clicking stopped, and the man's voice rumbled against the woman's words. John watched their shadows merge and walk into the street together.

He followed.

Because Ione and Jenny had both been attacked where he'd found them, John had assumed the man did the same with each woman. Some of the brutality had been extreme though. The pieces were coming together. He was taking her somewhere so he could take his time. He had to be able to know her face, her expressions, long enough to paint her. John's stomach roiled as he followed them across the street, away from the alley.

They went some distance. The woman's quiet laughter covered the sound of John's shoes, and for that he was thankful. She did most of the talking. John listened, determined not to miss a turn. He wouldn't let another woman be sacrificed to the man's perversion.

The neighborhood changed, it was nicer. The woman changed her voice accordingly. She quieted, and when she stepped into the glowing orbs of light, her shadow had placed a proper distance between their bodies. She knew the rules of the upper classes and was abiding by them in case Tate might run into someone he knew. The loss of her tainted laughter made it more difficult to follow. John tried to close the distance.

An arm reached out and pulled him off the sidewalk. John grunted in surprise.

"Shh," Michael said. The footsteps stopped.

"What is it?" the female voice asked.

"I don't know," Tate replied. After a few seconds, the footsteps resumed. "We're here anyway."

John couldn't see where they were going.

"I know which one is his, just relax." Michael pointed to the intermittently visible brick entryway. "It's his place."

"He's got a woman."

"I could see that much. What do you think we should do?"

"We can't just leave her in there."

"But we can't exactly barge in, either."

A lamp was lit in one of the main floor rooms. Slivers of light escaped from a small space in the closed drapes.

"That would be the library if I had to guess," Michael said.

"Do you think he has any servants?"

"I doubt it. This isn't a neighborhood where it would be strange if he didn't, and if he's leading the kind of life we suspect, I doubt he wants witnesses."

"There's no way we're going to find the police in time, let alone talk them into invading his house. Did you see if there is a back entrance? Or could you see in any of the basement windows?"

"I was going to walk around to the back when I heard them coming."

John heard the latch slide locked at the front door. "Did you hear that?"

"Yes I did. Let's find a way to see in."

Jenny woke to someone pounding on the door. Theo, sleeping next to her, mumbled and rolled over, snuggling deeper into the covers. She slipped out of the bed and tied on her robe when the pounding started again.

"Who's that?" Miriam stepped into the hall. She could hear Ione tell Maggie to stay in the room before she closed the door.

"Who do you think it could be?"

"I have no idea," Miriam said. The three women didn't move from their perch at the top of the staircase.

"You all stay up there," Mr. Butler ordered, crossing from the back of the house to the front door. "In fact, back up a bit, so you can stay in the shadows."

The women did as they were bid.

"I don't like it," Jenny said. "If it were someone we knew, and it was an emergency, they wouldn't be banging like that."

"Who is it?" Mr. Butler hollered through the door.

"It's the police."

Mr. Butler looked back at the women. Miriam stepped out of the shadows, ready to come down the stairs. Mr. Butler hurried to meet her. "Do you know what this could be about?" he questioned in a loud whisper.

"Not at all." Miriam shook her head. "Perhaps I should speak with them?"

"No. Take Maggie and Theo and hide. I know you have places where you will be safe. Take them there, and don't come out until I call for you."

Jenny was already on her way to get Theo. He fussed when she pulled him out of the warm bed, but he wrapped his arms around her neck and snuggled in. Maggie, who'd been waiting by the door, was already standing by Ione.

"Follow me," Miriam said. She headed up to the third floor and unlocked her studio. She then locked the door behind her while Ione lit a lantern. Miriam put her key in another keyhole, turned it, and pressed a wooden panel. It sunk into the wall and then eased out. Miriam pulled at the hidden door and gestured for the women to walk in ahead of her. Stomping feet and male voices thundered up the stairs as Miriam slid the door closed again.

"Where are we?" Jenny asked.

"There's a series of rooms my father had built into the house. Five in all, with connecting hallways. We're going to head down to the kitchen side of the house. In case we need to flee, at least we'll be near a door."

Authoritative, male voices reverberated through the walls. They were looking for something.

As they neared the kitchen doorway, Mrs. Maloney's voice answered back. "We told you Miss Beaumont isn't at home. If you want to question her, you're going to have to request her at a decent hour."

"We aren't looking for her, although we do need to question her. We're looking for the women under her *care*." The officer added a lascivious emphasis to the last word. "Yep, we know all about how she's *helping* these women."

"How dare you." Mrs. Maloney's seething voice rose at least an octave in pitch. Jenny looked back to Miriam and Ione. Maggie shirked away from the shared kitchen wall. "Get out of this house!" Mrs. Maloney shouted. "You get out right now!" She slammed what must have been an iron pot, hard onto the table.

"We'll be back, when the women return from their duties." one of the officers called back as he decided not to vex Mrs. Maloney any further. His voice, on the other side of the door, startled Theo. Jenny shuffled him in her arms and covered his mouth. He understood what that meant and was quiet. A tear slipped down his cheek to wet Jenny's fingers.

The women sat down in the tiny hallway. "I bet your father didn't anticipate his secret passageways would be used like this," Jenny said.

"Probably not," Miriam admitted.

"Why do you think they did that?" Ione asked. Her brows furrowed in concentration. "They're wrong about us, but what if they were right? There's any number of legitimate and known houses they could have raided. Why pick yours?"

"That's what we're going to have to figure out."

Jacob Tenney watched from the park across the street. He knew the women were home, but none of the officers had brought anyone out. If no one was arrested, it wouldn't get the attention he needed. After some shuffling, they climbed on their horses and headed into the fog.

They'd still be shaken up. They were women, after all. Jacob would continue with his plan. The woman had money, and lots of it, and he was willing to gamble that she'd pay a pretty penny for the rest of society to remain in the dark regarding the other women living with her. Rumors could be nasty...and started so very easily.

Chapter 30

Michael paced in the breakfast room, waiting for Miriam to descend the stairs. It was early, and she wasn't expecting him. He'd come over needing to speak with her about last night. Mrs. Maloney wasted no time telling him what had happened to Miriam while he and John were out chasing ghosts.

Michael had all he could do not to put his fist through someone's face, but there were no appropriate targets. He paced to the buffet table, to the hearth, and back to the buffet table again, where he considered a sausage but decided to reject it based on his need to continue walking. If he had known what was happening here, he would have been here. He should have never left her alone.

"Good morning, Michael."

"Are you all right?" He rushed over to her and gave her a fierce hug. Her arms dangled at her sides.

"I'm sorry." Michael took a step back and dropped his arms, trying to read her through her large gray eyes. He couldn't see anything helpful. "Mrs. Maloney told me. Why didn't you send for me right away?" He couldn't keep the chiding tone out of his voice.

"We did fine." Miriam picked up a plate. She chose toast and a sausage and a fruit jelly before finding a seat at the table. "Aren't you going to eat anything?"

Michael realized he was standing in the middle of the room, staring. Her dress was buttercup yellow, and it made him hungry. He grabbed a plate and piled it high before sitting next to her at the table. She had no idea the kind of danger she was in. He speared a slice of ham and shoved it in his mouth without cutting it first. What had she done to him?

"Are you all right?" Miriam set her fork down and turned to

face him.

"No. No I'm not all right." Michael picked up the pitcher of juice and poured his glass half full. He swallowed the juice in one gulp. "I'm not all right at all. I spent all night waiting for a man to kill a woman, only to watch her walk out, perfectly fine, in the wee hours of the morning. And while I wasted my time doing that, you were here being harassed by the people who should not only be helping you, but finding out who's killing the other women." He poured another glass, splashing some onto the white tablecloth.

Miriam set her hand on his forearm. "We were fine here last night. We hid in the secret rooms."

"You shouldn't have had to, though." Michael covered her fingers with his. He knew she had no idea how protective he felt, which was only right, because he had no right to feel so protective over her. She wasn't his wife, after all. He had no claims to her. Her fingers shifted under his, as if she wanted to move her hand, but he couldn't let go. He held her there. He wanted her to feel his tension. He wanted her to know. He felt her gaze shift to his face. He met her eyes, expecting confusion, but instead she smiled.

"You care for me," she said simply.

Michael dropped his gaze to his plate, trying to remember when he'd eaten the food.

"Am I wrong?"

"No." Michael turned to face her. His knee brushed against hers, and she didn't demure. "I've always cared for you. I cared for you when you were too young to care for. There wasn't a day that passed when I didn't worry about how you fared in that blasted warehouse."

"I liked the warehouse."

"I know. That's why it's the blasted warehouse."

She smiled and bit her bottom lip.

Michael lifted his hand to the side of her face. "Don't do that." He moved his thumb to her chin and put the slightest pressure against her skin until she released her lip. "Your mouth is perfect."

Miriam listened as Mr. Butler answered another knock at the

door. This time it was a note via a messenger. He carried it into the parlor where she was entertaining Michael, John, and all the women of the house. Theo sat at Jenny's feet, building with the blocks Mrs. Maloney had found in the attic. She'd also found wooden, painted animals. The zebra poked out of Theo's back pocket.

Miriam slid her fingernail under the seal and smoothed it out over her knees. "Mrs. Penn would like both you and me to visit." She looked up at Michael. "This afternoon, if possible."

"Does she say what she wants?" Michael asked.

"No. She only asks that we respond so she knows if we are able to visit."

"Do you have any other appointments today?"

"No. You?"

"No."

Miriam turned to Mr. Butler. "Would you send a return message that we will arrive early this afternoon?"

"If you both don't mind"—Miriam looked back to where Michael and John sat—"I will leave you so I can figure out what I'm going to wear to meet with Mrs. Penn. Unfortunately, this part of the process takes me a while." Miriam frowned. "I've now learned why women are often 'fashionably late.'"

John smiled. "I can't say I couldn't use the time at the cathedral anyway."

"How much longer until you take your vows?" Michael asked.

"Just a couple of weeks. Fortunately, Father Ayers has been more than patient with the unusual demands on my time and the sneaking into the night to watch the gambling houses." He looked to Jenny and Ione. "I think what happened to you both right outside his church really shook him. He's always asking if there's any new news."

John stood and walked over to Theo. He lifted him for a giant hug and set him back on the carpet at Jenny's feet. "You be the man of the house today, okay?" He ruffled Theo's blond curls.

Theo nodded. He held up the block with the letter "K."

"Did you see that?" John asked.

"Maggie's been teaching him his letters," Jenny explained proudly.

"Have we talked about what we're going to do with him

permanently?"

Jenny looked up, appearing shocked by the question.

"He's not saying we have to give him up," Miriam said. "Just that there is legal paperwork, and there are processes involved in adopting a child." Miriam confirmed the decision to keep Theo with a nod to John before he caused Jenny any further panic.

"I guess." Jenny nodded, her brows furrowed.

"Don't worry about it," Michael added, standing to leave. "I'll have an attorney draw up the appropriate paperwork. But we do need to know who will officially adopt him."

Mr. Butler carried the men's hats and jackets in.

Theo climbed into Jenny's lap and rested his head on her shoulder.

"I think we all know who that will be," Ione said. Jenny tucked his head under her chin and wrapped her arms around him. Michael nodded to her, sliding his arm into his jacket.

"Well then," he said. "I suppose we do." He bowed to Jenny and smiled. "I'll see what we need to do to make it official."

"Will you pick me up then after lunch? Or would you prefer to meet me there?" Miriam asked.

"No. I would not prefer to meet you there," Michael said, shaking his head. "I'll come back after lunch and we can go together."

"I know I'm not wrong about him," Miriam said. "Even if that woman did leave his house unharmed last night." Miriam and Michael shared the davenport in Mrs. Penn's sitting room. It was decorated in various shades of blue. Most of the furniture was painted white, some with carvings and gold leaf. Tall windows along one side of the room made the most of the views of the churning lake.

"I don't think you're wrong either, but it will be interesting to hear what Mrs. Penn has learned."

"Thank you both for coming. I wish we could be visiting under better circumstances," Mrs. Penn said from the doorway. "If you would like to follow me upstairs, I have something to show you."

"Certainly," Michael agreed. They both stood and followed Mrs. Penn up the curving staircase.

Mrs. Penn turned to watch them as they climbed together. "After I spoke with Michael, I talked with my husband and we came up with a plan. I never did get much of a chance to speak with Mr. Tate at the unveiling of the Renoir, but I do know he was anxious for me to examine his art." She faced them so they both could see her roll her eyes at the word *art*.

"My husband and I both thought it might be best to draw him out and find if this particular piece is one of a kind, or if there are others similar to it." They reached the top of the stairs and followed her into the ballroom. During the day, the room was just as beautiful as it was at night. The sun reflected off the lake, creating a sparkling blue background for the lush greens of the rooftop garden. Miriam paused, considering the play of light in the room.

"It turned out even better than I'd hoped when we designed it." Mrs. Penn stopped next to Miriam to consider the view. "You should see it on a stormy day, when the lake is gray and angry and the wind has its way with the plants. When we light the chandeliers on a day like that, it, well, it's hard to describe, but it's like I'm standing in a small, floating, jeweled haven. It feels delicate and temporal, and insufficient against the anger that whips the lake to a froth." They all stood, watching the water.

"But let me show you what I've collected." Mrs. Penn broke the spell and swung open the doors to her collection. The electric lights were already burning bright, and a collection of paintings stood on easels in the center of the room.

"I have them displayed only for you both to see. These will never be on display in my home. Not only are they violent, but they aren't even that good. This is a man who undoubtedly has some raw talent, but lacked the discipline to study and perfect his technique."

The weight of the subject matter pushed against Miriam as she made her way to the easels. Women in various poses screamed silently from the canvases. Michael picked up one of the paintings and turned it over so Miriam couldn't see.

"Jenny?"

He nodded. "I think we have our confirmation," he said to Mrs.

Penn.

She frowned. "I was afraid so."

Theo's mother's chin was tilted against a force just outside of the frame. Her blond curls were pasted with red paint to the side of her face and down, barely covering her breasts.

"These need to be destroyed." Miriam backed away. She shoved her shaking hands into the pocket slits of her dress. "There can never be any risk of someone seeing these. Poor Theo, what if Theo would see this?"

"Who's Theo?" Mrs. Penn asked, turning down the lights.

"Her son." Miriam pointed to the blond woman.

"Where is he now?"

"He lives with us," Miriam said.

"You've quite a collection in your home, haven't you?" Mrs. Penn gently took Miriam by the elbow and ushered her back to the ballroom while Michael turned down the lights.

Miriam could only echo Mrs. Penn's words. "Yes, quite a collection."

It was like some kind of macabre funeral parlor. Michael followed Mrs. Penn and Miriam out of the room, closing the door behind him. He was grateful Mrs. Penn had the foresight to escort Miriam out of the room. It was too much.

"There's no doubt, then," Mrs. Penn said.

Michael just looked at her over Miriam's head.

"Let's go back downstairs. I'll call for some tea."

"How did you get all those?" Miriam's asked, her voice shaky. Michael watched her closely as they descended the stairs. If it weren't so improper, he'd pick her up and carry her.

"I sent a message to Tate. It said I enjoyed his piece, and I wondered how many others he had. I hinted at possibly doing an exhibit. The rest arrived at my door last evening."

"What are you going to do with them?" Miriam asked. Michael backed her up to a chair and told her to sit. She complied.

Mrs. Penn rang a small bell and ordered tea when a maid appeared as if out of nowhere.

"That depends on his situation." Mrs. Penn sat across from Miriam. "My husband took one look at the paintings and started making phone calls. We know the police are turning a blind eye to some of the evidence, but we don't know why. We need to see what kind of money he has, and what, if any connections are in place."

"Frankly, the police have ignored our requests for assistance." Michael paced to the window and looked out, seeing nothing. "However, I still think, if we can get them to look at the evidence, they wouldn't continue to deny what we all know is happening out there."

"I would have to agree."

The maid carried in the tray and set it silently on the table between the women. Mrs. Penn poured a cup for Miriam, then crossed to the liquor cabinet and added a splash of whiskey before handing it to her.

"Drink up, dear."

Michael would have gladly skipped the tea part of the beverage.

"We should have some answers by tonight," Mrs. Penn said, holding out the plate of teacakes for Michael to choose from. He took one and forced it past the lump in his throat.

"In the meantime, we're going to have to keep an eye on him. We know where he lives, and we know where he prefers to gamble. It could be a problem though, because I think he suspected something last night. He had a woman with him, but she left, unharmed, in the pre-dawn."

Michael glanced at Miriam. Her color was improving. "Do you want to talk about last night at all?"

"What about last night?" Mrs. Penn set her tea down.

"My house was raided by the police. They were looking for us, but we hid."

"Good gracious! Why didn't you say something before now?"

"I guess I was more worried about the women upstairs," Miriam said. "We were left unharmed."

"What was their claim?"

"They hinted that I was running a brothel."

Mrs. Penn brought her hand to her chest. "This is ridiculous. What is going on here? We have a man who is killing prostitutes, and the woman who is helping his victims being investigated for a prostitution ring. This is going to end." She stood up and rang for the maid to come and take the tea tray.

Then she focused on Michael. "What are you doing to protect Miriam's house now?"

"I have a private investigator keeping watch. Unfortunately, he wasn't there last night, so I didn't hear about the police until this morning." Miriam looked up at him and he shrugged. "I forgot to tell you."

"That's all right."

"In the meantime, tonight I will visit your home," Mrs. Penn nodded to Miriam. "That will stop any potential gossip in its tracks. Whoever is stirring up trouble will have a much more difficult time doing so."

"Michael," she continued, "you will take a few of my men and spread them out in the city wherever you deem necessary. They are all incredibly discrete, and even more loyal." She turned to address the maid who'd come to collect the tray. "Mabel, please take Mr. Farling down to the kitchen and introduce him to Hans. Tell Hans I've asked him to do precisely as Mr. Farling asks of him."

She faced Michael again. "Get on, now, and take as many men as you need. I'll see Miss Beaumont to her carriage."

Chapter 31

Jacob watched a shiny black carriage roll to a stop outside Miriam's house. The footman hurried to open the door. Jacob craned his neck to make out who it was that could be visiting in such a well-appointed vehicle.

A woman's shoe found its hold on the step the footman had dropped. Next, a white-gloved hand, and finally, Mrs. Penn stood on the pathway to Miriam's house. The footman opened the iron gate and escorted her to the door. It opened promptly, and she disappeared inside. Mrs. Penn had put her stamp of approval on Miriam's household. It didn't go unnoticed by the twittering women standing across the street. No police officer in the city was going to step another foot in the place.

Jacob slammed his fist into the tree and swore. She'd outplayed him. He wasn't finished, though. She'd make a mistake, and he'd be there. No one had that much luck.

"From what we can gather, he has quite a bit of money but lives like he's on the fringes. I would think that's due to the lack of privacy required when one owns a home large enough to require servants." Mrs. Penn handed her cape to Mr. Butler and followed Miriam up the stairs to the private sitting room.

"I thought we could sit upstairs where it's a bit more private. You can also see a few of my mother's paintings in that room."

"That sounds splendid. I'd forgotten how beautiful this home was."

"You've been here before?"

"Yes. But you wouldn't remember me. You were far too young. By the way, did you call your butler Mr. Butler?"

A small laugh escaped from Miriam. "I'm sorry," she said. "Yes. His name is Mr. Butler."

"That's wonderful. What's your cook's name?"

"Regrettably, not Mrs. Cook." Miriam opened the heavy wood doors into the sitting room.

"I've never been in here before."

"This is the room that connects my parents' rooms." Miriam pointed to the doors on either side. "I thought you might like to see that, over there."

Mrs. Penn followed Miriam's gesture to the picture that hung over the fireplace. "Oh my." She took a step nearer. "Is that a self-portrait?"

"My father told her she had to paint a self-portrait. She had a rebellious streak."

Mrs. Penn smiled, staring up at the painting. "I'd say so. It's beautiful though. But so was she. She was the kind of woman you had to watch. Wherever she was, that was the center of the room. Your father loved her deeply. Do you remember very much about her?"

"I thought I did, but now that I'm back here, I remember more every day." Miriam studied Mrs. Penn's expressions as she studied the brushstrokes.

"Were you happy growing up with your father in the warehouse?"

"I was. He was a good man. I miss him."

Mrs. Penn continued to examine the artwork. Finally, she sighed and took a step back. "Well, as long as we're here, what would you think of letting me in on the secret of your dressmaker? Again, today, you look astounding, and I know I've not seen work like hers before."

"I think you might be surprised."

There were two men posted at Miriam's house, two at the gambling house, and one at the entrance of the alley next to the cathedral. Three more had the duty of creeping along in the shadows, looking for anything out of the ordinary.

Michael and John were standing across the street from Tate's house. A youth of about twelve was with them. He would act as a runner in case they needed to send for anyone.

The church bell rang out twice.

"He should be along soon now." John watched the dark windows of the house.

Michael nodded, not taking his eyes off the street. The air was nearly as thick as it had been the night before, blanketed in the odors from the slaughterhouses. The lack of wind didn't help.

"The smell is fitting," John said sardonically.

Michael squinted into the fog, waiting for Tate, hoping he chose tonight to make a mistake, and hoping he made the mistake where they thought he might.

"Do you hear that?" Michael said. It was the sound of metal on stone, an intentional tapping.

"What is that?" The boy crept closer to John.

"Shh." Michael listened to place the direction. "That way." He pointed down the street. They backed up behind a set of stairs, waiting to see if it was Tate, and if he was alone. A woman's soft voice answered the question.

"Is it the same woman?" John whispered.

"I think it might be. Her voice is familiar."

"She won't be nervous tonight. He was building her confidence. That's why he let her go last night."

"That makes sense. She'd be more willing to do things she might not like because she'll trust him more."

The fog swirled and parted, revealing the couple. She hung on his arm, pandering to his ego. He patronized her, carrying on meaningless conversation with a dead gaze. Michael glanced at John, and John nodded. She was in danger.

Tate pulled a key from his trouser pocket and pushed the door open. She walked into the dark room ahead of him. He turned and paused at the threshold, looking down the street. He stared, waiting for something, before he closed the door and locked it.

Michael watched for the light they had seen the night before. It slowly flickered to life. John let out a rush of air.

"What do we do now?"

"We wait, and hope."

"Hope for what?" the boy, now holding tight to John's arm, asked.

"That there's enough time to get to her after we realize she's in trouble."

"There will be," John said decisively. "No one else will die tonight."

John pushed away from the wall and disappeared into the fog only to return seconds later with two men in tow. They were the ones who had followed Tate from the gambling house.

Michael had forgotten they'd followed. The two extra men would be helpful. "John, you and I should go around to watch the kitchen door." He looked at the pair of formidable men. The Penns chose their employees well. "If she comes out unharmed, send the boy for us. If she exits in distress, or you hear anything else that concerns you, send the boy to find the police."

The two men nodded. One of them placed his hand on top of the boy's hat, reassuring him. The boy looked up and nodded, standing taller, understanding his responsibility. John started around the building. Michael followed.

Angelene couldn't sleep. Lucy was tucked into her own bed. She'd adjusted admirably to Maggie's absence, and from all she'd heard, Maggie was doing well too. It was good for her to be back by Ione. Maybe she could help her older sister. Maybe she could bring her to church. Maybe she could help her find grace.

That wasn't why Miriam was awake, though.

She sat in the dark, rocking back and forth, watching the black window and seeing nothing but her own reflection through the lace. Something else was at work.

Miriam was a good woman. She'd helped them, even though she had her own problems. She didn't want for money though, and that made everything easier. There was a cloud around her, and Angelene sent up a quick prayer, but Miriam wasn't the reason for her sleeplessness either.

"What's wrong?" Her husband leaned against the doorframe.

"Can't sleep."

He walked into the room, choosing the chair across from hers. "Me either. It's going to be hard to preach tomorrow if I can't get some sleep tonight."

"Something's wrong, and I can't figure out what it is, and there's nothing I can do about it."

She turned back to the window. A hack rushed by, with the horses' hooves clomping against the cobbles and the lantern swinging angrily. The light illuminated their fence and drew wavering lines along the path to their house.

"The Lord is my shepherd," he began, quietly.

Angelene paused. She took her gaze away from the black night and looked at her husband. "I shall not want." She watched him.

It was his turn to gaze out the window. "He maketh me lie down in green pastures."

There was always something she could do. No matter what was going wrong. She didn't need to know or to understand in order to prevail. She continued to rock, resting her head back against the cushion. "He restoreth my soul."

Light flickered from under the workroom door. As Miriam neared, she could hear Ione and Jenny's hushed voices. Miriam knocked and turned the knob.

"May I join you?"

"You can be so silly. Of course you can join us. It is your house, after all, and we were talking about you anyway."

"Me? What about me?"

"We were wondering if we should bother your sleep in order to go over numbers for some of the clothes," Ione said.

"Our clothes or the children's clothes we were discussing earlier?"

"Well, we have numbers for both, but the ones we're working on right now are the children's clothes."

"Let me see."

The lamps were already burning brightly. Miriam carried an extra bench over to the work table. Sheets upon sheets of paper were organized, some with drawings, some with lists, and some with rows upon rows of numbers. Ione pulled out one etched with miniature patterns and slid her bench over closer to Miriam's.

She pointed to the shapes. "Here is the best use for the fabric. If we buy it in seven yard lengths, we are able to cut fifteen pairs of trousers from the fabric. Otherwise it's two per yard."

"And," Jenny interrupted, "if we cut only the front panels of the shirts in a continuous line, and the arms from an entirely different piece of fabric, we can fit at least one more shirt out of about five yards of fabric."

"That sounds good, but how many people will you need to do this?" Miriam flipped through the pages to the ones with the costs. "Have you figured how much it will cost for the labor? How many women should we employ, and will we be able to use women who might not have experience as seamstresses?"

"I think if we give everyone small jobs at first, there will be fewer things to teach right away," Ione said. She flipped through a few more pages and pulled one with job names. "I think we might be able to hire four women to begin with, and those four should have skills as seamstresses. They will also have to be patient, as we will need them to teach the other women when we have enough orders to hire more people."

Miriam nodded. Although the numbers were large, the final figures seemed realistic. "Have you thought about how you will sell the product? How are we going to get stores to order from us?"

"That's what we're still trying to sort out." Jenny frowned and dropped her pencil onto the table. "I can't sell, and we'll need Ione to design."

"Maybe I can," Miriam said.

Ione and Jenny looked up, their shocked expressions unguarded.

"I said maybe," Miriam apologized, a bit disconcerted by their lack of confidence in her abilities.

"No," Ione said. "I just hadn't imagined you would want to do that. It's so...well...exposed."

"Are you sure?" Jenny asked. "You would have to talk to strangers, and go to places you haven't been..."

Miriam thought, picking at a nick in the tabletop. "Well, maybe

I'm not the best choice."

"No, no." The women said simultaneously.

"I think you would be great," Ione added quickly. "But I also think, if you do want to work, we could use you to help teach the women and to keep an eye on things at the warehouse."

"I'd probably like that more anyway. At this point though, if we don't have buyers, we don't have a business."

Ione picked up a pencil and drew a curved line on the back of another list. She feathered the line and flared the bottom, and suddenly it was the outline of a dress.

"We also have to give Ione time to design gowns. She's going to have a lot of that type of business too," Miriam said. "Wait. You know, Miss Vaughn was very interested in your kids clothing plan. She's already working with stores in the poorer areas of town to bring in healthier milk. Maybe we can get her to introduce some of our products. If I promise to help her with her project, maybe she'll help me with mine. Then I wouldn't have to do it alone, and she would have a good idea where to begin."

"You know, she also mentioned nursing uniforms when she was here. That's not a bad idea. It might help us to run profitably while we try to establish the children's clothing."

Miriam stared at the papers. They were beginning to swim together. "I want to stay awake to hear if they find Tate and confirm it's him, but I'm not sure I can."

"I agree." Ione stifled a yawn.

"If you two can get these papers together in a way that makes some sense, I can take them to Michael and have him run the numbers too. I want the warehouse to have three functions. First, to serve the community with jobs for women; secondly, I want it to be a place where we can train girls to work jobs that will give them a sufficient income; and third, to make inexpensive clothes for children who need them. Are we all in agreement?"

Jenny and Ione nodded.

"Then we need to make sure we can do it without losing money. We don't have to make a whole lot, but we can't lose it either."

"Agreed," Ione said. "We'll put it together after church tomorrow. Maggie and I will be leaving in the morning to join the Whitakers for the Sunday service."

"Oh," Jenny said. "That sounds nice."

"So you want to come with us?" Ione asked Jenny.

"I wouldn't want to intrude."

"It's no intrusion, I'm sure they'd love to have you."

Jenny looked down at her skirt. "It would be nice to go wearing one of my new dresses. I've never gone to a real service before. Pa said they were...well...I won't say what he called the church people, but he wouldn't let me go."

"Pastor Whitaker was nice, and I know Maggie likes Mrs. Whitaker. Lucy does too," Ione said. "I think you should come with us."

Jenny thought for a moment longer and then agreed.

"Miriam," Ione said. "You are welcome to come with as well."

"Thank you, but there are a few things around here I'd like to get accomplished. I went to church with my mother when I was young. My father didn't go, and he didn't take me, but I think that had more to do with losing my mother than with any unbelief. We still prayed at mealtimes and he prayed with me when he tucked me in at night. To tell you the truth, sitting in the pew makes me feel like I did at my mother's funeral, when everyone was watching, and I couldn't get away. It's a little too close right now. Maybe someday. Until then, my church is upstairs in my studio."

Ione nodded. "Let me know if you change your mind. You're always welcome."

Chapter 32

The windows upstairs remained dark. John wasn't sure if that was good or bad. When the basement window cast a square of light across his feet, he decided it was bad.

"Why would he be in the basement?"

"I don't know."

Michael crouched next to the uncovered window, ready to take a quick look in.

"What if he's looking out?" John asked.

"I don't see a shadow."

"But he could be waiting."

"Wouldn't the woman be suspicious then? Why haven't we heard her yet?"

"Maybe there's a wine cellar in the basement."

"In there?"

"Just because it would be unusual, doesn't mean it's impossible."

Michael sent John a tired look.

"Okay. Take a quick look."

Michael stooped, placing his hands on the dirt and spying as much as he could while staying in the shadows. "There's only a door, and some shelving, and the stairs leading to what I would guess is the kitchen."

John knelt next to Michael to look. The ceilings were low. One side of the box around the coal chute had disintegrated, spilling its black contents onto the dirt floor. Michael grabbed John by the shoulder and pushed him out of the way. "He's coming down the stairs."

Slowly, Tate descended. He walked into the open door and came back out with a medical bag.

"That's a bit ominous," Michael said.

"Where do you think the woman is?"

"If you stand on my knee, do you think you might be able to see in one of the main floor windows?"

John looked up. "Probably. Let's try it over there." He pointed to the one next to the kitchen stairs.

Michael brushed the dirt off and knelt again, this time under the kitchen window.

John stepped on his leg. "Sorry," he whispered. He pulled himself up on the window ledge and looked inside.

"She's not in there. He's not either. I'm going to step down."

"Did you see anything important?"

"No. It's a kitchen that doesn't appear to be used very often. There are no dishes or anything setting out. Let's try the window over there." John pointed to a darkened room with only ambient light leaching from a gap in the curtain.

Michael again knelt, and John stepped up. He paused and peered harder into the room.

"What is it?" Michael whispered harshly from his kneeling position.

"I think you need to take a look." John climbed down and took Michael's place.

"Sorry, I'm a fair bit heavier than you."

"That's fine. Just look." John pointed to the window. His pale face told Michael what he might see.

He reached up and pulled on the sill, trying to keep as much of his weight off John's leg as possible. At first he saw nothing—a room with little light, a cheap bed, an open armoire. A slender leg relaxed in a seated position, stretched out, naked. Michael craned his neck to see more, but the curtain was in the way. He watched her leg for movement. Nothing.

"You saw her leg, right?" he asked John.

"Yes. Is it still unmoving?"

"Yes."

The light intensified as Tate entered the room with a lamp in one hand and an easel in the other. Michael backed away as much as he could while continuing to watch. Tate set up the easel outside of Michael's line of vision, and then dragged a chain across the floor, closer to the woman.

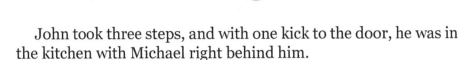

John took three steps, and with one kick to the door, he was in the kitchen with Michael right behind him.

They raced to the next room and stopped short. The woman was naked, slumped in a hard wooden chair. Her head was tilted to the side, and her long brown hair cascaded to cover her face.

"Oh, Jesus." John dropped to his knees next to her and pushed her hair off of her face. Purple bloomed under her pale skin from her temple to her neck. The smell of ammonia was overwhelming. Her body was cool. He pressed his fingers to her neck and waited for her fluttery pulse to surface. "She's alive."

The breath Michael had been holding escaped his lungs in a rush. He ripped off his overcoat and laid it gently across her chest. She looked like a child.

"One of us needs to stay with her," John said.

"I'll find him."

John turned back while Michael punched through the swinging door leading to the front of the house. The ropes tying her wrists had burned through her flesh. She'd struggled admirably. John felt a surge of pride that had nothing to do with him. These women, the ones who sold themselves to feed their families, were fighters. He pulled out the knife he'd carried and cut the rope. Her arms fell, dangling and bloodied at her side. He wondered if she had a child who would have been wandering the streets tomorrow.

Michael reached the front door. The other two men, having heard the commotion, had already broken in.

"You check this level. You, come with me to look upstairs." Michael was already taking the stairs two at a time.

"Is she alive?" the first man yelled after them.

"Yes. Find Tate."

The upstairs was almost black. A gas wall sconce at the top hung in the shadows. Michael nodded, and the man behind him lit it while he walked down the hall, swinging open door after door.

The middle door was locked. Michael kicked it open and walked into the black room. There were no windows. The light from the hall flickered weakly, revealing walls and floors, convulsing with color. Portraits hung in a frustrated rhythm, covering every available inch.

"Get a lamp." Michael walked back out of the room down to the end of the hall. He could see enough to know Tate wasn't in that room; nor was he in any of the others. "We need to find the attic access."

Michael opened the last door to a narrow set of stairs. The attic was completely open. There would be no way to hide, no wall of protection in case Tate had a gun or decided to attack. The man returned with a lamp and handed it to Michael. There was no sense going up in the dark. Tate would know he was there. He might as well be able to see the attack coming. Michael took a deep breath and started up, one step at a time.

There was a single dormer over the front of the house, and nothing else. The attic was empty.

"He's not up here." Michael swung the lamp around, taking in every dark corner. He walked the floor, searching for any irregularities, any place where a man might slip into and hide.

"Let's get back downstairs. He didn't come this way."

The man raced ahead of Michael, but stopped at the room with the paintings. He looked back, questioning. Michael nodded and followed him in, this time with the added discomfort of light.

The paintings—the samples—Tate had given to Mrs. Penn were mild. Beyond mild, compared to the monstrous screaming procession that waltzed around the room. The women's faces paraded in an exhibition of pain and panic, a study of the animal reflex. They looked like deer trapped by a mountain lion—the tendons of their necks contorted and stretched; their eyes rolled back to white; faces twisted into something unrecognizable. They were memorialized at the moment they'd abandoned hope.

Michael took a step back. Chains rubbed against the back of his head and shoulders. He jumped and turned, the bile rising as he looked up to where they were attached from the ceiling in an elaborate pattern of torture. He swallowed convulsively, willing his stomach to submit to the ungodly spectacle. The man who had entered the room with him stood bent, retching in the hall.

He pointed back toward the room. Michael followed his shaking finger.

He carried the lamp farther into the room. A chunk of hair was adhered to each frame. It was placed strategically, in the line of vision of each woman. Michael nearly pushed the other man over in his haste to get out. He slammed the door behind him and stumbled down the stairs.

"Did you find him?" The other men came running to meet them.

"No. Check the basement."

They all turned and burst into the kitchen, following one another toward the basement door. Michael, first, opened the door and took a step back, hacking at the stench that rose from the dank hole. Every man grabbed a lantern, and they sank into the darkness.

Gingerly, John picked the woman up off the chair. He carried her out of the room and away from the kitchen. He didn't want her waking up in the same place she'd learned she would be butchered.

His hands were on the bare skin of her back. John shifted, drawing Michael's coat between her soft skin and his rough hands. He couldn't imagine what her terror had been. They should have broken in sooner.

She moaned in pain when he set her on the chaise in the front room. John offered up a prayer of thanksgiving that she was alive and making noise at all.

"What's your name?" he whispered, tucking Michael's coat more securely around her. "Can you tell me your name?"

She began to tremble. Gooseflesh climbed down her legs. John took off his jacket and covered her knees.

"I need you to tell me who you are. Do you have a family?" He brushed the hair back from her face. It was hard to believe that an hour ago she'd walked into the house of her own free will. Now she fought for consciousness.

She moaned again and struggled to free her arm. Tucked

in tightly, she panicked at the restraint. John helped her, and she lifted a shaky hand to the bruise on her face. "What..." She stumbled through a few more syllables John couldn't make out, but he could understand.

"You were attacked. You'll be fine now."

"How..." She opened her eyes briefly and then squeezed them shut. "How did you...?" The sentence died off again.

"We found you. You're safe."

She dropped her hand to the jacket covering her. "Oh." She felt the rough fabric. John could see the instant when she became aware of her own nakedness. She bunched up the jacket and held it to her chest.

"Where..." She fought her eyes open, this time succeeding. "Where are my clothes?"

"I'm not sure."

She bent her head forward as if to get up. "He...he tried...he tried, and he tied my hands..."

"Lie back," John instructed. "You need to rest until we can get you to a doctor."

"And he made me..." She opened her eyes again to study John's face. She took in his collar and slowly turned her head away. "I shouldn't have been here." A tear wet her already tear-stained face. It glistened in her eyelashes before becoming too heavy and falling to her chin. "Where is he?"

"They're looking for him now."

Her eyes grew wide. She pushed herself into the corner of the chaise, pulling her knees up. She winced at pain in places John couldn't even imagine. "He's still here? He got away? I have to leave. I need my clothes." She was crying in earnest.

"He can't hurt you now. We're all here."

"You don't understand." She tucked the jacket further around her body. "He's not like bad people, or mean people, or even desperate people. He's not like people at all. I need my clothes."

"Just stay there. He can't hurt you now." John looked over his shoulder. The men were taking too long in the basement. "If you don't move," he conceded, "I'll see if I can find your clothes."

"No." She changed her mind. "Just stay with me."

John watched her tuck the jacket up under her chin. "My clothes are in the basement. I don't want them back."

Chapter 33

Michael took the last step onto the dirt floor, stooping under the low ceiling. One by one the other men crowded around him with their handkerchiefs pressed to their faces.

They'd covered all the exits of the house. Tate had no way out. The basement was the last possibility. Michael nodded for the men to follow him forward. They signaled to the man behind, even though there was no reason not to speak. The lamps that every last one of them carried illuminated the basement well past the point of a secret ambush—there was no hiding their presence, or their intention. Still, talking was somehow too normal, too temporal an activity for a place manifestly tainted by the unholy. This man's evil was a solid presence. Michael shivered in the damp heat.

There was a door. A steady, rhythmic creaking leached from the opening. Michael moved past the threshold, his lamp illuminating a network of tables and tools and jars and fabrics.

"He's not here," one of the men said.

"Check for other rooms, closets maybe."

"Already did. He's nowhere."

"Shh...do you hear that?"

"What is it?" The men split up, shining their lamps into the dark corners and shadows, ignoring for the moment what they found. "Where's it coming from?"

Michael stood in the middle of the room, looking up. "Here," he said, holding his lamp high into an open chute. Two feet dangled above his head, swinging slightly. "He hung himself in the dumbwaiter."

It was over. The men crowded around, staring into the cavern.

"Look over here." One of the men set his lamp on a table and pointed to a shelf full of fabric. "It's not fabric." He pulled one piece down. "They're all dresses." He laid it reverently on the table.

"How many do you think there are?"

"He must have kept them down here for a while." Another man stood by multiple pairs of shackles. A chamber pot was spilled near an empty corner, its contents staining the dirt.

"What do you think this is?" Another in their group pointed to jars lined neatly on shelves across the back wall.

"Don't…" Michael knew they contained things he didn't want to see, but it was too late.

They all stood together, lamps trembling, unable to look away from the hanging man's preserved mementos.

"I have to get out of here."

"Be quiet." Michael held up his hand. "Did you hear that? Someone else is down here."

They started ripping the basement apart. Tables were turned over, shelves emptied, boxes thrown to the side. They found nothing.

"Didn't you hear that?" Michael turned around. "It wasn't just me, was it?"

The men shook their heads, listening again. The noise grew louder—a mewling noise, like a kitten. They breathed a collective sigh of relief. They'd already seen enough to make sleep impossible, at least for the foreseeable future. They didn't need to stumble on another horror.

"Sounds like a cat." It was coming from outside the room.

"If the poor thing is stuck in this basement…"

The men went to work on a wave of sympathy for any living creature relegated to the dank space. If they had found a plant, it would have been saved. They searched every corner, discovering the truths behind the odors. They found reason upon reason to pray fervently. Finally, they stood at the base of the coal chute. Together they began to dig.

Michael jumped back. He'd uncovered a foot. "Get the lamp over here, quick."

He brushed off pieces of coal, trying not to scrape the delicate flesh. He wrapped his hand around a fragile ankle. The person didn't move, but the leg was warm. There was life. The men dove in and scraped the coal out from around the girl. At last Michael was able to pull her free. He scooped her into his arms and ran toward the stairs. Weakly, she wrapped one thin arm around his neck.

"Get a glass of water for her!" he shouted to the men tripping up the stairs ahead of him. "And a blanket. Find a blanket."

Her eyes fluttered open. "I hid," she croaked out. "He couldn't find me. He was mad."

She couldn't be much more than twelve.

"You're safe now. He's gone."

She took a deep, shuddering breath in and opened her eyes. "You look like an angel," she whispered.

The police arrived. They sneered at the bruised prostitute, threatening to arrest her. The brutal approach to law enforcement stopped when Michael took the lieutenant to the upstairs room. The basement nearly undid the man. Michael hadn't even considered how he would burn the images from his own mind.

No one offered the women clothes. How could they offer what was likely a murdered woman's dress? Michael paced in the open doorway; John stood over both of them. They huddled in blankets, the younger exhausted and sleeping on the warm lap of the older. Michael wanted to get them something to wear while they waited for the doctor. He glanced out the window onto the street below. It had begun to rain—the drenching cold kind that left the city, at least for a few minutes, smelling clean. He wanted to stand in it.

"I could get some clothes?" Michael slid one foot over the threshold.

The older woman shook her head emphatically. "The blanket will do for now." Her reaction said she knew about the dresses.

The police huddled in two groups: one at the top of the stairs, the other in the basement. They debated how to get Tate's body out of the dumbwaiter. Cut the rope and let him fall? Try to catch him? The overwhelming consensus was to leave him rot in the hole, and burn the place down.

Fire. Michael walked into the room with the women, averting

his eyes even though they were decently covered. The little girl... what was the man thinking? Michael wished he were alive so he could kill him again. He stoked the fire to roaring. It was a huge stone fireplace, much too big for the room, but it would be useful, nonetheless.

Michael marched to the foyer and back up the stairs. Not bothering to light a lamp, he sightlessly ripped a painting off the wall and carried it downstairs. John nodded, seeing his intention.

"May I ask your name?" Michael held the painting so the woman on the chaise couldn't see the terrorized subject.

"Lena."

"Lena, would you like to have the honors?" He held the back of the painting out for her.

She rose, fingering the buttons of his coat, checking to make sure she was covered as much as possible. Her legs were bare, her feet were bare, but she walked over and pulled the painting from his grasp. She put it face down in the fire.

It sizzled and popped. The flames licked around the edge. The weakening canvas softened, coating the logs in a sheet of disintegrating color. Finally, it crumbled and curled to nothing but a charred frame. Lena looked up and met Michael's eyes.

John returned to the room. Michael hadn't realized he'd left, but he stumbled in under the weight of four more portraits. Michael helped him stack them on the fire. This time, the acrid scent of burning human hair invaded the room as the long tresses curled into nothingness.

"What are you doing?" The lieutenant ran in. He bent to retrieve the pictures, but seeing it was too late, stood and faced Michael, hands clenched at his sides. "Those were evidence. You can't burn those!"

"Evidence against whom?"

The lieutenant crossed his arms over his chest. His mustache twitched as if it wasn't connected to his face. "We need to save the evidence."

"And destroy how many lives?" Michael nodded toward the sleeping girl on the chaise. Lena pulled the closed jacket tighter around her slender body. "He's dead. There's no justice for us to seek, no case to try."

The lieutenant nodded slowly, glancing at the crowd of other officers and Mrs. Penn's employees.

"Boss?" one of the men asked.

The lieutenant pursed his lips out and exhaled loudly. "Let's clean it." He motioned toward the staircase. "But if we do it, we do it all."

"Understood," one of the officers said, his feet already on the steps.

Michael stood back, watching as the men loaded the fireplace. With each trip in and out of the room, they nodded to Lena, as if apologizing for the experience. When the upstairs was emptied, they headed to the basement. John had already stoked the furnace to hell-like fury. The bright yellow flames licked the opening, and still he heaped in another shovel-full of coal. He'd removed his vest and rolled up the sleeves of his clinging shirt. Sweat dripped from his forehead.

The sound of shattering glass ripped through the room. One of the officers had thrown a jar into the furnace. They watched, standing in a half circle around the glowing box, as the fire ate the contents of the jar.

They fed the fire till early morning.

When the house was purged, they sent one of the officers for Dr. Pierce. He brought his carriage to take Lena and the girl to the hospital. Michael tucked his business card in Lena's hand as he walked her out of the house. The rain had stopped. Michael would have put his coat on the puddles so she didn't have to trudge through with bare feet, but she already wore it. Briefly, he considered carrying her, but she wore nothing under the coat, and the courtesy would likely embarrass them both. She didn't look back at the house; instead she focused warily on Dr. Pierce.

"I'll return your jacket," she said to Michael, shrugging apologetically.

"That's not why I gave you the card. You call on me tomorrow, after you've rested. I'll see about finding you a job." Michael glanced at the girl John cradled, carrying her past him to Dr. Pierce's carriage. "Do you know who she is?"

"No."

"We can figure that out tomorrow too."

"You mean today." Lena glanced up to the lightening sky.

"I suppose I do. There's some money in the left pocket of the coat. Use it as you see fit."

Michael watched John gather the blanket around the girl. He brushed her hair from her soot-covered face and bent to kiss the top of her head. Michael and Lena walked up in time to watch him reach into his pocket and pull out a tiny prayer card. He tucked it protectively into the folds of the blanket.

"I'll give you a report later today." Dr. Pierce picked up the reins.

John turned to walk back toward the house. Lena stopped in front of him, blocking his path.

"Thank you," she said, her chin tucked down. She wiggled her wet toes in childlike penance. "I know God don't like what I've done. And even if he just sent you for that girl, I'm sure thankful you came."

John paused. Michael watched his calling pour from his posture. He could see John wanted nothing more than to pick the woman up in a father-like embrace. John shoved his hands in his pockets and took a step nearer, bending down to talk to her. "God doesn't see the past. He forgives. He only sees the future."

Lena looked up, tears threatening to spill. John stepped aside, making room for her to climb into the carriage.

"You know where to find me?" he asked.

She nodded.

"Is there anyone you would like us to contact for you?"

"No. There's no one."

"And you know how to find Michael?"

"Yes, Father," she said. "He gave me his card and some money."

"Good. You call on him once you've rested, okay?"

She nodded again, glancing over John to where Michael stood.

"He's helped other women with the same kind of trouble." Dr. Pierce leaned in to explain.

Lena ran her thumb along the printed words of the card Michael had given her.

"Can you read?" John asked.

"No," she said, studying the black print.

"I'll help her find you," Dr. Pierce said to the waiting men. He turned back to Lena. "We'll make things better for you and the girl, won't we?"

She nodded.

He snapped the reins lightly, and the horses, used to transporting patients, eased forward.

"Don't worry, we'll find her if she doesn't come to us." Michael settled his hand on John's shoulder.

They turned back to the house together, back to the basement, where the officers stood in a circle around the chute listening to one of their members saw at the rope overhead.

With a snap, Tate fell in a heap on the floor. No one stepped in to break his fall. They dragged him up the stairs to the floor in front of the chaise and called the undertaker.

Chapter 34

Miriam hadn't slept all night. It was as if her old schedule of sleeping during the day and waking with the setting sun had taken over, leaving her fidgety and shaky.

She hadn't heard from Michael or John, and she didn't know if they were safe or what they were doing, and now the black hues of night had lost their grip, and lavender was sliding in. Miriam dropped her brush into the jar and wiped her hands on her apron. She crossed to the window that looked out at nothing but her own courtyard, and for the first time wished she could see to the street.

The painting on her easel was nothing but unearthed memories, resurfacing only long enough to make the imprint on the canvas and then move on. Miriam had spent most of the night standing there, thinking of nothing, her brush dipping and stroking with no more forethought as to what was being created than she put into her next breath. What she was left with was her mother's hand, holding hers. It was the child's perspective—the view looking up, the wonder and mystery and questions and answers all in the simple bend of the fingers. It was a painting of assurance and dependence, of security and reliance. There was still more work to be done, but Miriam closed the door behind her and walked toward the stairs.

She heard a soft, tentative knocking on the front door.

Miriam stopped, puzzled. It was far too early for callers. Even Mr. Butler wouldn't be awake yet. She knew, however, he would hear if the knocking grew any more persistent, and as she was already up, or rather still up, she hurried to the door.

"Who's there?" she said through the heavy wood, hoping they could hear on the other side. She didn't want to open the door to a stranger. She pressed her ear, listening for an answer.

"It's Michael."

Miriam rubbed her hands on her apron again and pushed her hair behind her ears. Her bun had been discarded hours ago. He always seemed to show when she was at her worst. She flipped the latch up and eased the door open.

"What are you doing here?" She moved back to give him room to step into the hall.

"Why are you answering the door? I was only going to knock lightly in case Mr. Butler was already awake; otherwise I was going to return later."

Miriam pulled him into the parlor and lit a candle. She held it up to his face.

"You look terrible."

"Thank you." He tilted his head sideways, his haggard appearance emphasized by his direct answer.

She pulled him to the chaise and sat down, tugging his sleeve until he joined her. He slumped to the seat and leaned forward, elbows on knees. Miriam watched him pull his glasses off his nose and rub his face.

She placed a hand on his arm.

"We got him."

"What?"

"We got him. He had another woman, and a girl. Dr. Pierce took them to the hospital."

"Did the police come? Did they arrest him?"

"The police did come, but he's dead. Hung himself in his house."

Miriam sucked in a shallow breath, bringing her hand to her mouth. "You were in his house?"

"Yes."

She couldn't imagine the nightmare. After she'd seen his paintings, there was no doubt of the emotion and anger Tate had dedicated to the task of tormenting his prey. She brought her hand to Michael's face and turned him so he looked into her eyes, anchoring him, bringing him back.

"Thank you," Miriam stated simply, holding his face in both of her hands.

Michael blinked. She could see the gradual return, the haunting slipping away as she kept him with her. Finally, he nodded.

"You're welcome."

She loosened her grip. She was sliding away. He covered her hands with his, held her to him, stopping the loss. He hadn't realized he'd needed her so desperately. He thought he'd only stopped to share the good news. But she'd opened the door, and everything that had held him upright drained from his body. Now, she sat in front of him, holding his face as she would a child's, looking into his eyes with her steel gray gaze, infusing her strength into him.

"Don't leave," he heard himself say, not really knowing what he meant. He was in her home. He would be the one leaving.

"I won't," she whispered, drawing his head down to her chest. She leaned back on the chaise, bringing him with her, and wrapped her arms around his shoulders. She held him, and he let her.

He lay nearly on top of her, both of them watching the colors at play in the garden. The sun was rising.

"I need to go to my place. I need to get some rest. I can come back later today to tell you all what happened."

"If you want."

He felt her shift underneath him, but he didn't move.

"Let's get you upstairs."

Michael nodded, pushing himself off her warmth, wanting nothing more than to climb into her bed. His need for her wasn't illicit, he rationalized. He'd just been near death for too long.

He forced himself to a standing position. Miriam came up next to him, taking him by the hand, moving him toward the stairs. She laced her fingers through his.

"I'll put you in my father's room. It's the quietest in the house."

"I should just go back to my own apartment," Michael said as they gained the second floor. He didn't mean it.

Miriam opened the door to her father's bedroom and walked him to the side of the bed. Michael sat and looked down at his shoes. She dropped to her knees before he'd gathered the energy to bend and untie them.

"Don't." He shifted back. "I can do that."

"Take your jacket off and lie down," she instructed—all business. He'd imagined her before, together with him. This was not what he'd imagined. He sighed loudly but followed her instructions.

She pulled off his shoes and set them neatly next to the foot of the bed. Taking a blanket from a nearby chair, she covered him. He prepared himself for the loss of her presence, held his breath for the click of the door latch. But she surprised him by sliding under the blanket next to him, molding her body to his back. She didn't hesitate or hide. Simply, she gave. Her warmth pervaded, melting away the night's images. Her breathing steadied him. Finally, he let his eyes close.

Ione shook Jenny awake. "Are you getting up for church?"

Jenny rubbed her eyes and sat up. Theo had climbed into bed with her again. It had been a late night. They'd all stayed up to hear of any news. When night passed into early morning they'd given up.

"Yes. How much time do I have?"

"About an hour. Mrs. Maloney is setting out a simple breakfast. Don't forget, we're invited to Pastor and Mrs. Whitaker's house for lunch."

"Is there any news yet?" Jenny dropped her feet into her slippers and reached for her robe.

"I think there must be, but I don't know what it is." Ione said, mysteriously. "Follow me."

Jenny scrunched up her eyebrows but followed Ione down the hall and into the sitting room between Miriam's parents' bedrooms. Ione pointed to her father's open door. Miriam slept soundly, tucked into the crook of Michael's arm, her head and hand resting on his chest. He was asleep as well.

"Well, I think someone has news of *something*." Jenny giggled.

"Jenny." Ione pushed her out the door into the hallway. She closed it behind them. "They both had their clothes on."

"Oh, I know." Jenny couldn't wipe the grin off her face. "I'm just happy for them."

"Why?"

Jenny looked confused. "What do you mean why?"

"Well, I, for one, have had my fill of men." Ione shook her head, pointing out what she thought to be obvious.

"That's not about men." Jenny stopped and faced her. "That's about finding someone to need, and someone who needs you back."

She was right, but Ione didn't want to think about it. "I need to make sure Maggie is awake," she said, walking around Jenny. "I'll see you in the dining room?"

"Yes," Jenny answered quietly. "I'll be down there."

Miriam woke in stages. She was warm and comfortable. She stretched her legs, halting when she remembered where she was. A soft, masculine chuckle had her scrambling.

"Oh." He moved his heavy arm over her waist, effectively pinning her to the bed. Lying on his side, propped on one elbow, he gave her a lopsided grin. He had obviously regained his footing. "I didn't mean to fall asleep." Miriam tried to sit up and straighten her hair, but he kept her pinned.

"How long were you watching me?" She turned toward him, suddenly aware that he seemed completely awake, whereas she still struggled through the haze of sleep.

"Not long," he blatantly lied.

"What time is it?"

"I have no idea."

Miriam saw a flash of curiosity in his eyes, but it wasn't enough to get him to move.

Then his grin faded. "Thank you."

"For what?"

"For staying with me. I came here last night because I thought I would be doing you a favor in releasing you from your wait. When you opened the door, I realized that was just an excuse. I came here to be with you. And you didn't turn me away."

Miriam rolled over to face him fully. "Why would I turn you away?"

Michael lifted his arm and gestured to their bodies in the bed.

"This isn't exactly what would be considered proper."

"And when have I ever cared about that?"

"I guess never."

"So why would I now?"

"You might when Mrs. Maloney finds us in here, together."

Miriam smiled and sat up. Mrs. Maloney would be angry with Michael. That much she knew. "I would be more nervous if I were you," she teased.

Michael grew serious. "I don't want to leave."

"I don't want you to leave." She crossed her legs on the bed and faced him.

She was honest with him, because he was honest with her. He'd been there for her and she'd been there for him, and that was the way it was.

"What?" she asked, for once unable to read his expression.

"I mean, I don't ever want to leave."

She knew that Michael watched her carefully; he measured her for signs of discomfort, shock, anything. But his revelation wasn't much of a revelation to her. "What do you want me to say?"

He sat up on the bed, facing her. Her hair still trailed down her back. He ran a strand of the brown honey through his fingers, tugging at the end, bringing her nearer.

She followed his tug, leaned forward into him as his other hand wrapped around to caress the tendons of her neck. "I want you to say you need to be with me as much as I need to be with you. I don't want to torture Mrs. Maloney with an affair, and I don't want to scandalize your reputation." He pulled her closer, until his lips met the tender curve of her ear. "Most of all," he whispered, "I don't want to wake up in a bed without you next to me."

Chapter 35

Angelene watched Maggie drag Jenny and Ione to the front row. Jenny sat down quickly with Theo in her lap. Ione whispered something to Maggie. Maggie nodded and turned, spotting Lucy. Lucy, sitting next to Angelene on the other side of the aisle, but also in the front row, hadn't seen them. When she did, she squealed and ran over, tucking herself between Maggie and Ione.

The three of them, so obviously sisters, belonged together. Angelene busied herself opening her Bible and sightlessly turning pages as if she searched for a passage. She didn't want to talk to anyone else. She didn't want to watch the families pour into the chapel. If she weren't the minister's wife, she could talk to her husband, occupy herself with thoughts of dinner that afternoon, but she was the minister's wife, and she sat alone.

Two small white patent-leather shoes stopped on the floor in front of her. Lucy took Angelene's hand in hers and pulled.

"Where are you taking me?" Angelene asked.

"You need to sit by us." Lucy stopped Angelene in front of the space she had occupied between Maggie and Ione, and pushed her back to sit. Then she crawled in her lap, turned to face the front, and folded her white-gloved hands in her lap to wait for the service to begin.

Angelene quickly glanced at Ione, relieved to see she shared Lucy's smile. She turned to steal a quick look at the pews behind. More than one woman dabbed her eyes. Angelene looked up at the ceiling, concentrating on anything but Lucy on her lap. She'd come back to her, and with a child's gesture made it apparent that Angelene was part of her life.

But Angelene wanted to be so much more than part. She sniffed in quietly, marshaled her thoughts, and prayed that the service would start soon so she could think of something besides the girl who sat in her lap with perfect posture.

Jacob Tenney sat in the park, considering the townhouse across the street. He'd watched the prostitutes leave in one of Miss Beaumont's carriages. Mr. Farling left shortly after. Jacob sneered. No wonder he wouldn't sell. He'd probably had designs for the warehouse himself. Obviously, he had designs on the woman who owned it.

Later, the maids left via the kitchen door. They swung their small purses, chatting as they walked down the sidewalk. Their stylish Sunday hats sported dyed feathers that bobbed with each giggle. Even her servants were well dressed.

If he calculated correctly, the only ones left in the house would be Miss Beaumont, the housekeeper, and the butler. Rarely were there so few people. If he had a chance, it was now.

Jacob took a step forward, checking down the street. A single carriage ambled forward. He moved back out of the line of vision. He would wait, and then the street would be his. It was Sunday morning, and things were quiet.

The carriage slowed in front of the townhome. Jacob swore, hissing through his teeth. The young driver jumped down from his perch and scurried up the stairs, knocking on the door before his feet even came to a stop. Miss Beaumont stepped out. Jacob, hidden by the hulking carriage, crossed the street and ducked behind a tree. He at least wanted to hear her directions to the driver. He wouldn't lose her today.

"Over to the warehouse." Miss Beaumont pulled on her gloves. "We're making some plans, and I need to count what we have, and what we might need."

The boy nodded, offering his arm. He escorted her and opened the door, dropping the step down. She thanked him and stepped up.

She was going back to the warehouse. Jacob waited for the driver to turn the corner. When they were out of sight, he strolled down the street in the direction of the docks. If a hack happened by—or better yet, if he could jump on a trolley—he'd get there faster. If not, he didn't worry. He knew where to find her now.

Michael dried his hair with a clean towel. After the past twenty-four hours, it felt good to bathe. He'd set his clothes—a brown suit and a vest—out on the bed. The vest had a strange swirl pattern the men at the clothier had talked him into. He'd not worn it before now, but today seemed a good day for it.

He buttoned his starched white shirt, enjoying the crisp, rough feel of the fabric against his arms. He'd woken next to Miriam. Her hair, with the sun glinting off the long strands, was the color of his vest. He ran his fingers over the silk, remembering her breath against his chin. It was so soon. Not really, he'd know her for most of their lives, but it felt soon. That morning he'd stopped short of asking her to marry him. He didn't know why. He lifted his chin to fasten the top button.

He disliked having things unsettled, especially in his own life. He had no doubt what he wanted, but she was so different, she required so much honesty, he knew his proposal would necessitate not a small measure of self-capitulation. He smiled. What a strange scene it would be.

He'd always imagined a proposal to go along the lines of *I can take care of you, I have money. You're beautiful. Will you let me in your bed for the rest of your life?* But this, this was more like *You don't need my money, you've lived satisfactorily by yourself for years, I will do my best to give you things you haven't yet imagined you might want, because I can't live without you. And, you're beautiful. Will you let me in your bed for the rest of your life?* Funny, the last sentence hadn't changed.

Michael caught his reflection in the mirror. He wore a stupid grin. He put on his glasses and tried to marshal his expression into something more reasonable and not so blatantly besotted. It didn't work. It was likely the first of many humiliations of the day, he reasoned. He might as well get used to it. If things went well after the late lunch Mrs. Maloney had planned, he'd get to look like that for the rest of his life.

John glanced out his window over to the warehouse. It was a habit he wished he could stop. Seeing it empty—it had always been rather empty, but seeing it and knowing she wasn't upstairs, possibly looking back at him—left a dark place where once there'd been light. He glanced down in time to see her alight from a carriage. The driver took the key from her and opened the door, letting her in. They spoke for a while, while John stripped off his service robes. He wanted to get there before she made it upstairs and he was left to pound on the locked door, hoping she heard him and would let him in.

He nearly stumbled out of the pants he wore under his robes in his haste to grab his other pair off the hanger. She'd still be there, he reminded himself, even if he took a few extra minutes to get changed. He didn't know why she'd returned though.

He put on a more dignified expression to walk the halls, but once outside, he jogged across the street, dodging horses and bikes. He tested the door and found it unlocked.

"Miriam?" he called into the dark, dusty cavern.

"John? Is that you?"

"Where are you?" He'd expected to hear her call from upstairs, but instead, her voice had echoed through the huge space, bouncing off the industrial rafters overhead.

"Are you standing at the door?"

"Yes."

"Go left, and walk down between the crates."

John followed her directions. She stood amidst dirty columns of sun. They jutted sharply at an angle from the small, clouded windows overhead. Dust floating in haphazard, lazy swirls, following invisible currents. She sneezed.

"Bless you," John said.

"That's funny." Miriam giggled. "What does one say to a priest when he sneezes?"

John stepped close to her, sending a tired look.

Miriam turned to face him fully, and studied his face. "Thank you."

"You're welcome," John said, his heart nearly breaking with

her beauty. Smudges of dirt scampered across her nose. His hands itched to touch her, to rub the dirt away. Instead, he looked down at the floor.

Miriam didn't back away. "God is lucky to have you."

John let out a snort at the ridiculousness of her statement, and looked up, expecting her to be wearing her teasing smile. But she was serious. She rubbed her nose, adding an extra smudge of dirt. John reached out, ignoring the warning screaming through his mind. He cradled her cheek in his hand. She covered his fingers with hers and turned her face into the hollow of his palm, breathing in deeply. He couldn't look away. It was a gesture of love, but the love of a sister. He blinked quickly and forced himself to take a step back.

"So what are you doing here?" His voice was hoarse, it sounded foreign in his own ears, but it broke the spell.

She dropped his hand and turned, ready to get back to work. She gestured to the mass of tarp-covered conveyors and machines. "I need to inventory what we have and see what we can sell so we can get the right kind of equipment in here."

John barely heard what she said. He knew Michael would have her, should have her. "What's in these crates?" He slid a wooden box across the floor, out of his way so he could get to another stack. Work was his path to sanity. He was weak today. He hoped it was just the effects of the day before. He would work until he was too tired to feel anything but exhaustion. Tomorrow would be better.

Church let out, and Ione and Jenny were immediately engulfed by the women. They loved their dresses; they made polite conversation about sewing and the weather and favorite desserts. They deftly avoided any mention of their ordeal, which everyone knew about, and their previous profession. Ione wore a brilliant smile. It was the first Maggie could remember seeing. Jenny, one of the few white people, stood wide-eyed in the center of the throng, holding Theo and trying for all she was worth not to stand out. Maggie laughed and reached for Jenny's free hand.

A man stumbled out from an alley across the street. It looked like he'd slept outdoors. He was dirty and huge. His waxy yellow complexion advertised his disease. He stood to his full height, which was considerable, and coughed loudly. "Keep it down, will ya?" he yelled through moist hacks and grumbling slurs. He spat on the street. The men of the congregation turned dead eyes in his direction. He scanned the crowd, weighing his options, counting how badly he was outnumbered. His eyes fell to Jenny. Her fingers slipped from Maggie's, and she ducked down to squat behind the women's skirts. She hid Theo behind the masses of fabric, and signaled for him to be quiet.

The women sized up the situation quickly and circled around her.

"It's her father," Ione whispered to Angelene. Angelene stepped sideways to whisper into her husband's ear.

"What you doin' back in this part of town, girl? Workin' for them now, are ya? Couldn't get along with them rich folk? They caught on to ya, did they?" He took a step forward, tripping over the curb. He stopped himself from falling and sneered at the women protecting Jenny.

Pastor Whitaker stepped forward. His deacons stepped in behind him.

Jenny's da shouted something incomprehensible, but the men didn't back down.

"It's time for you to be on your way," Pastor Whitaker said, using his preaching voice.

"You can't tell me what to do." The man had his feet planted wide on the cobbles. His clothes were filthy, the stench wafting from his hulking body. "You're just a..." He didn't finish his sentence but took a step back as Pastor Whitaker walked toward him.

"Of course, you are welcome to come in and pray. God might forgive you of your sins. It's worth a shot," the pastor offered, his tone flat and none too inviting.

Maggie watched Angelene send him a look. But he didn't back down.

Jenny slowly stood up. Her back straight, she asked the women protecting her to move aside. She handed Theo's hand to Maggie, and the crowd parted. She walked toward her father, gathering around her all the grace she'd found that morning.

"Da, you can come in and pray, or you can leave. You don't have any hold on me, and I don't have to worry about you, 'cause you make your own decisions."

He took a step back as if he'd seen a ghost. Finally, his shoulders slumped. "Nah, God don't want nothin' to do with me." He turned to leave but stopped. "You look like your ma, all cleaned up like that. She'd be glad," he said without looking back. Jenny stood still as he lumbered away.

The women slowly came around her, pressing in. When he turned the corner, they began whispering how good she'd done, how proud she should be, how pretty she was, and how Jesus was her real da. Ione, normally stalwart, didn't even hide the tears she shed for her friend. The group of trussed-up women carried on, bustling her back into the church, leaving the men outside to deal with their own worries. Maggie followed them in, knowing they wouldn't let Jenny go until she had a smile back on her face, at least enough of one to see her through the week.

Chapter 36

Miriam pulled her father's watch from her pocket. It was nearing lunch. She wished the warehouse had one of the telephones that Michael kept threatening to install so that she could tell Mrs. Maloney she might be a few minutes late. She clicked the watch closed, chuckling to herself. She'd open her father's warehouse back up, and with a phone. He'd be proud.

John was working with her. He was a beautiful man. She knew that men didn't like to be beautiful, but he was anyway. When he'd turned away from her hand he was the man in her painting. Everything was right—the sun streaming down, the colors behind, the tilt of his head, and the purpose and stalwart dependability communicated in the angle of his shoulders—it was as it should be. Miriam took a deep, dusty breath and exhaled, satisfied. She brushed her hands together, resolving not to be late for lunch. She'd done admirably with her list thus far; she deserved to sit next to Michael for an hour that didn't have to be spent calculating their next move against a madman.

Sliding her clipboard off the table, she tucked it under her arm and stopped. There was a rustling on the other side of a high stack of crates. The hair on the back of her neck stood up. Miriam told herself it could have been an animal, but the cascading tarps and sheets, the covered tables, the myriad of places anyone or anything could hide, had her wondering where John had gone.

Backing down the aisle, Miriam watched the shifting shadows and the swirling dust, looking for some clue that she was indeed alone. Her own breathing became the loudest sound, drowning her ability to differentiate other, more ominous noises. A sickening thump hammered down behind the crates, and Miriam ran to the stairs.

"John!" she yelled, tripping up to her apartment.

"Down here. I got him," he shouted back.

Miriam stopped. "What?" She started back down the stairs.

"Here. I saw him sneak in. He's been hanging around off and on for a while. Didn't like the looks of him, but when I saw him sneak through the door, I knew he wasn't up to any good."

Miriam skidded to a stop when John came into view. He hovered over the unconscious man.

"He was going to push a box over."

John knelt to rifle through the man's pockets. He pulled out a small stack of business cards. They were bound in twine, rather than the typical small leather wallet. "Jacob Tenney," John read out loud, scrunching his forehead. "Isn't that the man who Michael said kept bringing offers for the warehouse?"

"Yes. But why is he here?" Miriam stepped closer. An angry welt had formed on his forehead. "He's going to wake up with quite a headache."

"He was probably trying to convince you to sell."

"But I thought we'd figured it was Tate who had wanted the warehouse."

"This poor sap probably had no way of knowing he's dead."

"You know, it wasn't very priestly of you to hit him so hard." Miriam raised an eyebrow.

"Yeah, well today, I'm not feeling so 'priestly.'" John chuckled. "Don't you have to go back to your house for lunch?"

"I was going to, but now what do I do about him?"

"Don't worry. I'll take care of it. I've been looking for a reason to visit the police again anyway. I'll bet they're singing a different tune after last night." John smiled. He grabbed a piece of rope off a nearby table and bound Jacob's hands. The man groaned, regaining some consciousness. John picked him up by the back of the collar, and the man's legs scrambled for footing.

His eyes opened wide when he saw Miriam standing in front of him.

"I'm not selling the warehouse, and the man who hired you to convince me to sell is dead."

He swung his head around to see who held him. Taking in John's collar, he groaned and dropped his head back down.

"How does a trip to the police station sound?" John escorted him out the door.

Miriam followed, locking the door behind her. Her driver dropped down, his mouth hanging open at the view of the priest dragging the bound man out of her warehouse. "Are you okay, Miss Beaumont?"

"I'm more than okay, Jonah." She settled her skirts on the cushion and smiled widely, knowing beyond doubt that she was more than okay.

The Whitakers' dinner table had grown comfortably quiet. Forks clinked against plates, and the fire in the stove crackled only occasionally.

"What did Mama look like?" Lucy interrupted the silence.

Ione stopped and glanced at Maggie. Jenny, sitting on the other side of the table, set her glass back down without taking a drink.

"She was beautiful. She had silky hair, and her skin was the same color as yours. She was always smiling, always singing." Ione moved a piece of roast across her plate, suddenly not very hungry, surprised by how hard she had to work to recall her mother's face even after such as short time.

"Did she look like Mrs. Whitaker?"

Ione glanced at the woman to her right. Angelene's lip trembled. She tightened them to a smile that didn't reach her eyes.

"A little, yes. She was pretty like Mrs. Whitaker."

All eyes were on Lucy. Her tiny forehead creased with thought. "Do you think Mama would mind if I called Mrs. Whitaker mama?" she whispered the question across the table to Ione, as if no one else in the room could hear her.

Ione looked at Maggie, and Maggie nodded, reading the question in her eyes.

"I think Mama would be glad to know you found someone you loved enough to call mama," Ione said back to Lucy, continuing the ruse of no one else in the room. Pastor Whitaker pulled a handkerchief out of his pocket and blew his nose, then rubbed his eyes. Mrs. Whitaker had tucked her face into her apron. Her shoulders shook, but no sound escaped. "But I think you're going to have to ask her." Ione nodded toward Angelene.

Angelene stilled and lifted her gaze to Lucy. Lucy hopped off the big book on her chair and walked over. She wiped a tear from Angelene's cheek with her finger. "Can I call you mama?"

Angelene looked at Ione once more. Ione nodded. She looked at Maggie. Maggie nodded. She looked down to Lucy. "Yes, sweetie, I would love for you to call me mama." Lucy crawled up into her lap, wrapping her arms around her new mama's neck. Then she stilled, her mind again at work. She looked across the table.

"Does that mean he's my daddy?" she asked, her mouth close to Angelene's ear. She pointed to Pastor Whitaker.

"If you'll have me," he croaked out, giving up on hiding the emotion.

Lucy patted her new mama's hand, signaling she needed to get down. Once her feet were planted back on the floor, she scampered over to the only man at the table. "I never thought I'd have a daddy," she said, eyes focused on his huge shoes under the table. "Are you sad?" She looked up, waiting for his answer.

"No, honey. I'm not sad."

"Would you like a little girl? I know mens like boys. I can act like a boy sometimes," she offered.

"You know." He picked her up under her arms and settled her into his lap. "Just the other day I was talking to God and I asked him for a little girl. What do you think of that?"

Lucy gave him a brilliant smile. "I think God picked me."

Her new daddy laughed. "I think so too."

Michael paced the front hall of the townhouse. She'd not told him she'd had plans. Mrs. Maloney said she'd gone to the warehouse. He didn't like it.

Carriages raced up and down the street. He watched from the parlor window. Finally, hers slowed in front of the gate. Michael kicked off the wall he'd been leaning against and met her with an open door.

"I didn't know you had plans." He tried to keep his voice even.

She paused, listening to his tone, and then continued to

remove her shawl. "I'm sorry, I wasn't aware I needed to tell you everything I did." She met his eyes, waiting.

He took in a deep breath. "You don't. I just overreacted. I'm still a bit nervous about everything that's happened."

"Apology accepted. And I'm sorry too. I should have known you'd be worried if you didn't know where I'd gone."

He looked down, studying her. Her honesty diffused him completely. He smiled. She stretched up on her toes and planted a light kiss on his lips. "Do we have a few minutes before lunch?" She stepped back, leaving him bereft of her presence and his arms fighting not to snatch her back to him.

"I think so." He glanced into the dining room, wondering what she had planned.

"Good. Follow me."

She led him up the stairs, then up to the third floor. Halfway up, he'd caught her fingers in his and slowed her down.

"I need my hand back so I can unlock the door." She led him to her studio.

She turned the key and pulled him inside, jumping when he kicked the door closed behind them.

"Well." Her heart started drumming in her chest. He stood entirely too close. "I've some numbers for you to go over." She backed up a step. "I was at the warehouse, seeing what equipment we would need, and what we could sell if we were to open up another business in that location." She tried to keep business on her mind, but his eyes were watching her lips, and it was distracting.

She escaped to her stack of paintings.

"We want to do this." She picked up the large canvas and held it up in front of her face. It was the painting of the women standing outside the warehouse. He covered her hands with his own, as if he were going to take the picture, but he held her there instead.

"I want you to look." She poured her exasperation into her voice.

"Fine." He lowered the painting. "You talk first, and then I want a turn."

She nodded, quickly explaining their plan, promising figures for him to go over, and finally pointing back to the painting.

"Did you think I wouldn't like the idea?" he asked.

"Well, no. But you know what it would take financially. I'm not fully versed in either that or what my resources are."

"Ah, yes." Michael sat on a nearby chair. The sun played with his hair, and Miriam knew she'd paint him next.

"John caught Jacob Tenney at my warehouse."

"What?" He stood.

"I thought I'd better tell you before you thought I was hiding information. You weren't very happy about me going at all." She frowned at him and crossed her arms, matching his expression.

"Is there anything I have to do?" he said flatly.

"No. John's taking him to the police station. I'm sure he'll stop by later to give us all the details."

Michael sat back down, appearing less than ecstatic. He leaned back, his long legs stretched out and his shoulders concealing the back of the chair. She smiled. From her angle, he appeared to be floating in the middle of the room. She leaned the painting on the floor against her easel and walked over to him. He looked up.

"Your turn," she said. "What is it you want to discuss?" Before she could think, she was in his lap.

By the time they returned to the main level for lunch, it was to face Mrs. Maloney's dark glare and cold chicken.

Michael and Miriam shared the davenport. Jenny, Ione, Maggie, and John sat in various other chairs. Theo sat, as usual, at Jenny's feet. The two were inseparable.

They'd just finished a late dinner. Maggie, growing more comfortable, was the only one who could describe the lunch they'd had with Pastor and Mrs. Whitaker without crying. Both Ione and Jenny had tried first and failed. John had recounted the scene at the police station. Vindication was not a very heavenly word, but it fit. The rest of the time had been spent discussing the potential business. It was going to be quite an undertaking. Now, they sat in comfortable silence.

"When is the ball for the hospital?" Ione was working out her schedule.

They all looked at Michael. That was his primary involvement.

"Oh," he said. Miriam tried to hide her smile. Ever since they'd snuck back down the stairs for lunch, he'd been beyond distracted. John sent Miriam a questioning glance that she deftly avoided. "It was moved out due to a change in venue. It will be two weeks from yesterday."

"Saturday night?" Ione liked precise details.

"Yes." Michael offered nothing else in the way of conversation.

Miriam picked up the slack. "If possible, I'd want us all to go."

Ione and Jenny looked up. "I don't know how to dance," Jenny panicked.

"We have two weeks. You'll learn."

John leaned forward in his chair, looking at Michael and Miriam. "What's going on here?"

Michael cleared his throat. "What do you mean?"

John pointed at Miriam and speared Michael with his eyes. "Here, between you two. What's going on?"

Michael smiled like a guilty schoolboy, and Miriam blushed.

"Ohh," Jenny said. She started to cry. "I've been crying all day," she lamented. "This has got to stop."

"What?" Ione asked, looking from person to person. She'd been nose deep in her schedule. "What did I miss?"

John stood up, appearing ready to throttle Michael.

"Whoa," Michael said, holding up his hands. "Sit down." Miriam started laughing.

Mr. Butler peered from around the doorway.

"Mr. Butler," Miriam said, between giggles. "Would you and Mrs. Maloney please join us?" She glanced at John's dark expression and tried to stop smiling.

"I'm right here." Mrs. Maloney poked her head out from behind Mr. Butler.

Michael rolled his eyes and waved them in. He waited for them both to find a chair.

Then he took a deep breath. "Today, I asked Miriam to marry me."

Jenny clapped her hand over her mouth, her eyes welling yet

again.

Miriam smiled at the people surrounding her. She glanced at Michael, remembering how he'd knocked and knocked on her warehouse door after her father had died. Michael reached for her hand. She'd found a purpose. One that went beyond her own tiny world. When her gaze rested on John he nodded, wordlessly communicating his approval.

"Well?" Maggie asked, losing her battle with patience.

Miriam glanced at Michael again. "I said yes."

Sweet Mountain Music
by Suzie Johnson

Chloe Williston will make a name for herself...
no matter what beast she must track to achieve it.

Hidden Faces:
Portraits of Nameless Women in the Gospels
by Golden Keyes Parsons

A compilation of four biblical novellas.
Trapped: The Woman Caught in Adultry
Alone: The Woman at the Well
Broken: The Woman who Anointed Jesus's Feet
Hopeless: The Woman with the Issue of Blood

CPSIA information can be obtained at www.ICGtesting.com
Printed in the USA
BVOW08s1927100216

436279BV00004B/140/P